COMRADES

Comrades

A novel
by

BARBARA BORST

BOOKS

Adelaide Books
New York / Lisbon
2020

COMRADES
A novel
by Barbara Borst

Copyright © by Barbara Borst
Cover design © 2020 Adelaide Books

Published by Adelaide Books, New York / Lisbon
adelaidebooks.org
Editor-in-Chief
Stevan V. Nikolic

For any information, please address Adelaide Books
at info@adelaidebooks.org
or write to:
Adelaide Books
244 Fifth Ave. Suite D27
New York, NY, 10001

ISBN: 978-1-953510-22-8

Printed in the United States of America

For David

August 1988

A shroud of smoke from thousands of coal fires drifted over the streets of Soweto. It lurked among the concrete bungalows and the shacks patched together from corrugated metal and scrap wood. It haunted the lines of black men and women trudging in the last hour before day toward the buses that would take them to work as laborers and factory hands and maids.

The smoke spread across the vast township, seeping in at the windows of Sandile Malindi's bedroom. It began to rouse him. He rolled over in bed, pulled the quilt up onto his shoulders, and closed his eyes against the hints of light coming through the curtains.

But the smoke sneaked into his thoughts, too, reminding him of the challenge ahead. Nearly conscious, he eyed the clock: 5:57. Fear jolted him awake. He popped out of bed and shut off the alarm just before it was set to ring. He walked across the room to his closet, pulled out his school blazer, shirt and tie, folded them swiftly, slid them into his pack along with his books and homework and an apple, slipped on his uniform pants and a second pair of slacks over them, and pulled a polo shirt and then a sweater over his head.

Stepping into the upstairs hallway, Sandile glanced at the open doors of the other bedrooms. He felt late already; everyone else was out. He barely glanced at the reflection of his dark face and buzz-cut black hair in the bathroom mirror, quickly rinsed his mouth at the double sink, then sprinted down the stairs two at a time.

As he dashed through the front hall, his mother's voice calling from the kitchen startled him. He thought she had left for work.

"*Molo*," Grace Malindi said. "Sandile, you must have tea. It's cold outside."

He stopped and paced the hall floor thinking 'good morning' didn't cover what lay ahead for him. "No time, Mama."

"Ready just now. And where is your uniform?"

He leaned in the kitchen doorway as she turned toward the steaming kettle. "In my sack. There's a boycott," he said, stepping from one foot to the other, frustrated that she had forgotten why he was in a hurry.

"I know. For township schools, not yours," she counseled as she poured boiling water into a teapot.

"Doesn't matter to the comrades."

"Stay at the shop with us."

Sandile saw his mother make her daily check to be sure her pistol was loaded, then tuck it into her bra and adjust the neckline of her dress. He couldn't understand why he was barred from guarding the family's grocery overnight like his brother and father, but he was expected to stay in the shop all day and miss school.

No time to reopen that debate, so he answered her simply, "Big exam today. I won't miss school because they hate theirs."

"At least eat," she said, turning to offer him a bowl of apples. "Fresh shipment."

"Got one," he called back as he ran out. Checking for his house keys, he pulled the front door closed behind him and then launched himself over the three front steps. He crossed the barren yard, stepped over the ruts that his father's and his brother's cars had carved into the earth and dashed out through the gate.

The smoke tasted dead in Sandile's mouth as he hurried, on the watch for young men. He knew hardly any neighbors, having moved just a few months before from the Orlando East section of Soweto to Diepkloof Extension. Everything about his new neighborhood – the double-story homes, some with swimming pools, the cars parked inside security gates – marked him as a target for the comrades, he believed.

The bus depot was more than two miles away. He wanted to run but thought haste would draw attention, so he strode westward for the first mile, determined not to let his fear show. He understood that he was too tall to look like a primary school pupil, too young to look as if he were headed to work; he was exactly who the comrades wanted to pressure into joining the high school strike.

Peering through the shreds of smoke that hovered over the hostels for male workers and the rows of low houses, Sandile surveyed the rolling land ahead of him for any danger. A few adults walked toward the bus depot, many of them wrapped in blankets against the chill. Sandile watched for boys his own age who might be strike enforcers – teen-agers, not in school uniforms, usually in pairs, often armed with sticks. He looked down each street as he crossed it. A few stray dogs appeared, but no teens.

He thought about swinging north past his old house where his father and brother were working at the shop, but that route would have nearly doubled his journey. Instead, he continued southwest for another mile, zigzagging toward the bus depot. Twelve more minutes of watching, watching, watching, and walking fast, but the journey felt endless.

At last, he joined the back of the queue, which already stretched beyond the metal fences that slotted everyone, like cattle, into the right chute. He eyed the lines of men and women who stood on the dirt waiting to crush their way into one of the buses or the mini-vans. A corrugated metal roof covered only a part of the line; there were no walls to protect them from the cold breeze.

Breathing hard, not from exertion but from fear, Sandile took off his backpack and set it between his feet, to look less like a student. Without noticing it, he began again to shift lightly from one foot to the other, like a defender bracing for an attack on the soccer field. He pulled his collar up and tucked his chin to hide his face a bit, but still he kept his eyes open for trouble. He did not feel safety in numbers. If the comrades came, he thought, people were likely to scatter. The lines made him feel trapped; his best defense – a swift escape – would be cut off by the crowd around him and the railings that kept them in line.

Sleepy commuters shuffled forward. Aching to jump the line, Sandile shifted in place, not speaking to anyone, on guard. At last, it was his turn to board. He paid his fare. Dozens rushed him toward the back of the vehicle, which soon filled to capacity with commuters.

As the bus pulled out of the terminal and rolled along Potchefstroom Road away from Soweto, Sandile looked back in relief. He could see the first group of comrades, some with sticks in their hands, grilling commuters as they neared the depot.

His bus rolled along the highway, jockeying for position with other early morning traffic on its ten-mile trip northeast into central Johannesburg. As it emerged from the smoke of Soweto, the sky brightened with the rising sun. Sandile saw that it would be another cold, sun-filled August morning, like every day of the long, dry winter.

Trying to collect himself after the morning ordeal, he glared at the landscape he saw from the highway every day – white neighborhoods filled with pastel-colored houses that sat like eggs in a carton, each boxed in by a tidy garden and a wall or fence; the towers of the gold mines where black mine workers had blasted South Africa's wealth out of the Earth; the skyscrapers of Johannesburg rising straight up beyond the artificial hills made of mine tailings. Looking over the shoulders of other passengers, he seethed with anger at what was officially off limits to him because he was black; he banished the fleeting thought that his anger might be a mask for envy.

The last street lights flickered off as the bus plunged into the canyons of the downtown streets and stopped at one traffic light after another before reaching the terminal. Sandile filed out with the rest of the passengers, then hunted for the next bus, the one that would take him four miles north to his school in Houghton Estate. He stood in line in the open air among black women wearing maids' uniforms with ruffled aprons and black men in rough clothes who were headed to work as gardeners. He didn't notice any other students. He boarded and the bus started on its twisting, halting journey through downtown toward the first of Johannesburg's northern suburbs.

Sandile anticipated the signs that they were entering the lavish neighborhood surrounding his school: first, the barks of guard dogs demanding to know who was passing, then the scent of flowers from the gardens behind security walls. He peered through the ornate gates of mansions, watched for his stop, got down and walked the last few blocks while devouring his apple.

Sandile paused at the open gate in the tan brick wall that surrounded Saint Andrew's Academy and its manicured playing fields. Shifting slightly from side to side, he breathed deeply, stretched to full height and centered himself as he prepared for the switch from evading the comrades to taking his algebra test. He held his head high with pride not so much in himself as in his family, his clan, his people, who had made him who he was, who expected so much of him. Composed, Sandile headed straight for the lavatory to change into his uniform.

The little house was so quiet that Kagiso Mafolo could hear her heart pounding as she lay awake waiting for dawn. When the curtainless window began to brighten, she rose gently from the bed she shared with her little sister. Taking her hand towel from a hook on the wall, she squeezed past the cot where her younger brother sprawled on a mattress in the same room. She entered the kitchen, pausing to push the embers in the coal-burning stove into a heap, and slipped out the back door to the bathroom her father had built around the water and sewer pipes provided by the township. No one stirred in the one-room shacks in the backyard that her father rented to people even poorer than her family.

The washroom was barely big enough to turn around in, and it was cold, but the cracked mirror strapped to the ply-wood wall let her check her face for any blemishes, cover the few she found with medication, see that her eyelashes curled up just so, fluff her Afro. She pouted, smiled, batted her eyes, turned solemn, headed back to the house, towel in hand.

She took the kettle and went out to fill it with water at the tap. Back in the kitchen, she placed it on the stove and poked the fire again.

While the water heated, Kagiso went to her room and slipped into a pair of jeans and a long-sleeved red T-shirt, pulling her bracelet of red-and-white beads out from under the cuff. Next, a thick navy cardigan and over it her school uniform jumper. Checking her jeans pocket for her favorite earrings and her house key, she opened the bedroom window two inches.

"*Dumela,*" she whispered as she bent over her sister, Tiny, who curled herself tighter into the blanket. Kagiso tugged slightly at the covers and added, "Time for school." She lifted Tiny out of the tangle, set her on the edge of the bed and patted the top of her head.

"*Dumela,*" Tiny said through a yawn as she flopped against her sister's thigh. Kagiso made her stand up, handed her a wash cloth and sent her to the outdoor bathroom. "Let's move," she said, anxious to get started on her own plans. She turned to her brother's bed and put a hand on his shoulder. "*Dumela,* Mike."

Still asleep, he batted her hand away. "*Tswaya,*" he ordered.

"Up, up, now."

Suddenly, he jumped out of bed and started boxing her hands with his skinny fists. Ignoring his harmless morning ritual and satisfied that he wouldn't fall asleep again, she set his uniform on the bed, then sent him to the washroom after Tiny. Returning to the kitchen, she poured hot water over teabags and added powdered milk from a can. While the tea cooled, she helped Tiny into her school uniform. Despite her efforts to speed Mike along, he insisted on dressing himself, even if that meant his belt was twisted and his black leather shoes were laced wrong.

As they all stood at the small kitchen table, Kagiso cut two thick slices of bread and spread them with margarine and a just a hint of strawberry jam.

"I don't want...," Mike protested.

"You must," she instructed him. She checked their school bags for their homework. As soon as they had finished eating, she said, "Let's move," and swung both hands toward the front door to show the way.

As they entered the main room, Kagiso saw their father's powerful left arm extended beyond the back of an upholstered chair, holding some kind of paper. He was home early from his night job. She waited to see if he was awake. He turned slowly toward them, his eyes half shut.

"*Dumela, Baba.* We're going that side just now. For sure we have to hurry to school," she added brightly, leaving her father no time to reply as she quickly walked her sister and brother outside. As the door shut behind them, she heard him ask a question about the school strike – a question she didn't want to answer. Instead, she shooed the little ones off on the ten-minute walk to their school, rounded the corner of the house, pulled off her uniform and slid it in through the bedroom window. Then she walked swiftly along the street, passing crowded little one-story houses like her own, until she felt sure her father would not come after her.

Despite the chill, she unbuttoned the top of her sweater so that the red shirt showed, to show off her figure. She reached into her jeans pocket for her earrings. The dangling strings of red and white glass beads glowed against her dark skin. Shaking her head to make them swing, Kagiso freed herself from her father's opposition to protests. He was overprotective, she told herself, and what good did that do? He couldn't shield his family when it mattered. He was too cautious to challenge the system, but the students were fearless. That's where she wanted to be.

In three minutes, Kagiso arrived at the edge of a squatter camp that spilled down a slope toward a streambed filled with garbage. She picked her way along a crooked path among the shacks, which leaned on one another for support, their wood frames and oddly shaped panels of corrugated metal spreading in a patchwork. Halfway down, she stopped to knock at a rough door.

"Palesa, it's me," she announced. A key turned in the padlock on the inside of the door.

"Tea will be ready just now," Palesa Mhlongo said as she opened for her best friend. She spread margarine from a large tin onto two slices of bread. A saucepan of water began to boil on a kerosene burner.

"Your mother leave early, too?" Kagiso asked as she surveyed the one-room shack.

Palesa nodded.

"I am very much hoping he doesn't come," Kagiso added as they blew on the scalding tea so they could drink it. She knew Palesa understood that 'he' meant T.S. They both knew he wouldn't miss the protest; he was one of the instigators.

Palesa looked sideways at Kagiso and said, "You know he's in love with you, right?"

"No." Kagiso squirmed at the memory of the tall skinny classmate with his uninvited hands on her shoulders, talking down to her about politics. "In love with himself, for sure."

"Thinks you're his girl."

"Or plaything."

"Handsome," Palesa taunted.

"Yeah," Kagiso said slowly, looking at the corrugated ceiling and smiling just a bit. "But, at the end of the day, he tries to boss me. No chance for that."

"Take your pick. They're all at your feet."

"You're imagining. They're little boys."

Palesa changed the subject. "Love your earrings."

Kagiso tossed her head to make the red-and-white strings dance below her Afro.

"But a red shirt?"

"What's wrong with matching?"

"Yeah, catch a policeman's eye."

Kagiso chided herself for letting vanity supersede caution. "Lend you a shirt?"

"Too tall and skinny," Kagiso replied as she buttoned her cardigan to cover the red neckline, pulled the left sleeve over the string of beads tied around her wrist and then stuffed her earrings back into her pocket with her keys.

The two quickly finished their tea and set out for school, climbing the tangled path up to the street above the shacks.

At the top, Kagiso looked out over the township of two-and-a-half million people that had always been her home and saw other students emerging one by one, gathering in small groups, converging on the high schools of Soweto by the hundreds, by the thousands. This, she thought, this is how we will win, not cowering like our parents but united in protest. She breathed deeply, ignoring the smell of coal fires and the chalky odor of uncollected trash that had dried up in the African sun. She stood on her toes and smiled big and softly as her hopes rose with the gathering light.

Palesa spotted their friends Sonny Boy Gumede and Lawrence Sithole; the two girls ran to catch up. They joined more and more classmates along the way, saluting each other with clenched fists and shouting hello in a jumble of languages – Zulu, Tswana, English, township slang. Ahead, they saw a small cloud of khaki-colored dust rising near the schoolyard and they sped up their steps to reach the demonstration sooner.

Kagiso waved to Mrs. Ndlovu and Mr. Rachidi, the only teachers the students felt were on their side. She could see that the two had chosen their spot well: not so close to the protests that they could lose their jobs in a government school but close enough to monitor in case of violence.

Kagiso admired the discipline among her classmates: They all wore jeans and sweatshirts or jackets or sweaters. No one wanted to be mistaken for a sell-out who would break the boycott, so no one wore the usual black-and-white uniform or entered the school building. Instead, they gathered just outside the wire fence that surrounded the dry schoolyard, grassless from too many feet tromping it daily. They turned their backs to the red brick school that stole too much of their lives in what seemed futile efforts.

Let the school sit empty, she thought, its broken windows bearing witness to the students who had escaped its cold concrete rooms and gone out to protest in the sun. They wouldn't be sorry to miss a day crammed three at a desk, sharing textbooks and pencils, trying to learn enough of the government's propaganda to pass the final exams. This would be a much better lesson in how to change the world. She hurried to get into the crowd of students stomping in place to the beat of freedom songs. The dust rose around her feet, around all their feet, sprinkling their shoes and pants with fine tan particles, rising into the air in a signal that the Earth heard their protests, alighting on their hair and faces. They stamped and shook their hips as they chanted 'Liberation Before Education' and other slogans

Kagiso saw their numbers keep growing. The demonstrators spread beyond the shade of the one tree that survived on the edge of the school yard. They danced in the parched grass that clung to life outside the school fence. The whorl of dust and the gusto of their voices seemed to draw students like a magnet. She could feel them unify like an army slowly assembling and beginning to feel its might.

Beyond the dust, she noticed that the neighborhood was unusually quiet; the stream of children heading to school or play had disappeared behind closed doors. She knew, everyone knew, what to expect, what it was the students wanted: confrontation with the authorities, a chance to show their courage and their rage. The police would be there soon enough, she calculated. She turned her thoughts back to her classmates, savoring the freedom to sing and dance and protest while they could.

The muffled thumps sounded to Peter Seibert like teammates banging on the side of the bus, trying to drum up excitement for the coming soccer match. He rolled over in his sleep, dreaming of goals scored. But the thumps persisted, half woke him, turned into shouts from his mother to get ready for school. He opened his eyes just a little and tried to figure out where he was. The room was not familiar. It was littered with large open boxes whose contents were spilling out. Clothes draped over chairs and suitcases and drooped from bureau drawers. He rolled onto his other side and caught a glimpse of a poster on the wall. That much he recognized: the great Dutch striker Marco van Basten in a bright orange jersey curving a shot into the goal mouth in the European Football Championship just two months earlier. The one thing he had found a place for in their new home.

"Please, Peter, get up now," his mother pleaded from outside the locked door.

Peter groaned and began to untangle himself from the covers. He lay on his back trying not to think about the day ahead.

"OK," he assured her, spying around the room for the clothes he was supposed to wear. Not seeing them, he lumbered out of bed and looked under a suitcase and then behind a brown corrugated mover's carton. There they were, in a heap: gray flannel trousers, white shirt, navy blazer with gold stripes, and a tie. A *tie*. A tie to go to school. With gold lions on a field of royal blue. He picked it up and shook it, as if he could persuade it to become something else. Then he dropped it on the floor again and headed for the bathroom to wash up.

"Come on, Christina. My turn," Peter told his sister through the closed door.

"You have your own bathroom," she reminded him pertly.

"Oh, yeah," he said as he slouched down the hall to a big blue-tiled bathroom with turquoise and green fish on the wallpaper. He splashed his face. He looked from under a mop of wavy blond hair, staring at his reflection, without his game face, letting his nervousness about entering a new high school show for a minute. He would have been the star striker on his soccer team at the International School of Kenya had they stayed there, but here he didn't even know if he could make the squad. He let that thought hover briefly, then told himself to lighten up. Saint Andrew's Academy had every possible sport. If he didn't make the soccer team, he could take up cricket or fencing or rugby.

But, arriving in the middle of the school year, would he find new friends? And what would it feel like being white in South Africa, a country he knew was violently divided by race? He set those thoughts aside and put his game face on.

"You're a star," he said. He flashed a self-mocking grin at the mirror as he took exaggerated bows before an imagined audience. Laugh at yourself before the others do, he told himself. It had helped him when his family had suddenly moved from the United States to Kenya four years earlier; it might work again here. The best defense is a good offense, he parroted some coach. He ran a comb under the faucet and then tried to pull it through his unruly hair. Padding back to his new bedroom to get dressed, he perked up at the scent of bacon, scrambled eggs and toast wafting from the kitchen.

Riding in the backseat of his mother's secondhand Mercedes, Peter munched on his bacon-and-egg sandwich, hastily wrapped 'to go' in a paper napkin after he showed up late at breakfast. He fidgeted in the unaccustomed uniform.

"Still wish you'd send us to the American school like in Nairobi," he told his mother one more time, as if the choice could be unmade at that late point.

"Peter, we've been through this a thousand times," Ann Seibert said as she drove south along the four-mile, unfamiliar route, looking for the turn. "The American school is halfway to Pretoria. We need to live where your dad and I can get to work. And stop talking with your mouth full."

"But look at these prissy uniforms," Peter complained, pulling one lapel to emphasize the point while clutching the remains of his breakfast in his other hand. "And girls in ties!"

"It's the only multi-racial school that takes both girls and boys and has room for the three of you. And they all require uniforms."

"Not the American school," he mumbled loudly as he wolfed down the last of his sandwich. He was resigned to his fate, but he liked trying to score points on her.

"You hate the clothes because they disguise you as a gentleman," she teased. "Besides, the sports are better here."

He had no comeback, since sports were the center of his life, so he picked at the uniform and then tickled his younger sister, Megan, to distract himself from thinking about how to fit in.

"You wrecked it," Megan wailed, looking at the purple streak across the picture she had been drawing with markers. She turned and punched her brother in the stomach.

"Now look what you've done, you little creep," he shouted back when he saw the purple streak on his shirt. Just like this pugnacious squirt in pigtails to get him started on the wrong foot, he thought.

"Your fault. Mommy, it was Peter's fault."

"Stop it, both of you. We're almost there. And Peter, wash that out as soon as you can."

The car – bright green like South African Granny Smith apples, Peter had heard his mother claim, but he thought it was gaudy – pulled through the school gate. Peter, Megan and Christina climbed out, shouldered their school bags and walked slowly toward the main administration building with their mother. He got a glimpse of the soccer field, with its crisp white lines defining the goal area and its benches for spectators. That at least looked inviting.

"Welcome to Saint Andrew's Academy, children," said Mrs. LeGrange, the school secretary.

"Thank you," Christina said, as if she were the family's official voice.

"You remember where to go?" Ann asked the girls, They nodded. She hugged them and sent them off, then pointed out a washroom for Peter.

"Cold water and soap," she recommended. "I'll pick you three up in the front parking lot after school. Take care of your little sisters, please, Peter."

"Yes, Mom," Peter said, ducking into the boys' room to escape her farewell hug. As he set to work scrubbing the purple streak out of his shirt, a tall black boy entered the lavatory. Peter noticed in the mirror that the other boy stripped off his pants, revealing a second pair in the gray flannel of the uniform trousers.

"Nice to see someone who hates these stuffy outfits as much as I do," he called out to his new schoolmate.

"What do you mean? I am proud of this uniform," the other student declared. In silence, the boy put on his white shirt, tie and striped blazer, placed his ordinary clothes neatly in his bag and walked out, holding his head up as if it bore a crown.

Peter looked in the mirror and rolled his gray-blue eyes in mock horror. What a prickly guy, he thought. In Kenya, he had heard many Africans speak stiffly in English, their second or third language. Was that it, the language difference? Or was there something else? No way to figure it out yet. He rinsed his shirt, looked around for paper towels to dry it, checked to see that his hair wasn't too badly out of place and went to his classroom.

"Good morning. I'm Mrs. Nel," his teacher said.

"Good morning," Peter replied, then remembered what his mother had coached him to add, "Ma'am."

"Pleasure to meet you. Please take the empty seat at the end of the center row, next to Sandile."

"San-DEE-lay," Peter heard. Following her directions, he found himself sitting beside the boy he had seen in the washroom. Peter grinned in greeting. Sandile offered no sign of recognition.

"Class, let's welcome our new member, Peter Seibert from America," Mrs. Nel said, rolling all the 'r's. Everyone turned to look at Peter, who stood up and took a ceremonial bow. The class laughed; the teacher tried to scowl through a smile.

"Peter, today we have an exam in maths," Mrs. Nel said, striving to recapture her audience. "I would like you to take it, even though you've just joined us. To give me an idea of your level."

What a start, Peter thought.

Adding her two small shoes to the hundreds of feet stomping in the dust, Kagiso felt like part of a many-legged creature that could not be stopped. Even the ground seemed to feel their power. As the big beast took up another song, she lent her scratchy alto to the rolling verses of *"Nkosi sikelel' iAfrika* (God Bless Africa)."

"Maluphakamis' uphondo lwayo (Let its horn be raised)," the circles of protesters sang out through the chill morning air, turning the anthem of the outlawed African National Congress from a hymn into a call to action. Kagiso listened as Palesa's luscious soprano soared over the others and Sonny Boy's bass underscored it. Then she heard T.S. somewhere behind her punctuating the song with rhythmic grunts in a voice too big and deep for his frame. She tried to ignore him. OK, he had brought her into the student movement, helped her find an outlet for her anger when she moved up to the high school, but that didn't make her his pet.

As the songs poured on and on, something else began to unsettle her. She began to notice that the air reverberated not just from their singing but also from a deeper rumble. She detected, underneath their voices, the drone of heavy machines approaching. She stood on tiptoe to see over the taller students around her who were all facing inward. Thwarted, she ducked away from Palesa and dodged among classmates to reach the edge of the group. As she popped out of the crowd, she caught her breath: four armored vehicles, Casspirs, in the South African Police colors of sickly yellow with a wide blue stripe, fast approaching across the neighborhood, crashing through shacks and backyards. She shouted and pointed frantically. The singers hesitated as more and more of them saw what was coming.

Then a few students took up the hymn again more defiantly. "*Yizwa imithandazo yethu. Nkosi sikelela. Thina lusapho lwayo.* (Listen also to our prayers. Lord, bless us. We are the family of Africa)." They rallied their classmates and prepared for battle.

Kagiso heard T.S. push his way through the crowd, shouting, "Get the rocks. Now, now, now."

She saw a group of boys obey his command and rushed to warn them, "Stop. You know they'll shoot."

The boys were bent over their work piling up jagged tan and gray rocks they found scattered in the dirt outside the school fence. They looked up at her. She could feel their gaze not on her face but on her breasts.

T.S. slung his arm around Kagiso's shoulders. "Don't listen to a scared girl," he said. "I'll take care of her."

The boys laughed as if they were not afraid.

Kagiso felt T.S.'s long fingers – warm despite the cold morning – clutch her upper arm. She quickly spun to free herself from his grasp, but she did not back off. "It's a non-violent protest," she insisted, tossing her head to show her independence – not scared in the way that T.S. meant. More excited than afraid. Part of a movement, and that made her feel invincible, even with the Casspirs coming.

"Let's move," T.S. ordered the boys.

"It's not *your* protest. It's all of us," she shouted at him, struggling to be heard over the chanting. Yes, she admitted, he was handsome. But wrong.

Lawrence and Sonny Boy and Palesa rushed to her side. Kagiso was ready to argue the point with T.S.

But the police were coming. She saw, they all saw, the Casspirs advance swiftly from the west, knocking down fences and shacks in their way.

Suddenly, Kagiso and the others heard the classmates behind them scream. They spun around to see a team of black men from the Soweto Police running out from the cover of houses east of the school and attacking the students on the edges of the protest with four-foot-long sjamboks. The young people shielded their faces as they backed away from the hippo-hide whips.

"Almal van julle huis toe gaa," they heard a bullhorn bark from a vehicle approaching from the west, demanding in Afrikaans that they all go home. Kagiso turned quickly again and saw that the Casspirs were nearly upon them, looming large. She could not see the police officers inside, but the barrels of their guns poked out through narrow horizontal windows high on the vehicles.

Kagiso could feel the many-legged creature coming apart under assault from two directions, the feet scattering, the fear rising. She wanted to rally the group, but she was surrounded by taller students, Sonny Boy and Lawrence and Palesa and T.S. and others. Hoping her voice would carry over the deafness of fear, she thrust her fist into the air and shouted, *"Amandla."*

"Awetu," came the reply from just a few.

"Amandla, she stamped and shouted, making her voice as big and deep as she could.

"Awetu," came the reply from a hundred.

The rest of the protesters quickly joined in the call-and-response, punching the air with their fists and repeating, *"amandla"* ("power") and *"awetu"* ("to the people"). Kagiso, in the thick of the crowd, urged them on.

The bullhorn blared again. *"Gaan nou of ons sal jou skiet."*

The students understood the order to disperse or be shot, but they were united again in defiance.

T.S. stepped out in front of the group, faced the vehicles and shouted, "*Viva*, Comrade Nelson Mandela. *Viva.*" Kagiso and Palesa and all the other students quickly took up the salute, although they knew the government had made it a crime to mention the name of the imprisoned African National Congress leader. There was urgency in their voices because he had just been moved from prison to a hospital. They chanted the names of other ANC leaders – Walter Sisulu, Oliver Tambo, Govan Mbeki. The protesters taunted the police. They were electrified and strong together, despite the weapons in front of them.

Still encircled, they heard the pops as the police launched tear gas and the hiss as the canisters released vile plumes. Protesters began to choke and cough and cry. Kagiso held her breath and closed her eyes as she hunted for her bandana. Not finding it, she pulled the neck of her red T-shirt up over her nose and mouth. Palesa tied a handkerchief over her face. Others pulled up scarves or collars.

The students tried to hold their ground in the confusion and the swirl of tear gas and dust, but the group gave way, backing up to the school fence as the Soweto Police advanced on foot in front and the South African Police vehicles rolled forward on each side to box them in. The foot patrol beat the trapped students, girls as well as boys, lashing them with whips and cracking them on the head with sticks until blood ran down some of their faces.

Kagiso dodged and ducked; still, the whip caught her more than once, a hot flash of pain running through her back and legs as it stung her even through thick clothing. Spotting an escape route, she pulled Palesa down to the ground with her to wriggle under the V-shaped belly of a Casspir, which rode high on big tires. A policeman beat them on the legs and tried to pull them back, but Kagiso and Palesa and other students who had followed them clung onto wheels, axels, any handhold to pull themselves through.

"Come under," Kagiso shouted back to students trapped and screaming on the other side as she grabbed the hands of those who were on their bellies squirming beneath the Casspirs.

"Help me," shouted Sonny Boy, who was big and struggling to get through with a policeman pulling him backward by the ankles. Kagiso and Lawrence dragged him to safety. The legs of his pants were torn and spattered with blood.

T.S., skinny but strong, got under easily. He stood up on the other side and called for a counter-attack.

"The rocks. Throw them," he barked at his lieutenants.

Kagiso braced for worse trouble as they followed his command, targeting the Soweto Police on foot, hitting a few officers and diverting police attention from the students under the vehicles.

The foot patrol whirled and came after the rock throwers, who ran away. The Casspirs revved their engines. Students scurried from underneath just before the vehicles began to move. Kagiso watched in horror as the bristling guns fired at the rock throwers, who were darting among houses. She saw a boy trip and a vehicle nearly roll over him. The rock throwers fled through a pocket of tightly packed concrete bungalows where the Casspirs could not pass. Their fallen comrade fell into police hands. She could not see whether anyone had been shot.

Kagiso and Palesa and the other escapees scattered, running hard, but stopping a short distance away to catch their breath, regroup in clusters and belt out "*Nkosi Sikelel' iAfrica*" to antagonize the remaining police.

Surrounded once more by classmates, Kagiso shivered with excitement.

"We showed them," she shouted.

"*A luta continua,*" Palesa responded.

As the police departed, the students began to chant again, not wanting to let go of the moment.

Later, the excitement eased, and Kagiso began to feel the pain in her legs where whips had struck her and to feel the gouges in her hands from grabbing the metal underbelly of the Casspir. She saw that her sweater was torn, buttons were missing and her clothes were covered with dust. Palesa was coated in dust, too, and her jeans were speckled with someone else's blood. They headed home to clean up so that their parents wouldn't see that they had been at the protest.

At lunch time, Peter followed his new classmates to a dining hall with a lofty ceiling, wood paneled walls and pointed windows like a cathedral. Standing in the cafeteria line, he eyed steam trays of roast beef and mashed potatoes.

"Come join us," a white boy told him, speaking with a vaguely British accent. "I'm Tom. This is Vusi." Tom pointed to a black classmate who smiled and shook hands with Peter. "You play football?" Tom said as he sized Peter up.

"Soccer?"

"Of course. None of that American stuff," Tom sniffed. They headed to a long wooden table where Sandile was tucking into his meal. "You've already met our star sweeper," Tom added, pointing to Sandile.

Peter nodded at Sandile but got no reaction.

"And that's Andre Malan," Tom said, pointing to a stocky student at the far end of the table. "Poor sap plays rugby instead," he added in a loud voice.

Peter wondered about the way Tom took charge. Must be class president or soccer team captain or something. Vusi and Tom quizzed Peter about America; he didn't want to disappoint them by admitting that he wasn't up on celebrity gossip and hadn't spent much time in the U.S. since he was eleven. So he repeated a few things he had read about.

"Yeah, so in California there's this place with lots of empty swimming pools, like a swimming pool store that closed, and the surfer guys got skateboards and went in there and invented new moves. They come straight up the sides," he explained, using his hands to show how they did 180-turns above the lip of the pool.

His listeners were rapt. Of course, he had only seen it in a magazine, so he covered up by asking them a question. "Say, I want to learn rugby."

"South African Springboks are best in the world," Andre bragged from several seats away.

Peter decided not to mention that South Africa was banned from the Rugby World Cup because of its racist apartheid system. The way Andre rolled his 'r's made Peter wonder if he was an Afrikaner, and the boy looked beefy enough to bulldoze his way through a scrum. Instead, he said, "So, there's this funny fashion in the States where everyone's wearing rugby shirts but nobody actually knows how to play."

The students laughed. Andre said he could teach Peter the game.

"Football starts next week," Tom countered.

Peter crossed his fingers in hopes of making the team. He felt he'd been a fraud so far in the chatter with these new classmates. Something wrong here, he thought. You don't get included just like that.

The bell rang and they returned to class for lessons in Afrikaans, which Peter found out was the language that Dutch colonizers of South Africa had developed. He used the period for concentrated daydreaming. He was more than ready to go home and get out of the uniform by the time his mother came to pick them up.

"Shotgun," he called to claim the front passenger seat. He outraced his sisters to the car.

When their mother asked about their day, the girls dutifully described their teachers and classmates.

"Well, I've had a big day, too," Ann said as she drove them home. "I've been at protests all morning. Thousands of high school students on strike all over Soweto. I was in Orlando West, near Mandela's house." Then quietly, so Peter would hear but his little sisters in the back seat would not, she added, "The police attacked them from armored vehicles. Dozens arrested and many badly beaten, though no deaths reported so far."

And then she said to all, "I called my editor. He wants the story. So, I'll have to drop you and rush downtown to file."

"Cool you got a story," Peter said, sounding upbeat to mask his feelings. He was too big to admit to her or to himself that he would have liked her to be with them that first afternoon. "What're they protesting?"

"Sixty kids in a class. History lessons that claim the country was empty when whites arrived, so blacks are not citizens," his mother said.

Peter felt guilty for complaining about his new school, but glad it had some black students at least. Maybe he could even make friends with them, if Vusi and the others weren't as stuck up at Sandile seemed to be.

"So, we haven't heard about your day, Peter."

"I was the center of attention," he joked, with the tip of an imaginary hat.

"Aren't you always?"

When they reached their new home, Peter, Megan and Christina crossed the freshly mowed lawn on a wide slate path as their mother sped off.

"Hello, children. How was your first day?" Ellen Dlamini greeted them, her arms stretched wide to hug the girls.

"Fine, Mrs. Dlamini," Peter said, cheered by this woman who had come to work for them only days before.

"Call me Ellen. It's easier."

"Mom says it's rude for us to call you by your first name," Christina informed her of the rules.

"But 'Mrs. Dlamini' is too formal. You could call me 'Auntie' or 'Auntie Ellen.' Perhaps your mother won't mind that."

They followed her into the kitchen where the aroma of freshly baked cookies perfumed the air. She served them all at the breakfast table in the long, sunny kitchen and listened to their stories as they ate.

"Your mother said to ask if you have any lessons to do," Ellen said as she cleared the table after their snack.

"Later, Mrs. Dlamini. I mean Auntie," Peter replied.

"Beat you at tennis," Christina challenged Peter.

"I'm playing, too," Megan added.

"Last one out is dead meat," Peter shouted as he ran to his room to change into shorts and a T-shirt, collect his racket and head to the tennis court in the backyard. For him, it was the perfect way to put off thinking about the challenges of his new school.

Sandile climbed the footbridge from Baragwanath Hospital back over Potchefstroom Road. He walked a mile and a half north through the neighborhoods of Soweto, watching for comrades but not expecting any in the late afternoon.

"Hello, Mama," he said as he entered his old home, the one-story orange house that his parents had transformed into the only real grocery store in eastern Soweto.

Grace turned from her work directing shop assistants who were stacking supplies.

"You're back safe. Did you see my mother?"

"For sure."

"And?"

"Sitting up now and then." Better than last week, he thought with a heavy heart, but not by much.

"Thank the Lord," his mother said, pausing for a long moment with her hands pressed together in front of her lips.

Then she added, "George is getting his car repaired. Would you please take a box to Josephat Dube's?"

Sandile nodded. He chose an empty carton and filled it with supplies – a large bag of cornmeal, a big pumpkin, dried beans, margarine, cooking oil, two loaves of bread, powdered milk, sugar, tea, and two boxes of chocolate cookies for the six Dube children, who had been hungry since their father lost his job. He hoisted the box onto his left shoulder, walked the few blocks to the two-room shack the Dube family rented in the backyard of another house and knocked on the door.

Ezekiel Dube, the eldest child and about Sandile's age, said nothing when he opened the door for Sandile. His brothers and sisters cheered and danced around Sandile as he set the box on a rough table. Ezekiel chased them away, keeping the cookies out of their sight.

Sandile felt Ezekiel's silent stare as an accusation, as if it were his fault that his own family was comfortable while Josephat Dube was out of work. He couldn't decide which was worse, Ezekiel's anger or Josephat's humiliating gratitude when he was home to receive a delivery. His own father would never abandon the Dubes who had found him a room to rent when he first arrived in Soweto to look for work. Sandile sighed and tried to shake off his discomfort as he headed back to the store, picked up his school bag and went to the office in what had once been his bedroom.

"*Kunjani, Tata,*" he greeted his father in Xhosa.

"Hello, son," Stephen Malindi replied, looking up from his papers. He stood, clasped his younger son in a bear hug and pulled up a chair so they could sit together at the big, cluttered desk. He adjusted the pistol tucked into his belt as he sat down to continue checking the store's finances.

Sandile delved into his homework on quadratic equations, the history of South Africa's colonization and Shakespeare's "Romeo and Juliet" before going out to work the cash register. The wave of commuters stopping to buy cornmeal, tea, bread, soap and a little meat or vegetables on their way home from work kept him busy for most of the evening.

When sales calmed down, he went to talk with Abel, a new shop assistant. He had seen the man stack cans and boxes upside down.

"Let me show you," he said as he found the man unloading canned tomatoes.

Abel looked up, surprised, nervous.

Sandile squatted next to him. "You take your tins and put them like this. Do you know why?" he asked as he turned the can right side up.

Abel said nothing.

"Can you read the words?"

No reply.

"May I teach you?"

Abel remained silent.

George walked into the store, laughing as he called out, "Greetings, everyone."

"Maybe another day," Sandile said to the assistant. "You let me know. *Yebo* (Yes)?" He walked over to hug his brother, who smelled of beer.

Stephen Malindi came out of the office so that he and George could close up for the evening. Sandile asked his father once again if he could stay with them to guard the shop that night.

"Not after your grandmother. George and I will…"

"But I want to help catch the *tsostis* who shot her."

"I have other plans for you."

Sandile knew his father's word was final. But he felt crushed. He wanted to be treated like a young man, not a schoolboy. At fifteen, he was five years younger than his brother, but taller and a better athlete. Of course, George had their father's gift for gathering friends around him. Sandile thought of himself as reserved and serious. But didn't that add to his qualifications? It made no sense to him why he wasn't allowed to help protect his family.

He wished he could go back to Baragwanath and talk to his grandmother, the only one in the family who really listened to him. She would have heard him out, guided him through. A traditional healer, she had the wisdom of the ancestors to share. But she was lying in a hospital bed and struggling to breathe. And he was headed to an empty house to spend another night alone.

While cooking supper for her family, Kagiso heard a knock at the door.

"It's me," Palesa said softly from outside.

Kagiso unlocked the door and went out.

"They came for him," Palesa whispered.

Kagiso understood: the police were after T.S. The girls left out specifics because their secrets were at risk from busybodies and informers and strict parents. "Did they take him?"

"No. He wasn't home. Broke down the door. Grabbed his brother. Said they would take him to John Vorster. His mother pushed them out."

Kagiso winced at the thought. She knew how protective T.S. was of his younger brother. "Know where he is?" she asked.

"No. But he can hide."

Kagiso nodded.

"What if they come for you?"

"Me?" Kagiso asked, surprised. "Don't think they saw me. I'm so short."

Palesa shrugged her shoulders. "Not even the red shirt?"

"They take the boys," Kagiso replied, though she wondered if that made her safe.

Palesa touched her hand and then left.

On the stoop, alone for the first time that day, Kagiso shuddered to think that T.S. could be taken to the infamous police headquarters at John Vorster Square or even to a Soweto police station. That scared her right through. She remembered the warmth of his hand on her shoulder. Then she remembered her cry of "*amandla.*" She tried to dismiss any thought that she, too, might be marked.

September 1988

The sound of breaking glass woke Kagiso at two o'clock in the morning. She sat straight up in bed and peeked out the window, fearful that the police had come for her.

"*TSWAYA!*" a woman ordered from ten feet away, in the house next door. A man shouted back at her, slurring his threats and knocking things around.

Danger, but not for her, Kagiso realized. Another drunken fight in the shebeen. No matter how many times her mother had begged their neighbor to stop selling liquor, the woman kept on because she had no job and four children. There was always trouble.

Kagiso lay down again and pulled the blanket up to her chin and over her sister's shoulders. She tried to go back to sleep, but it was no use. She wanted to shout at them to stop the noise. She wanted to smash the racist system that kept her neighbor poor. Images of all that was wrong with Soweto, with South Africa, flipped through her mind like photos in a magazine. She clenched her fists in frustration.

At least the students were doing everything they could to protest.

But thoughts of school led to thoughts of the student the police had killed three days earlier: Sipho. She hadn't known him well. He was a class ahead of her. Small for his age, with a sweet tenor voice that she remembered from his solos in church. But he was really dead, shot in his own home. The police said he had pointed a gun at them. His mother said he never had one. The whole school was going to his funeral later that day. They would sing. They would dance defiantly in front of the police. They would not be able to bring him back.

Kagiso felt hot tears run down her temples as she lay on her back. The noise next door had not awakened Tiny or Mike, who snored like a person much bigger than he was. It was a rare moment when Kagiso had the house to herself, in a sense. But that was not how she wanted to be alone. It was not private; it was lonely. She wiped her tears and turned to cuddle with Tiny in their shared bed.

As the little girl turned over, she unclenched her fist. Kagiso saw that her sister had taken the red-and-white beaded earrings to bed with her. She pried her favorite earrings out of Tiny's hand. She got up and tucked them in a new hiding place inside a red sock that had lost its partner and put it in the back of her drawer in the bureau they all shared. Then she opened Tiny's drawer and pulled out her sister's T-shirt featuring Hello, Kitty with a red bow. She concealed it in a fashionable oversized green shirt her mother had brought her from the garment factory, a shirt she would never wear because she thought it made her look chubby, and hid the two shirts in her own drawer. Satisfied, she crawled back into bed and fell asleep.

Kagiso kept telling herself that she didn't mind shopping for her mother. It was normal for parents to send their children on errands on Saturday mornings. The streets were full of young people scurrying off to make purchases or dallying instead of doing what they'd been told or meeting up with friends along the path. Besides, she knew how hard her mother worked at the factory bent over a sewing machine stitching uniforms.

No, it wasn't the idea of errands, it was the particular errands. Her mother wanted things that weren't sold at any of the nearby informal shops in the front rooms of people's tiny homes. No, her mother wanted a particular brand of skin cream, a certain kind of tinned sardines, a decent piece of beef for her father's dinner, even though there wasn't enough money for anyone else in the family to have beef, and two cans of her father's favorite snack – *phane*. The very idea of buying *phane* made her skin crawl, even though the four-inch long caterpillars inside the cans would be dead. She could hear her father's voice praising them as full of protein and very nutritious, whether stewed with vegetables or served dry and crispy. He said they were real African food, that they tasted of his childhood home in Bophuthatswana. But to Kagiso, Soweto was home and eating bugs was disgusting.

With a shopping list like that, there was only one place for her to go: the big store in Orlando East. And that was the other problem. She needed to finish these errands quickly so that she could join her classmates at the funeral for Sipho, at Regina Mundi Church, four miles west of her home. To save time, she had dressed for the funeral already in black jeans and a dolman-sleeved sweater in goldenrod. She hurried along the one-mile route north into Orlando East, greeting friends quickly along the road, not stopping to chat.

Kagiso reached the store and made her way among the many Saturday customers inside. Searching the aisles, she turned a corner and stopped short, looking up at a boy she didn't know. Dressed in new blue jeans and a maroon polo shirt, he was instructing a shop assistant to read the labels aloud, as if the man were illiterate. She was shocked to hear a boy speak that way to a man twice his age. Was he the owner's son? She looked at him a little too long, staring at the side of his buzz-cut head. He turned and looked straight at her, a long angular face with flared nostrils and thick arching brows. He just looked, unblinking, unreadable, a mask. She turned quickly and went into another aisle.

Kagiso finally found the sardines – pilchards, she called them – paid for all the goods and headed home with her bundles. While she was fishing in her jeans pocket for the front door key, she heard a voice she thought she recognized.

"Fine. Just fine. Even tries to help with housework. Gets in the way. But it is better to work for Americans."

Kagiso hoped it was her mother's older sister who had come to visit. She was about to enter when she heard her mother speak.

"I am very much worried for Kagiso. She is getting into politics."

Kagiso waited to hear more.

"What has she done?"

"That's it. I don't know. She's always out."

"She's clever. She will not go wrong. Our children are going to make us free."

Then Kagiso knew for sure it was her favorite aunt and smiled to hear Ellen Dlamini defend her.

"Humph," Kagiso's mother said. "Too clever. Her father will stop her."

Alarmed, Kagiso wanted to hear more, but she was already running late. She opened the front door and acted as if she had heard nothing.

"Dumela," she greeted Ellen, bowing respectfully so her aunt could pat her on the head.

"Ahe," Ellen replied.

Kagiso saw her mother fold her arms across her chest, bunching up the sleeves of the bathrobe she still wore at midday. Given what her mother had just said, Kagiso read it as an assertion of authority. She took the parcels to the kitchen, where she put the sardines, beauty cream and *phane* on the table, and the packet of beef in the tiny refrigerator. She stepped out the back door to wash up, moving quietly so as not to attract the attention of her father, who was working with his brother Amos on an addition to the house. As she came through the front room again, she spoke to Ellen.

"Auntie, I am very much happy to see you, but I have to run. Will I see you later?"

"I have made my bed," Ellen said, gesturing toward the sofa where she usually slept on visits to her sister's house.

"Where are you going?" Sally demanded.

"Just out with friends," Kagiso answered, trying to sound nonchalant.

"I do not want you to go to Regina Mundi."

Instead of answering, Kagiso opened the door and looked out impatiently.

"They're here," she said and left.

Her friends were not at the door. She hurried to meet them at Palesa's shack so they could go as a group to Sipho's funeral. Kagiso, Palesa, Lawrence and Sonny Boy walked together through the streets of Soweto under a bright sun that did not lighten their spirits.

By the time they reached the modern wooden church, it was ringed by Casspirs carrying white policemen and by Soweto Police in their pickup trucks with grills over the windows. Kagiso sucked in her breath at the sight. No matter how many times they had done this, there was always a clutch of fear at the start. Passing single file between security vehicles, the four friends reached the church entrance just as township leaders and foreign diplomats in expensive suits began to lead the congregation inside. Hundreds of students filled the pews behind the dignitaries.

Members of Sipho's choir sang hymns from the steps in front of the altar. Kagiso imagined she could hear his pure voice emerge from their song. When she couldn't bear the thought of it any longer, she leaned close to talk with Palesa about anything else. The boys in the pews around them stomped in place and grunted in unison.

With her heart heavy, like a weight pulling her under, Kagiso watched the ritual begin: A group of priests and ministers, some in white cassocks over black pants, others in black suits and black shirts with their clerical colors stiff around their necks, swooped in the main entrance. Behind them came Sipho's father and his mother, held up by her husband and one of her remaining sons, another son and three daughters, all in new suits and dresses.

The choir began to sing "Amazing Grace." The congregation joined them; it seemed to Kagiso to be the best way to keep from crying. They sang seven verses as the procession moved slowly up the main aisle and into the space behind the communion rail. It was especially sad, she thought, that they all knew this routine so well.

Bars of sunlight streaked with the colors of the stained glass windows seemed to poke into the somber crowd. She listened as the ministers and priests proceeded through prayers and eulogies and hymns, blessing the silver coffin with the white roses perched on top. They did not mention politics or police shootings; they did not need to.

When the service ended and the pall bearers carried the coffin toward the door, the choir sang "Ave Maria." Kagiso and the other students stood and sang, their voices mingling with the whole congregation, but their thoughts leaping ahead to the coming confrontation with the police who surrounded the church.

Once the family and the religious leaders had passed through the doorway, many of the young men waiting inside the church began to stomp again, pumping up their courage. Kagiso could see through the wide doors that the Soweto police had emerged from their trucks and the white police were readying tear gas canisters. She and her friends and classmates launched into *"Nkosi Sikelel' iAfrika."* She could feel the tension as the crowd ahead of her pushed up against the black police, who stood shoulder to shoulder, guns drawn, and gave no ground.

Kagiso sensed the hard eyes of the police on them all as they filed out. The officers who had killed Sipho were sure to be right there at his funeral, neither to mourn him nor to regret their terrible deed but rather to intimidate his friends and family. That thought turned her heart cold.

The police won't fire yet, she reminded herself; too many diplomats and journalists watching. They would wait until after the graveside gathering, after the dignitaries and photographers had left and the students had moved onward to Sipho's parents' home for the funeral meal. She felt guilty about having to abandon her friends before that point, but also worried because she was under her parents' surveillance. When the students began to board the buses that would take them to the cemetery, Kagiso said farewell to Palesa and the others, then hurried back to her house.

Sandile was about to take his seat in class on Monday morning when Mrs. Nel approached him with Peter in tow.

"Good morning, Sandile," she said.

"Good morning, Mrs. Nel." He tried always to be polite, but he couldn't bring himself to say "ma'am" or "sir," as if he were a servant.

"The history exam is next week," she said, "and I'd like you to help Peter catch up."

Sandile understood it as an assignment, not a suggestion. He gave Peter a hard glance but tried not to let the teacher see. He hoped he had been chosen merely because his grades were good and not as some sort of test. "Yes, of course, Mrs. Nel," he replied.

"And please help him in maths, too."

"I will."

During the study period later that day, Peter took a seat next to Sandile and said, "You can be glad I know more about Africa than most Americans. I can find it on a map."

Sandile figured it was meant as a joke, but he didn't find it amusing to think white people knew little about Africa. Without replying, he opened the South African history text-book to that week's lesson: a long series of wars in the 1800s in which European settlers conquered the Xhosa people and claimed their lands along the Indian Ocean.

"I don't get it," Peter told Sandile. "How come the Xhosa – how do you say that again? KOH-sah? – just committed suicide by killing their cattle instead of fighting the settlers?"

"It was not suicide," Sandile retorted, defending his ancestors. "They were determined to drive out the colonialists and believed that the sacrifice of cattle would make them invincible."

"That's silly."

"No. It is a strategy that failed. Like the Crusades." Sandile hated this chapter more than any other in South African history, not only for his ancestors' defeat but also for the mockery of their beliefs. To him, Peter was just one more white who looked down on blacks, on Africans, without trying to comprehend.

"But, if there were all these battles, why do whites say the country was empty when they arrived?" Peter asked.

"To justify apartheid," Sandile said, thinking that the point was obvious: false history to explain racism. He was unwilling to credit Peter at least for probing. He returned to the text to get this lesson over with.

"Sandile, how come you don't join the township strikes?"

Sandile narrowed his eyes to slits. He tried out replies in his mind: that the strikers had no right to force him, that he would not be bullied, that he was working for freedom, too, that he was meant to be a leader. He didn't want to go into any of those explanations with someone he barely knew. Finally, he replied through almost clenched teeth, "That is Soweto; I am here."

"But my parents say the high school boys, the ones into politics – the ones they call comrades? – beat up strike breakers."

"How would they know?"

"My mom's a news reporter and my father works for a charity, so …"

"There have been troubles," Sandile allowed, trying to cut off the exchange.

"Don't you support the boycott?"

"We will not liberate ourselves by ignorance," Sandile said, deliberately reversing the slogan of the student movement. He spoke as coldly as he could to make it clear the subject was closed.

He wanted to stalk off. Instead, shackled by Mrs. Nel's assignment, he opened the math textbook to the day's assignment.

"Yeah, I could use the help," Peter admitted.

As they finished the study session, Peter asked, "Show me which field the soccer's on, OK?"

"I thought Americans only played baseball and that other kind of football."

"Some of us play soccer, too. Besides, I went to school in Kenya and that's about all they play there."

Sandile bristled. Playing soccer was the one luxury he allowed himself, the one time when he could be at peace, without having to explain himself to anyone. And here was this oaf trying to barge onto his team.

Peter sat on a bench in the locker room to put on his soccer cleats, wrapping the long laces underneath and tying them on top in double knots. He could hear Vusi and Tom joking on the other side of the room. But he had made Sandile angry by asking questions meant to show an interest in African cultures and township troubles. That perplexed him. Wish we'd stayed in Kenya, he thought. He would miss the annual high school trip – a week with Maasai warriors hiking through the savannah and hoping, or fearing, that they would see wild animals. Instead, he was here in this hostile environment.

He watched in silence as Sandile, at the other end of the bench, stomped his feet into his soccer cleats and laced them so tightly it looked painful. Peter secretly studied his classmate – long, angular features made more prominent by the shortness of his hair, nostrils perpetually flared as if in judgment, a broad mouth he had yet to see smile.

When Peter trotted out to the field, Coach Haverford asked what position he liked to play. "Striker," he replied, "or anywhere you want me. Sir."

As the coach ran them all through drills – dribbling around cones, taking corner kicks and penalty shots, running laps – Peter strived to earn a spot on the squad. Then the coach split them into teams for a practice game, making Sandile the sweeper on one side and Peter a striker on the other.

Peter saw that Sandile, so stiff in the classroom, came alive on the field – directing the defense, boldly confronting attackers, making powerful and precise clearing kicks to launch his team's offense. Inspired by the challenge, Peter ran his heart out – sending cross after cross through the penalty area, masterfully dribbling past other defenders, squaring off against Sandile. The game became a test of wills, an epic struggle between personalities, although there was no trophy, no official score. It was just a scrimmage.

At the end, they were both exhausted. Sandile walked up to Peter, smiling for the first time, and declared, "Good to know you're on our side against Redhill next week."

"Thanks," Peter puffed.

After showering and changing, all the players waited in the parking lot. Parents drove up to collect one student after another until only Peter and Sandile were left.

"How're you getting home?" Peter asked.

"My brother fetches me."

"My mom must be working," Peter mused as darkness crept over the school grounds. "She always forgets us when she's on a news story."

Finally, Ann Seibert wheeled the old green Mercedes through the gate, opened the window and called out, "Hi, Peter. Sorry I'm late. How was the practice?"

"Fun," Peter said, exasperated but not wanting to argue with her in front of his classmate. "Can we give Sandile a ride? His brother's even later than you are."

"Of course."

"I am not stranded for transport," Sandile declared.

"It's no trouble. Where do you live?" Peter's mother persisted.

"Diepkloof Extension."

"Where's that?"

"Next to Soweto."

"OK. Let's go."

"No, thank you. If you take me into town, I can make my way."

"All right. But you better call and see if he's on his way."

Peter and his mother waited while Sandile went to the pay phone outside the school office.

"I'm glad to see you're making friends," she said.

"I don't really know if he's a friend."

Careful not to catch any splinters, Kagiso slid onto the wooden bench at the crooked desk she and Palesa shared throughout the school year. She looked in disgust at the decrepit place – walls pocked by crumbling paint, windows opaque with grime, tattered textbooks to be shared. The lesson was about Mafikeng. Or rather, a lie about Mafikeng, Kagiso fumed. The history textbook focused only on the British soldiers who outlasted a 217-day siege by Afrikaner forces in 1899. Stuff of legend to the British. But the town was the capital of the Tswana people's land.

Kagiso raised her hand. She had to make a point. "What about the Tswana people?"

Mrs. Ndlovu gave her a long, pained look. "This is the part of the story you all need to know for the exam."

Kagiso felt bad to have put her favorite teacher on the spot, but she had to raise the issue. She wished she could go to university and become a history teacher so that she could correct all these lies with the harsh truth of conquest and injustice. Every time her father took them to visit family, it reminded her that the Tswana people were pawns of apartheid, living under a dictator chosen by the South African government.

Kagiso squirmed on the bench, then felt a splinter stab her thigh. That brought her back to the task at hand – learning the lies of history well enough to master the exams, without letting them seep into her soul.

With T.S. on the run from the police, Kagiso and her classmates decided it was safer not to call a big student meeting but to gather in small numbers in separate places. Each group would debate the next steps and then choose a representative to go to an executive meeting.

Kagiso and Palesa and Lawrence and other students assembled after school in the shed behind Sonny Boy's house, arriving in pairs or one-by-one, so as not to call attention to the gathering. Kagiso relaxed in this shed stacked with broken chairs and tables that Sonny Boy's father planned to fix for neighbors in the evenings after work. She liked the sense of purpose, and the shelter from her parents' suspicions.

Still in their uniforms, the students perched on two rough saw horses or leaned against the walls, careful not to dislodge

---

the saw, screwdrivers, hammer and rasp hanging on nails, each outlined to show its proper location. The boys joked around, pushing each other off the end of a saw horse. Then Sonny Boy stood up and called the meeting to order. The agenda: What form should the next protest take? He sat down.

Lawrence quietly called for a student strike in more townships around the country.

"Liberation before education," one of the girls added, as if a slogan explained everything.

"We need a stay away," Sonny Boy said a little too loudly, then dropped his voice to be more discreet, "so all the parents strike, too."

"Burn the houses of the collaborators," a boy named Zwele insisted.

"Burn the collaborators," another boy, Thabo, urged in a muffled shout. He leaned back, arms folded across his stocky chest as if he were in charge of the meeting.

Kagiso was startled. She had never seen either of them at a meeting before, and she hated their ideas.

Lawrence tried to stand his ground, calling for non-violent action.

Zwele lunged at him, his pointy chin thrust forward as a threat. "You sell-out."

"Doctor Motlana says…" Kagiso asserted before she was drowned out by boys who shouted, "Leave the old people out…" and then argued among themselves over which township councilors to attack.

Palesa warned, "Shhhhh. Talk soft."

"One settler, one bullet."

"Don't talk shit here."

"Stop," Kagiso begged, struggling to halt the barrage of insults spilling out in simplified Zulu with swear words in

English, bits and pieces of manifestos, interruptions. The argument spun on.

Because of Sipho's death, they were nervous. She even admitted to herself that she was a little scared, and deeply angry. Better to wait until all the students had let their feelings out, she reasoned; then they could make a real plan.

Eventually, Sonny Boy stood up again, his big frame seeming to fill the small shed. Acting as host and moderator, he raised his arms to hush them. "OK. We heard from everyone," he said. "Now, we must work together." He summarized the proposals and said they could take turns calmly presenting their reasons.

The arsonists insisted on revenge for the students killed. They wanted to make the townships ungovernable.

Their opponents agreed on the goal, but they argued that violence gave the police excuses to kill and torture more of them, and non-violent resistance gave the protesters the upper hand.

"Think of Madiba," Kagiso advised, referring to Nelson Mandela by his clan name.

"Think of MK," Zwele said. They all knew he meant Umkhonto weSizwe, the armed wing of the African National Congress.

"That's for trained fighters, not students," Kagiso countered.

Zwele patted his chest as if claiming to be a guerrilla.

She assumed he was just bragging. "We need to be disciplined," she insisted. "We need a clear plan. Start with a bigger school boycott, like Lawrence said. Later a ..."

"Lawrence is a coward," Zwele charged.

"You're the fucking coward," Lawrence shouted as he jumped up to go after his accuser.

"Fuck you."

Sonny Boy held them apart but argued Lawrence's side, saying it takes courage to hold a position without using violence.

Zwele did not buy it. He rocked on the saw horse as if he were about to leap at Lawrence.

"We are sitting with all these problems, and you attack a comrade?" Kagiso demanded, shaking her finger in Zwele's face.

Looming large over the group in his black sweater and pants, Sonny Boy steered the argument back to the main points. They went through the debate several more times. The arsonists calmed down enough for the group to agree on a school boycott first, with a possible general strike later. The group discussed ways to get students across the country to join. Kagiso said she could ask for help from a party leader she sometimes saw when she volunteered at a community childcare center. The arsonists refused to vote, but the rest of the group selected her and Sonny Boy to take their ideas to the executive meeting.

"Comrades, *amandla*," she saluted in a whisper before they split up.

"*Awetu*," they replied in hushed tones before they dispersed across the township.

Kagiso and Palesa left together, shaking their heads over the argument.

"Poor Lawrence," Palesa said.

"I'm telling you, that boy is stupid," Kagiso said of the accuser.

"But Lawrence takes things serious."

"You like him, don't you?"

Palesa averted her eyes.

Seeing her friend's bashful response, Kagiso didn't push the issue. "I'm going to the crèche," she said, pointing to where their paths diverged. "Tomorrow?"

They waved goodbye.

The sight of the child-care center lifted Kagiso's mood. The abandoned public bus, light blue like the rest of the fleet, sat parked on its axles next to the community-run health clinic. Wire fencing stretched around the playground swings donated by charities. The sounds of children's laughter poured out into the township.

Kagiso had loved this "crèche" when she was a child and her mother dropped her off on the way to work. In her imagination, the bus had taken them on magical trips, despite its lack of wheels – or maybe because it didn't run on roads. She wondered how many times she had come back since she graduated into government schools – first to collect her brother and sister, and later to volunteer whenever she could.

As she climbed the steps into the bus, the children's singing was deafening in that small space. After shouting 'hello' to Mrs. Van der Merwe, a white retired school teacher who also volunteered, Kagiso greeted each child with a gentle pat on the head and a big smile, then squatted next to the makeshift desks to help them color or count or write while their parents were at work.

She thought of how T.S. had often followed her to the crèche and felt glad he wasn't around. But thinking that way when he was in danger made her feel guilty. She was grateful he had brought her into politics. And he really was handsome, she admitted, just not the guy for her.

In the early evening, Kagiso walked home to make dinner on the coal-fired stove that provided the only heat for the four small rooms of her house. She assembled her ingredients on the kitchen table: a sack of cornmeal, beef bones wrapped in paper, two bunches of carrots, four fat onions and a pumpkin. Next, she needed a salt shaker and a skinny bottle of piri-piri hot sauce that sat close to the *phane* on one of the two shelves. She took a rough cutting board from a nail on the wall and two sharp knives from the one drawer in the table.

Standing over the pumpkin and using the ten-inch knife, she pressed with all her force to cut down through the hard golden flesh. She scooped out the seeds and saved them to be roasted. With the six-inch knife, she swiftly removed the white peel from the pumpkin, peeled the carrots and the onions, then returned to the big knife, rocking it back and forth to chop the onions into a fine mince, the carrots into slices and the pumpkin into one-inch cubes.

Humming "Let me Be Free," a favorite song by Yvonne Chaka Chaka, Kagiso stepped out the rear door to fill a bucket at the tap next to the bathroom. Back in the kitchen, she took out two big pots, poured a bit of oil into one and began to cook the onions. She practiced a dance step as she waited for the onions to turn golden. Then she added water, pumpkin, carrots and beef bones to simmer slowly for an hour. She filled the other pot with water and set it near the back of the stove to warm until it was needed to make the cornmeal into porridge.

Kagiso checked on her brother and sister, who lounged across unmatched armchairs in the living-and-dining room as they watched Inspector Gadget cartoons or whatever was on television, in English, Afrikaans, Zulu or Setswana. She sent Mike and Tiny out to buy bread for the next day's breakfast at a nearby shop. When they returned, she coached them through their homework and worked on her own. The math was easy for her; so was the English homework. But the history made her angry again, especially the map of "native reserves" to which Africans had been confined. Still, she made herself learn it.

The three of them waited for their father to wake up or their mother to come home from work.

Returning to the kitchen, Kagiso scooped a portion of the stew into a separate pot for Mike, who didn't like spicy food, and poured a large dose of piri-piri sauce into the main pot. Tasting the broth, she smacked her lips and added a bit more piri-piri. She stoked the coal fire, then ran back to the living room when she heard Brenda and the Big Dudes on television singing "Izolabud."

Patrick Mafolo emerged from his bedroom, yawning and stretching his body-builder arms as he prepared to work another night shift at the hotel garage.

"*Dumela, Baba*," Kagiso addressed her father respectfully.

"I heard there was more trouble yesterday."

"Oh?" she answered as if she were unaware.

"Comrades hitting workers."

"Did you see it?" she asked, not wanting to start another argument, not wanting to leave his claim unchallenged. She was confident that she and the other students were fighting for everyone's freedom. She wished her parents would try to understand and to help. "Maybe that's what the authorities...."

He bent down so he could look her straight in the eyes.

"Do not join protests," he warned.

"I was at the crèche," she said as she turned to go back to the kitchen to check on the meal.

"You will not walk away when I am speaking," he commanded.

She turned in the doorway and waited, her face as innocent as she could make it.

"You're a smart girl," he said, standing tall and talking from above her, "but you don't see. You were a baby when we brought you here. You didn't see the riots."

She waited through a lecture she had heard before. He always talked about how the police shot three students during a peaceful protest, how that ignited riots that spread across the country, killing hundreds of young people, driving thousands into exile. The Soweto Uprising of 1976, the year after her family moved to the township. She knew her father would remind her that he did everything to protect his family from the violence.

She didn't trust protection, however well intended. It was his inability to protect her that had driven her into the protest movement. She wanted to stand up for herself. She believed it was he who could not see that these strikes were going to change the system.

"But, *Baba,* I know you want...."

"If I find you in politics, I will send you to Mmabatho," he declared in a big, tired voice.

"No, *Baba,*" was all she could say, shaking her head in disbelief. It was a new threat. She prayed it was an idle one. She did not want to be exiled to his homeland, to the fake capital next to Mafikeng in the fake country of Bophuthatswana.

"I will eat now," he declared, ending the talk.

She returned to the kitchen to stir the stew and prepare the cornmeal pap and try not to think about his threat.

"Better get moving." Hearing his mother's warning, Peter increased his pace from a snail's to a turtle's, sleepily pulling a T-shirt on inside out, then struggling with a pair of patched jeans.

"We'll have to leave without you," Ann declared as she walked away from his room.

Peter opened his door and hopped after her, trying to pull a worn-out sneaker onto the wrong foot as he said, "I want to go but why so early?"

"I told you we have to meet the church group outside Alexandra. We don't know our way around every township yet," she replied while collecting her jacket, notebook and camera bag

"Don't be harsh on him," Richard urged, adding to his son, "It's great that you want to join us."

Peter sorted out his shoes, dragged a sweatshirt over his head and started for the kitchen.

"No time for breakfast. We'll just eat apples in the car. Go climb in," his father told him.

As they roared away, Peter wondered what the big deal was. They were always late for everything, so why the rush today? He shivered in the cold car and almost wished he hadn't asked to come. But he was curious to see what a township was like; it might help him understand Sandile and this strange country.

They munched on the apples while his mother searched the road signs, identified the correct one and told his father where to exit.

"Think this is the wrong place?" she asked when they pulled into an empty parking lot. "They said right by Dion's." She pointed at a huge blue and orange sign on the department store.

"We're too early," Peter groused. He stretched out on the back seat. Some way to spend a Saturday, he thought.

Richard read the instructions aloud and concluded that they were in the right spot. They waited. Peter dozed. Twenty minutes later, the car doors slammed. He sat up and caught the conversation between his parents and someone standing beside a half-size school bus.

"Are you here for the clean-up?" Richard asked.

"Good morning. Yes, we are," said a wiry man with a nearly British accent, a pointed blond beard and a clerical collar. Peter couldn't hear what he said his name was.

"Very nice to meet you. I'm Richard Seibert with International Child Aid."

"Only a pleasure. ICA. You have some programs in Soweto, don't you?" the minister asked.

"We support two day-care centers, I mean crèches."

"And I'm Ann Seibert," she said, thrusting her hand toward the minister. "Free-lance reporter for the *Dallas Morning News*. Thanks for including us and our son."

"Ah, 'Dallas' – we're all watching it on the telly."

Peter saw his mother head back to the car.

"Come out and meet Reverend Jeffries," she said.

"Too cold," he said. "I'll stay by the heater."

"Well, I'm not leaving it on."

Peter waited inside. A half dozen other cars arrived. When Reverend Jeffries asked everyone to board the bus, Peter climbed out, locked the door and shut it. His father lifted the garden shovels from the trunk and they joined the others.

"Ever been to a township, Mrs. Seibert?" Reverend Jeffries asked.

"I've been to Soweto, but not to Alexandra. How are they different?"

Peter tried to wake himself up enough to learn from their conversation. The hard, cold seats of the bus helped him stay uncomfortably alert.

"Alex, as we call it, is older. It started early in the century when a white farmer sold the land to black families. Government's been trying to remove them ever since."

Ann took notes. "How old is Soweto?"

"Started in the 1930s when government forced blacks out of mixed neighborhoods. But it really grew fast in the '50s, and got its name – South Western Townships – in the 60s."

"Here they own, right?" Ann asked. "I've been working on a story about the Soweto rent strike."

"That's right. Alex is black-owned. In Soweto, they have to rent from government." He paused to correct himself, "Except for one section, Diepkloof Extension, where they can get a long lease."

Peter tried to remember if that was Sandile's neighborhood.

The bus halted abruptly just outside Alexandra township. Peter was startled to see a rifle-toting white soldier who didn't look much older than he was quiz the driver. Another white soldier on the opposite side of the bus peered in at Peter, his parents, the minister and a dozen other white people. Sandbags and coils of barbed wire blocked the other lane. After a few minutes, the soldiers waved the bus through.

"Why are there soldiers here?" Peter whispered to his mother as they pulled away.

"People in Alex refused to be forced out. They fought a 'six-day war' a couple of months ago. But it's calm now and the army has promised to withdraw," she whispered back.

Peter's eyes bugged out. Were they in danger?

The driver stopped again a few blocks inside the township at an open square strewn with litter. Peter climbed down behind the others. About twenty black people had gathered, mostly women and older men. He was one of only three young members of the cleaning crew.

Peter listened to the ministers, black and white, and the township councilors, black, welcoming people to the Alexandra Clean-Up. Looking beyond the speakers, he could see young men in nearby doorways and yards staring at the visitors, definitely not interested in joining the project. He surveyed the shacks made of sticks and trash bags, the sheds of corrugated metal jutting from dilapidated brick houses, the garbage on the unpaved streets and the black plastic stalls of the communal latrines. He tried not to breathe in the township smells of old trash, coal fumes and outhouses.

When the speeches were over, Peter's mother whispered to him, "Try not to gawk. They may not be palaces but these are people's homes."

"OK."

"Not so different from Nairobi's slums."

"But you never took me there. And why are so few township people helping?"

"Touchy subject. I'll explain afterward," she said. "Let's join the group."

The organizers distributed piles of trash bags and told everyone to climb aboard the two dump trucks that would take them to the streets they were to clean. Peter, Ann, Richard and others were assigned to work in Fifteenth Avenue. They slipped on heavy rubber gloves supplied by an older white woman who said she had been on township clean-ups before.

For two hours they shoveled every manner of refuse into the bags, then heaved the bags onto the truck. Buried in the debris and mud, Peter found old running shoes without partners, plastic bags from Dion's department store and Wimpy's hamburger shop, ragged T-shirts in many colors and sizes, a television with its glass front bashed in, a filthy doll with no hair, a deflated soccer ball, and endless amounts of refuse that he couldn't quite identify. He didn't really want to look that closely. He definitely didn't want to touch the stuff. He was thankful for the gloves.

How did Sandile manage, waking up each day in a place like this? Maybe that explained why he was so stiff.

Inspired by what he imagined of Sandile's life, Peter pushed himself to work hard and not to stare at the shoeless toddlers and mangy dogs playing in the rubbish, or the wrecked cars and the discarded bits of other people's lives that slid down the slope and collected in the ditches of Alex. His mother stopped periodically to peel off the gloves and take photographs and notes. His father struck up conversations with the work crew, white and black. That reminded Peter to talk to the people, instead of focusing on the trash.

"Can you help with this?" he asked the one township boy in his group. Peter pointed to a ruined tricycle half-buried. The boy, who looked about ten, stepped right up.

"You play soccer?" Peter asked him as they tugged at it together.

"*Yebo.* For sure."

"What position?"

"Me, I am the best keeper in Alex."

"Name's Peter. I'm a striker." He lifted his hand to shake, but withdrew it when he realized how filthy his glove had become.

"Tshepo," his co-worker said, lifting his right hand and laughing at the sight of the mud on it. He wiped it on his tattered pants, two sizes too big. He didn't have gloves, or shoes.

"School team?"

"No. We don't have. But me, I am playing every day just there." Tshepo pointed to an open area of bare earth that was far from level. Two stones at each end indicated goals.

By that time, the project was winding down. The dump trucks were nearly full. The clean-up organizers had run out of trash bags.

"Nice to meet you," Peter told Tshepo as they headed back to the main square.

"Pleasure."

"Next time I'll come and score on you," Peter threatened.

"Never," Tshepo replied, giving a little salute before he pranced away into the township.

Back in the Dion's parking lot, Peter dumped his gloves into a trash can and stomped some of the mud off his sneakers. But the sense of being unclean ran deeper; he couldn't wait to take a long shower.

"Who's the boy you were talking to?" Richard asked as they drove away.

"Said his name was Sheppo or something and that he's the best goalie in Alex," Peter replied, trying to sit so that his hands didn't touch his dirty pants or sweatshirt.

"Maybe he and his friends'll join if we launch a sports program," his father speculated. "I talked with some of the ministers about supporting one."

"Great. But they don't seem like joiners," he replied. "Mom, you were gonna explain, right?" He figured he'd better learn how South Africa worked so he could stop getting things wrong at school.

"Oh, yeah," she said. "The clean-up was organized by the black township councilors. The anti-apartheid organizations see them as stooges of the government. They don't want do-good projects that make the townships livable. They want freedom."

"What about the guys glaring at the clean-up crew?"

"You've got a good eye if you noticed that," she said. "Most likely activists – comrades."

"I see," he said. "So, what you gonna write?"

"I want Alex people tell their stories. Then I need comment from anti-apartheid groups."

"Isn't that confusing?"

"I try to give all sides so people can understand the complexity," his mother replied.

"You saying apartheid has a good side?"

"No, of course not," Ann said. "Apartheid robs black South Africans of all their rights, even citizenship. And anyone who protests can be detained or even killed."

"Then what's complicated?"

"People. How they react. Like the anti-apartheid groups – there are so many."

"What'ya mean? There's Mandela's group."

"That's right," his father joined in. "The African National Congress. But there are others, like Pan Africanist Congress."

"What's the difference?"

"Their ideas about how to fight apartheid and what they want after," his mother said. "Sometimes they fight each other. Or attack informers and collaborators."

"Really?"

"And some blacks profit from apartheid, like township councilors and dictators in the 'homelands' and criminals."

"Now I'm confused," Peter lamented. Couldn't she give a simple answer so he'd know how to act around here?

"Real life is complicated, especially when there's conflict," his mother replied.

That wasn't a lot of help to Peter. Fidgeting as he tried to keep his hands sort of clean, he didn't reply.

"I'm inspired by courage," his mother started up again. "The leaders – Mandela, the Sisulus, the Motlanas, Tutu and a few whites like Beyers Naude and Helen Joseph. But also ordinary people who struggle to protect their families or risk everything to protest."

She turned to her husband and asked, "Will you stop at the photo shop? Got to get this film processed today."

They pulled into a shopping center and Ann ran inside for a few minutes.

"You think we could find the boy again?" Richard asked Peter.

"Sheppo? He said he's out there every day. But did you see how bad that field is?"

His father nodded. "That might be the thing to start on."

Peter had more questions for his mother when she returned. "Is it dangerous for you?"

"Sometimes. But it's dangerous for the activists all the time."

"How'd you learn all that in a month?"

"Studied before we came," she said, indicating his father, too. "And talking to everyone here."

"And it's all going in one story?"

"No," Ann acknowledged. "I plan to write a lot of stories."

"You covering the protest Monday?" Richard asked her.

"Yep, after I drop the kids at school."

"What do you guys want for lunch?" Richard asked as they pulled into the driveway.

"Whatever you got," Peter answered, "but first I wanna wash." He stepped out of his sneakers at the kitchen door and made a bee-line for the bathroom. Scrubbing everywhere and triple shampooing, he let the water wash over him as he tried to figure out how Sandile managed without a shower.

Another school boycott. Sandile was on his way earlier than usual. He walked fast and followed a new route, just to be sure. Watching intently, he crossed a major road and then wound through a maze of lanes lined with two-room brick houses. About a mile from the bus depot, he turned a corner and found himself on a street that ended at a steep streambed.

Two boys jumped out of a doorway as he retraced his steps. A wiry little guy trying to look tough, wearing black pants that were too short, too wide and held up by a rope belt; a taller boy in a navy sweatshirt with several holes and frayed edges who shifted like a prize fighter. They looked ready for action. Sandile backed away, keeping his eyes on them.

"*Yima!*" the smaller one ordered, rushing toward Sandile.

Sandile turned and took off, his legs strong, but his heavy book bag slowing him down. The coal smoke coated his throat as he huffed onward. He thought he lost them.

Suddenly they darted from between shacks on opposite sides of another narrow street.

"Where you going?" the smaller boy demanded.

"Baragwanath to see my grandmother." Sandile tried to sound casual as he lied, but his eyes narrowed and his face hardened as he prepared to defend himself.

"This early? Bullshit."

"She's only awake now and I …."

"What's in the sack?"

"Sweets for an old lady," Sandile claimed as he stepped lightly from side to side, readying his getaway.

"'Sweets for an old lady,'" the bigger one mocked from the left.

"Give it," the smaller one said, grabbing at Sandile from the right.

Sandile swerved away from the smaller boy.

The bigger one bent to pick up a rock. Sandile prepared to topple him with a take-out slide, as if he were defending a soccer goal.

But the smaller one pulled a six-inch knife from his pocket and came in quickly, shouting, "Give it or I'll cut you."

Sandile felt a streak of pain as the rock grazed his temple. Still, he dodged the smaller boy deftly. But that maneuver put him too close to the bigger boy, who rushed in and got a hand on the backpack. As Sandile twisted and kicked at them to free himself, the two strangers yanked the pack off his back. They slashed it open and flung his uniform and books into the heap of garbage on the edge of the street.

"Better than us – private school?" the bigger boy sneered.

"You break the strike, we break you." The smaller boy flashed the blade at Sandile's face, then threw the bag at his head as the two attackers walked away.

Sandile scrambled to collect his uniform and books from the trash, stuffing them in the sack as he ran away. Leaping over a fence, he dashed through backyards to reach another street and then crossed into Diepkloof Extension. In the middle of a familiar street, adrenaline pumping through his veins, he tried to catch his breath and calm his thoughts. This was halftime in the soccer match, he was down a goal, but he had to win. There was much more than a game at stake. But it required a new strategy.

He went to his house and sat on the steps while he sorted out what to do. Going inside was not an option. It would upset his grandmother, who had only been home from the hospital a few days, and the girl his mother had hired to care of her. Instead, he set the ruined backpack on the front stoop, took out his homework, folded it neatly and slipped it into his pants pockets. He refolded his white shirt, tie and blazer together, then slid them inside the front of his polo shirt like a chest plate and tightened his belt to hold them in place.

Sandile reasoned that, without the burden of his schoolbooks, he could outrace almost anyone in the township, if it came to that. He left the books behind as he set off through the neighborhood, walking to conserve his energy. Soon after he left Diepkloof Extension and entered the main part of Soweto, he headed across an open field beside an abandoned men's hostel. There was no hiding place for ambushers; there was no one at all around. At the far western edge of the field, he took a street along the fringe of the residential area where it bordered open land split by a gully flecked with litter. He felt more secure in the open, with an escape route in sight. Reaching the road that crossed over the stream, he sprinted the last several blocks to the bus terminal.

Lines were shorter than usual that morning. Sandile waited impatiently, gripping the fence as if to hurry the process. When at last he was able to board, he moved all the way to the back of the bus. The compartment was airless. His knees turned rubbery. A wave of fear washed over him; he had won, but victory showed him how close he had come to injury or death. He reached over a short woman to grab a handhold quickly before he collapsed.

Sandile clung to the bar as the bus swayed around a bend and then rocked along the highway. The crowd of people pressing against him helped to keep him upright. His empty stomach seemed to suck the energy from his limbs. His apple was in the trash heap. Clutching the bar, he set his mind to staying upright for the ten-mile ride.

When he filed out of the bus at the Johannesburg transfer depot, Sandile stumbled toward an open space and squatted to collect himself. Deep breaths began to clear his head, but his thoughts kept returning to the attack. It played over and over in his mind. He was angry at himself for not fighting harder, not knocking them down, not showing them how wrong they were, how ignorant, that liberation wouldn't amount to anything if everyone was a thug like them, that they had no right to tell him what to do.

Fear and anger twisted together inside him until anger won the battle and renewed his energy. Sandile stood up and shook himself all over as if to shed the attackers. He got in line for the bus to Houghton Estate. By the time he reached Saint Andrew's, half an hour late, he was pumped up with rage, ready to take on the day. He went straight to the lavatory to clean up his clothes.

Peter and two other classmates came in. They said hello. Sandile continued to scrub.

Peter was still washing his hands when the other two had left. "You OK?" he asked.

Sandile looked up from the sink but he didn't reply.

"You're bleeding."

Sandile looked in the mirror for the first time. There was dirt and blood smeared across his left temple.

"I'm fine," he said, splashing some water on the scrape.

Peter grabbed some paper towels and gave them to Sandile to wipe his face. "What happened?" he asked

Sandile glared into the mirror. "I slipped," he said, not bothered that it sounded like the lie it was. He finished washing his shirt and patted it dry with more paper towels.

Peter headed out of the lavatory, then paused and said as an aside, "You know, if there's ever another boycott, you could stay at my house." The door closed behind him.

Sandile didn't know what to make of an offer that seemed at once presumptuous and generous from a boy he hardly knew.

"Next week I'm off to Namibia," Ann Seibert told her children at the breakfast table on Saturday. "So I need you all to help your father and Auntie Ellen keep things running here."

"OK," Peter agreed, "as long as you go see the Finger of God."

"The what?"

"This enormous natural stone pillar. Mrs. Nel told us about it in geography. But there was this big sandstorm couple months ago. Broke it right off. Imagine if you'd been there when this thing older than the dinosaurs came down with a crash." He gave a dramatic simulation with the cereal boxes, spilling corn flakes onto Megan, who leapt up and flung them off her shirt at her brother.

"And I thought the news was Namibia finally getting independence from South Africa," his mother said. "Peter, Megan, stop that."

"And you should go to the meteorite. Bigger than a car," he added as he dodged his sister. "She recommended that, too."

Ann said she'd try. Then she stepped into the kitchen for a second cup of coffee.

"Mrs. Dlamini, I can give you a ride home, if you don't mind stopping at the photo shop on the way," she offered. "Can you be ready in a few minutes?"

Ellen paused over the mop to catch her breath before replying, "Yes, of course."

Peter slid into the kitchen in sock feet to ask, "Can I come?"

"You're all coming," his mother said. "Your dad's going off to play tennis with a friend."

Peter was eager to visit the biggest township in South Africa. He wanted to see where all the action was – the protests, the comrades, Sandile's other life.

The three kids piled into the back of the car while the women took the front seats.

"Mrs. Dlamini, I'm afraid I didn't give you a chance to let your family know we were coming," Ann said.

"My sister may not be up yet," Ellen cautioned. "But, in Africa, guests always bring honor."

"In America, guests should bring gifts," Ann replied. She stopped at the photo lab and then darted into a supermarket to buy a big box of chocolates for Ellen's sister and her family.

As Ann turned the car onto the highway and headed southwest toward Soweto, Peter studied the Johannesburg skyline of stone and glass and steel towers that gave way to modest white suburbs with their concrete bungalows, flower beds and security fences. The car sped across a kind of no man's land – strange artificial hills covered with dry grass, metal towers for some kind of industry. His mother saying it was mining.

The car rounded a curve in the highway. Peter suddenly saw Soweto sprawled before them, bigger than he expected. Thousands and thousands of small concrete houses with wisps of smoke curling over the rooftops. The sun bleached the scene into a pale yellow.

They turned off the highway onto a major road flanked by a half dozen towering eucalyptus trees, and then north into the residential area. At mid-afternoon on a Saturday, it seemed to Peter as if everyone was in the streets, going somewhere on foot or just gabbing with friends. Men were sudsing down mini vans and buses. Children pushed handmade toys along the streets or lugged parcels.

Peter checked out the houses – brick or stucco in drab colors that hadn't been repainted in decades, many with additions or shacks built in the backyards. The property lines were marked by rusting fences, barbed wire, corrugated metal or old boards. The breeze lofted empty plastic bags into the fences or tumbled them along the roadside.

The neighborhood was poor, he could tell, but it didn't seem shocking, not after Alexandra township with its landslide of rubbish.

"You turn to the right just there," Ellen showed the way down unmarked streets to her sister's home. "Then you go with that road for some time."

Ann stopped as instructed in front of a modest stucco house in early stages of do-it-yourself expansion. She pulled the car to the edge of the road, partly into the drainage ditch, although there wasn't much traffic.

Neighborhood children rushed up and stared at Peter and his sisters through the car windows. As Ellen opened the passenger door, the group of children jumped back and asked, "Where did you get the fine car, Auntie?"

"Madam is just bringing me home," she told them, laughing.

The boys ran their fingers admiringly along the rounded green fenders. The girls stood in a cluster for solidarity, hands at their sides.

Peter got out on the street side and stretched after being cramped up for an hour of errands. A toddler ran up and touched his hand, as if on a dare. Peter laughed. It reminded him of trips to the countryside in Kenya where white people were a novelty.

"Come meet Mrs. Dlamini's family," Ann prodded her daughters, who were squirming under the unwanted attention. They clambered out, locked the doors and followed Ellen and their mother toward the house.

"Very smart car," a middle-aged man called out drunkenly from the front step of the house next door. "You must give it to me," he informed no one in particular.:

Peter heard Ellen scold the man in an African language, then turn toward her employer and say, "Sorry for that, Mrs. Seibert." She placed herself protectively between the man and the Seibert children as she shepherded them toward the house.

Staring at the man, who was waving a bottle in the general direction of the car and muttering under his breath, Peter didn't see a threat. Never seen anyone so drunk before, not even at his parents' New Year's Eve parties, and certainly never at mid-day.

As Ellen and the Seiberts approached the front door of her sister's house, it suddenly popped open and a girl came dashing out, nearly bumping into them.

A girl with a deep, soft Afro, tight blue jeans and a red T-shirt hugging her figure. Peter couldn't take his eyes off her as she excused herself for barging through and quickly said "*dumela*" to Ellen.

"*Ahe.* Where are you going, Kagiso? I wanted the Seiberts to meet you."

"I have to see some friends."

"Just for few minutes?" Ellen turned to Ann and said, "Mrs. Seibert, my sister's eldest daughter, Kagiso. She's in Form II and a very good student."

"Delighted to meet you, Kagiso. Mrs. Dlamini talks a lot about you. She's very proud."

"Pleasure," Kagiso replied.

"These are my daughters, Christina and Megan," Ann said, pointing to the two girls immobilized in front of her. "And this is my son, Peter, who is about your age, I think. He's a very good athlete."

Peter cringed at the form of introduction and couldn't come up with anything better to say than 'hi.' To make up the difference, he stuck out his hand to shake hers. She seemed surprised. She looked at his hand for a moment before shaking it. Her touch was light and brief. She tossed her head to make a pair of long red-and-white earrings dance as she turned back toward her aunt.

He felt ridiculous. He saw that his hand was big, pale, hairy, splattered with freckles – a bad comparison with her small, smooth, dark fingers. He had caught a glimpse of dark eyes surrounded by tightly curled lashes, rounded cheeks framing a small chin and pert mouth. He thought how absurd he must seem wearing his beat-up tennis shoes and a green-and-black striped rugby jersey, just because it was the style, when he still didn't know how to play the game. No one had told him she would be there. He just felt large and awkward, hoping for an interruption to relieve his tension, hoping for another look at her.

"*Eng?*" a voice cried out from the doorway. Peter turned quickly to see a woman in a nightgown retreat into the house.

"Sorry for that, Mrs. Seibert. My sister works hard all week and likes to be lazy on weekends."

"Kagiso," the voice called from a window, "run to the shops and get some cold drinks."

Kagiso sighed, took the money her mother handed her through the window and did as she was told.

Peter watched her sway gracefully as she hurried down the street and out of sight.

Ellen invited them all into the Mafolos' house.

Peter realized he was staring after the girl. Trying to renew his interest in his first visit to a black South African home, he turned to follow his sisters indoors. The front room was filled with furniture. Bulky upholstered chairs and sofas, some olive green and others gold, lined the walls. A dining table and wooden chairs occupied the center. There was little space for someone his size to navigate. The whole house seemed to be about as big as the Seiberts' living room.

Ellen indicated that they should take seats. Two children who were watching an old "Airwolf" show on a television at the end of the dining table occupied the nearest seats. Peter edged around the far side of the table, getting a good look along the way into a kitchen with a massive stove like in a Western movie; there didn't seem to be a sink. Finally in a seat, he promptly stood up again when a woman entered from another room.

Ellen introduced the Seiberts to her sister, Sally Mafolo, who was tucking a black T-shirt into the waistband of a green skirt.

"This one is Mike, a nine years boy," Sally told Ann. "And Tiny, seven years."

Sally patted the little girl and sent her to the kitchen. Tiny returned carrying a tray with a small dish of peanuts and a plate with four cookies. She offered it to the Seiberts, lifting it out of Mike's range when he tried to grab a share.

As Peter reached for a cookie, Kagiso came back with a large bottle of Sprite. He watched her pour it into unmatched glasses, a full one for each guest and the remainder split among her family. She didn't pour one for herself.

"Excuse me but some friends are waiting for me. Nice to meet you," she said as she made for the door.

"Kagiso, wait," her mother called after her, to no reply. Sally spoke to her younger children in her native language, ending with the directive, in English, "and switch off the telly and take your guests out to play."

The girl in the red shirt had slipped away again. Peter felt as if the tide had rushed out, leaving him aground. He watched, detached, as Tiny cleaned up the plates and glasses. Mike turned off the TV, showed Megan and Christina his collection of toy cars made from tin cans, bottle caps and wire, and then ran off to play with others. Peter caught himself staring out the door as if Kagiso would flash across his life again. As if he could think of anything to say to her if she did come back. He could hear his mother talking in the carefully enunciated manner she used with people who spoke English as a second language. Something about chocolates for them. Oohs and aahs and thank-yous. Then a gift for her, a beaded necklace in blue and orange that Sally had made. More oohs and aahs and thank-yous. He didn't care what they talked about; he just hoped they would stay until the girl came back.

October 1988

Peter sat on the bottom step of a pale blue bus that was long out of service and resting on concrete blocks. It was supposed to be a nursery school, his father had said, but this was Saturday, so only a few children played on the swings. Peter tuned out most of his father's discussion with a teacher about International Child Aid's support for the project. Staring across the smashed cars tipped on their sides that encircled the property next door, he focused on trying to figure Sandile out.

What did it mean, he asked himself, that a boy so aloof had started to turn friendly? Was it just because Peter had scored a crucial goal in a soccer match that Friday? Or because Peter had offered him a place to stay? Did it mean they really could be friends? Did he even want that friendship? There were other boys at school who seemed much more approachable, easier to know. And, of course, there were some girls who caught his eye; he just hadn't had the confidence to do anything about that yet. But Sandile was a puzzle. Although everyone admired him, it didn't seem that he was close to any of his classmates.

Maybe Sandile's real friends were here in Soweto, Peter mused. He thought about what he had seen of the townships. On the visit to that beautiful girl's house – how did they say her name? Kah-HEE-soh? – the week before, he had seen what he guessed was a typical Soweto house: little rooms crowded with people and furniture, television but no kitchen sink, shacks in the backyard and neighbors practically on top of each other. And before that, at the Alexandra Clean-Up, crumbling houses and shacks crammed together on a steep slope, wreaking out-houses, alleyways and gullies filled with trash.

In each place, he had tried to picture Sandile's day starting and ending in poverty, with a slice of Saint Andrew's luxury in the middle. He had admired Sandile's dignity in adapting to those contrasts.

But when he and his dad had arrived at Sandile's that morning, Peter was stunned that the house was big and comfortable. Perched on a rise with a view over the highway. OK, the yard was tiny and really needed some grass or bushes or something. It was just dirt. But the house looked new.

Sandile's mother had welcomed Peter and his father inside. They had sat on overstuffed armchairs and sofas, all upholstered in matching salmon and soft blue. Curious but not wanting to look like a spy, Peter had glanced around and seen a separate dining room and a modern kitchen and a grand staircase. He had guessed that the house had a full upper story. Maybe not as big as the crazy place his parents had rented, but plenty large enough, Peter thought.

He was even less sure what to make of the pistol. He had seen the handle of it at the neckline of Sandile's mother's dress when they first came in. It was gone when she brought the tea out. Maybe she had left it in the kitchen. But why did she have a pistol at all, he wondered His father had been a pacifist since the Vietnam War, so there had never been any guns in their house.

Mrs. Malindi had urged her son to pull out photo albums to share with their guests. Sandile had showed them pictures

Barbara Borst

from his childhood, including a photo with him dressed in a black jersey with a white skull and cross bones, his right foot atop a soccer ball.

"Future Saint Andrew's all-star," Peter remembered having said.

"Future Pirates all-star," Sandile had corrected.

And there were photos of beautiful green hills dotted with thatch-roofed African huts painted in turquoise. It was a village south of Umtata, Sandile had said. Peter wondered where that was. Sandile had added that he would be going there at Christmastime to see his "other mother."

It dawned on Peter that if Sandile had an "other mother," it meant Sandile's father had two wives. Peter knew that was common in Kenya. He just didn't see how it fit in with the urban life that Sandile's parents had made, with their new house and their grocery store and their cars.

"You all right?" his father interrupted the reflections.

"Yeah. Just thinkin'."

"Let's head back. We can talk on the way."

Peter wasn't sure he was ready to talk. He didn't quite know what to say. They climbed into his father's white Toyota minivan with the words "International Child Aid" painted on the side in primary colors and headed for the main road out of Soweto.

"Great game. And cool to see you get MVP," Richard began.

"Thanks, Dad."

"But I missed the beginning. How did Sandile end up at our house last night?"

"He asked to come," Peter said.

"Not that I'm unhappy to have him. I just didn't know you guys were friends."

78

"Me neither. I think it was the only way he could stay for the awards ceremony."

"I see."

Peter didn't see himself as a gotta-talk-about-feelings guy like his dad. No need to pin things down when he hadn't figured them out yet.

"Invite him to something. That may help you find out," Richard suggested. "I think there's something your mom wants you to help with. Maybe Sandile could help, too."

Peter dismissed the idea, assuming she wanted to put him to work around the house.

He changed the topic. "Who are the Pirates?"

"Must be Orlando Pirates – pro soccer team with a huge Soweto fan base. Archrivals of the Kaizer Chiefs."

"Can you get us tickets?"

"I'll see what I can do."

They pulled into the driveway and walked in the front door to the sound of Ann shouting, "Whoever's tapping this phone, you can get off now. I'm done with that call."

"What was that about?" Richard asked when she joined them in the kitchen making sandwiches.

"Invitations to Thanksgiving."

"The part about tapping the phone."

"Sometimes, you can't hang up 'cause they're on the line."

"Again? I thought you called the company."

"I did. They deny it but they tap all the journalists' phones."

"Endangers every political activist you talk to, and my work."

"They think it's worth the risk."

"We could get thrown out," he warned.

"Chance we have to take."

Peter finished making two overstuffed turkey-and-cheddar sandwiches and took them and a tall glass of milk out to the poolside terrace. He had enough things to think about without sitting through their discussion.

Kagiso had just started for school when she saw a big girl with a slight limp running toward her as fast as she could. She quickly recognized Snowy, an older cousin of Lawrence's who had come to Soweto to take care of his mother. Flustered and near tears, Snowy panted out the news that there was an emergency, but she wouldn't say what it was. Kagiso decided school could wait, even though it was a day for planning the next boycott.

Snowy and Kagiso ran for ten minutes to the Sitholes' house. Inside, they found Sonny Boy alone in the main room. Lawrence was nowhere to be seen. Snowy led them into a bedroom with dark fabric pinned over the one window. The air was stale, as if the window had never been opened. Sonny Boy took a seat on one of the chairs near Mrs. Sithole, who was unable to sit up in the bed.

"I don't know what to do," Mrs. Sithole said in a hoarse voice, her face contorted with pain. "They took Lawrence this morning."

Kagiso slumped onto a wooden chair next to Sonny Boy's, too shocked to say anything. She couldn't imagine why the police had taken Lawrence. He was just one of many student protesters, not a firebrand, not a leader. A gentle boy in a violent place. A big brother to her. But then she remembered that they had killed Sipho, another peaceful boy. She prayed that the police wouldn't hurt Lawrence to make him betray friends.

Mrs. Sithole began to cough. Snowy brought a glass of water for her. Sonny Boy took Mrs. Sithole's gaunt hand in his big paw.

"They banged on the door before daylight," Mrs. Sithole began again. "Then they forced it open and dragged him away." She coughed and then took a drink of water. "His father is away. Help me, please."

Sonny Boy and Kagiso looked at each other. They agreed to help. They didn't know how they could.

Snowy led them back to the living room so that Mrs. Sithole could rest.

Kagiso said they could try calling a group she had heard of, the Detainees Rights Committee. They returned to the bedroom to check with Mrs. Sithole, who agreed with the plan.

With no phone at the Sithole's, Kagiso and Sonny Boy went to his house. They left messages for Lawrence's father and some of his older brothers at the places where they worked. They waited to hear back from them and from the committee. When the phone rang, Sonny Boy picked up, then handed it to Kagiso.

"Good day," the caller said. "This is the DRC returning your call."

"Thank you," Kagiso said. "Is it safe to talk?"

"Is this an emergency?"

"Yes."

"I'll put you through now now."

Kagiso waited for a moment.

"Reeva Jameson speaking. How may I be of help?"

"My friend was taken this morning."

"Please give me all the information you have."

"What can you do for him?" Kagiso asked, beginning to question the wisdom of calling the committee.

"We make formal inquiries with police headquarters and every police station in the area. We work with human rights lawyers to begin investigating the case so that we can bring it to the authorities. If he is not released immediately, we talk to the newspapers."

"Does that help?"

"Many detainees have been released after we asked about them."

Worth a try, Kagiso thought, and more than she and Sonny Boy could do on their own.

Sandile closed his eyes and swayed to the sound of Youssou N'dour's pleading, haunting, glowing voice as it floated over the national soccer stadium in Harare, in the neighboring country of Zimbabwe. He could hardly believe that he was cocooned in such beautiful music, that he was hearing it live. Never mind that he had not known N'dour's music before he went to the concert and that he did not understand any of the languages that the Senegalese singer and drummer incorporated into his songs.

There was something so vibrant in the sounds, so African, so unspoiled. It lifted him to his feet. He forgot that he was dancing in the grandstands in the middle of the afternoon next to Peter and Peter's mother. They were sitting, but he was standing in the sunlight, eyes shut, heart open to the real Africa, the dream of Africa. All the cruelty of South African racism washed away. The music spoke to him of birdsong at first light, of drums in the evening by a roaring fire, of peace and wholeness and hope.

It reminded him of his grandfather's village in the Transkei, but that brought Sandile back to a bitter moment earlier in the trip. He had been surprised when Peter invited him to the concert. Peter had said his mother needed company for the long drive to Zimbabwe. Sandile hadn't wanted to turn down such an opportunity, even though he thought Peter and his family were white do-gooders with simplistic ideas about South Africa. Then Peter's mother had decided the drive was too long and that they should fly to Harare for the "Human Rights Now!" concert.

Sandile remembered his excitement at the thought of taking his first ride in an airplane. But his pleasure had been spoiled by having to produce his travel documents. Peter and Ann had used their U.S. passports. But Sandile couldn't get a South African passport. The government had declared that people like him, from the Xhosa tribe, were no longer citizens of South Africa; they were citizens of the Transkei or the Ciskei tribal areas. Sandile had felt humiliated to take out a Transkei ID in order to enter Zimbabwe. Neither Ann nor Peter had remarked on it, but it had stung him all the same.

He turned his thoughts back to the concert. N'dour finished his set. The program moved on to Western stars – Peter Gabriel and Sting and others delivering loud rock, jumping as they played, lights flashing. They were good, Sandile thought, but he sat through their music. Only Tracy Chapman's clarity and heartache made him rise and dance again. After the big sound, there she stood, a small black American woman with an acoustic guitar on an enormous stage by herself. The packed stadium hushed as she launched into "Fast Car," lingering on the lines "I had a feeling that I could be someone, be someone, be someone" and "leave tonight or live and die this way."

Then the concert turned loud again. When Bruce Spring-steen started his set with "Twist and Shout," Sandile saw Peter jump to his feet and dance through the whole set, shouting the words to "Born in the U.S.A."

Suddenly, the concert ended, though the power of the music seemed to hover in the air. Sandile and the Seiberts filed out through the massive concrete structure into streets filled with concert-goers, black and white, singing, laughing. Ann could not find a cab to take them to the Meikles Hotel, so the three of them walked through the night, along with thousands of other people.

"Wish there were more African singers," Peter said as they strolled in the balmy darkness.

"But Youssou N'dour was amazing," Ann replied. The two of them chatted about the concert and racism in America and South Africa and whether Mandela would ever be released and the music they had liked during their years in Kenya.

Not what Sandile expected to hear from white Americans. He felt a little bad for having judged Peter harshly before.

When they reached the hotel, Ann went to her room to write her news article, and Peter and Sandile settled in the room next door, where crisp white sheets carried the scent of ironing. They were too excited to fall asleep, though it was well past midnight. Sandile was in a generous mood and, as they talked, he made allowances for Peter's clumsy questions.

"Are your parents the richest people in Soweto?"

Sandile told him that they didn't live in Soweto anymore; they lived in Diepkloof Extension. "At the end of the day, if they were rich, they would move to the white areas."

"Isn't that illegal?"

"That is one of South Africa's funny, funny things," he explained. "It *is* illegal. But wealthy blacks *do* live in white neighborhoods. The walls are so high that no one sees."

They both laughed at the self-defeating segregation.

"We also stay in the township to guard the shop," Sandile added.

"That's why your mom has a pistol?"

"My father and brother also have. They sleep at the shop. *Tsotsis* can come to rob at any time."

"Really?"

"Shot my grandmother. She was in hospital for two months." Sandile could hardly believe he had said that out loud.

"I'm really sorry. She OK now?"

"Getting better." How he missed the long conversations they used to have about Xhosa traditions and her mother's mother's mother's legends of how the world was formed. He wanted her guidance, the wisdom of a traditional healer, a *sangoma,* on how to navigate the modern world. His parents were too busy to talk, and his brother was a great guy, but not the model Sandile wanted to follow.

Those thoughts hung in the quiet of the hotel room for a moment before Sandile started asking his own questions. "Why did your mother buy that color car?"

Peter laughed. "Gross, isn't it? She says other journalists said to get a car that no one would mistake for an undercover cop."

Sandile nodded approval for the logic, if not the shade. He posed one more question: "Do you know who put Kaizer Chiefs stickers on my notebooks?"

He didn't get an answer.

November 1988

"Where's Sonny Boy?" Kagiso asked Snowy when they entered the empty front room of the Sitholes' house.

"He asked for you first," Snowy said. She opened the door to a darkened bedroom where Lawrence lay awkwardly splayed across a mattress with a blanket over him. He did not stir. The two girls retreated to the living room.

"They dumped him early this morning past Soweto," Snowy began in a shaky voice. "He reached here this afternoon. I washed him."

"Can I speak to him for a minute?" Kagiso asked.

"I'll check." Snowy went into Lawrence's room and quickly came back for Kagiso.

Slowly, painfully, Lawrence turned on his side. Kagiso hardly recognized him. His lower lip was fat and split. His eyes were nearly swollen shut. A ring of chafed skin encircled his neck. His hands were puffed up and covered in small cuts.

"Kagiso," he mumbled through sluggish lips.

She squatted next to his bed and placed her hand gently on the mattress, afraid to add to his pain by touching him.

"I'm very much happy to see you," she said softly.

He closed his eyes and seemed to sink deeper into the mattress. Snowy signaled to Kagiso that they should leave the room. They sat in the front room again, saying little.

An hour or so later, a cry from Lawrence's room startled Kagiso. She dropped her books and reached his room at the same time as Snowy. They went in together, fearing the worst.

"Drink?" he asked through bloated lips that slurred his speech. Snowy ran out to get him a glass of water.

"Stay," he said to Kagiso, lifting his hand to signal for her to sit.

She sat on the floor.

Snowy came back with the water, which he struggled to swallow. He slumped back, half awake.

Kagiso got up to leave and let him rest, but he roused himself enough to indicate that he didn't want to be alone. She sat back down, not knowing what to do as he drifted in and out of sleep. She couldn't just sit there; it depressed her to stare at his battered face. She didn't have Snowy's skill at talking to invalids. To fill the emptiness and fear, she began to hum "Amazing Grace." But a couple of lines in, she stopped. It reminded her too much of funerals.

Another song came to mind. She wished she had Palesa's beautiful voice instead of her raspy one, but she decided to sing Brenda Fassie's "Izolabud" anyway. Not loud and sassy like the original, but something with a little pep.

"Heading for the city. Looking for a ride..."

Next she did what she could with "Let Me Be Free," but toned down the feistiness of Yvonne Chaka Chaka's version.

"You watch every move I make. Don't give me time to breathe..."

Lawrence stirred. He opened his eyes. Kagiso stopped singing immediately and asked if he needed anything.

"Show you," he mumbled, gesturing for her to pull back the blanket.

She winced as she did what he asked, fighting her desire to turn away. He described what the police had done to him.

"Around here," he said, touching the raw marks on his neck where they had tied a rough cloth bag over his head. He showed her his wrists, bruised and chafed where they had been bound together behind his back. They had made him stand for days and beaten him on his back and legs, with sticks and whips, he thought; he had not been able to see, with the bag over his head. Nor had he seen their faces.

Kagiso felt his many pains as if they ran through her own body. She wanted desperately to close her eyes. Feeling helpless, she tried to offer a remedy.

"You are suffering too much. You must tell what they did to you," she urged him gently. "Detainees Rights Committee can …."

"NO!" Panic flashed across his face.

"They'll help protect you."

"No," he insisted, clutching at her arm. "Say nothing. Only Sonny Boy."

She looked at him in confusion.

"People will say I informed." His eyes were wild with fear.

"No one will say that. You're a comrade."

"Zwele."

Suddenly, Kagiso remembered the arsonists' accusations. Would Zwele really turn on a loyal member of the student movement like Lawrence? She knew that mobs could target anyone, guilty or not, as a collaborator. Hot words between them, but there was no reason to believe Zwele had it in for him. Lawrence was more scared than he should be, she thought, but she couldn't take a chance.

"Only Sonny Boy," she vowed.

He nodded and closed his eyes to sleep.

Kagiso got up, gathered her things and told Snowy she was leaving. Lawrence's dark secrets weighed on her as she walked home. She tried to compress them deep inside so that her family and friends would suspect nothing. Speak to no one. Except Sonny Boy. Did she have to keep the secret from Palesa?

December 1988

Squeezing onto a seat in a public bus along with Ellen and Mike, Kagiso slid the three flimsy plaid bags that held their belongings under the seat. Then she made room for Tiny to climb onto her lap. Ellen said they were lucky to sit together, that the bus was full for a Sunday, but not as crowded as it would have been on a work day.

Kagiso dreaded her first trip to Johannesburg in years. Her parents had insisted that she go. What sense did it make? They trusted her to get Tiny and Mike off to school each day, but not to stay in Soweto where her friends were during the long vacation? She had to be sent off with her aunt to the servants' quarters in some white neighborhood?

How could she abandon Lawrence? He was gaining strength, and she had persuaded him to let Palesa as well as Sonny Boy visit, but he was still scared. She would miss out on planning the protests for January, when the exam results were to be published. And how could she get along without Palesa to talk to about everything? Kagiso stared out the dust-covered window and fumed at her parents for sending her away.

The bus sped across the gold mining area and entered the maze of streets in downtown Johannesburg, passing close to police headquarters at John Vorster Square. Suddenly, her frustration with her parents seemed minor. Fear vaulted into

her throat, choking her as it had on that day five years earlier, salty and hot like a mouth full of blood, impossible to
swallow. She had told herself she was over that fear. That was
not true. She could see again the desperation in her father's
eyes.

Kagiso searched for actions she could take to fight back.
Unsure what Tiny and Mike remembered, she wrapped her
arms around the two of them to shield them from the past.
Mike wriggled in her grasp but she did not let go. When the
driver pulled to a stop in the depot, Kagiso got up and put
the straps of a plaid bag over each shoulder so that her hands
were free to grip her sister and brother. The three of them
edged sideways together along the aisle of the bus and down
the steps. Their aunt followed close behind them with the
other bag.

When Ellen signaled that she had found the bus that went
north to the Sandhurst neighborhood, Kagiso marched Mike
and Tiny to it and they boarded quickly as a team. Kagiso kept
watch in all directions even as she secured the bags under their
new seat.

The second bus emerged from downtown, bringing a
change in scenery from office towers and apartment buildings
on city streets to small shopping centers and restaurants along
a suburban road. The driver turned onto side streets lined with
security walls draped in bougainvillea vines with magenta and
tangerine flowers. The fear in Kagiso's throat began to ebb
and she relaxed her grip on Mike and Tiny, who leaned across
Ellen's lap for a better look. She even tried to get a glimpse of
the mansions, the swimming pools glimmering in the midday
sun and the lawns bounded by vibrant gardens.

A dog lunged at a closed gate, snarling at the passengers, all
of them black, who descended at the bus stop. Tiny, Mike and

Kagiso leapt back from the window at the sound of the growling and the sight of the fangs. After several more stops in Sandhurst, Ellen told the children they should prepare to get off.

"No dogs," Mike argued, crossing stick-like arms on his chest. "Not getting down."

"You can't stay on," Ellen pointed out.

Kagiso turned her little brother's face toward hers and reassured him, "Mike, we are going that side – together." He glared at her but didn't resist when she took his hand, and Tiny's, too, and led them down the steps to the side of the road.

Two lean black-and-tan dogs leapt at the gates nearby. Mike ducked behind his big sister. These were not like the stray dogs of Soweto that slunk away when ordered. She channeled her own fear into taking charge. Keeping Mike to her left, away from the gates on the south side of the road, she picked Tiny up. Ellen took two of the plaid bags.

The four of them walked along the edge of the grass in the partial shade provided by feathery mimosa trees, red-topped poinsettia bushes and eucalyptus trees with their drooping, silvery dark green leaves. Looking up through the canopy, Kagiso felt she had entered an alternate world, spacious and blooming, but one designed to exclude people like her.

"Stop that," Ellen instructed Mike, as he stripped the leaves from a drooping branch. Kagiso breathed in the cleansing scent of crushed eucalyptus leaves as it overpowered the perfume of the flowers.

Ellen paused at a gate and called out to a man who was raking leaves on the lawn, "*Dumela.*"

"*Ahe,*" he said, setting down his rake and brushing off his hands as he walked toward her.

"Simon, these are my sister's children – Kagiso, Mike and Tiny."

He reached through the wrought iron gate to pat each of the smaller ones and shake hands with Kagiso, his left hand supporting his right elbow. She mirrored his hands in the traditional greeting. "Welcome," he said. "Are you staying for the holidays?"

"For a week," Ellen said. "Then we go to my mother's place. Kagiso has just finished Form II."

"Congratulations," he said.

"Thank you."

"Last year, she was near the top," Ellen added, beaming at her niece.

A small, woolly dog came yapping up to the gate. Mike retreated.

"Don't be afraid," Simon said. "This one does not bite." He picked it up and offered Kagiso and Tiny a chance to pet its curls of scratchy gray fur. Mike kept his distance.

The group stopped at four more houses to exchange greetings with the workers, all of them black. Kagiso thought it odd that they had yet to see any white people, although the government designated the area for whites only. They stopped on the south side of the street at an elaborate double gate with a heraldic crest on each side. Ellen pushed a button on one of the pillars. When a man came to open up for them, she introduced the three children to the gardener, Huntington, before she led them inside.

So this was the place of exile, Kagiso thought. As the gate clanged shut behind them, she felt as if a prison door had slammed. She looked out through the grill. What was she doing in this strange place – her own country – that she had never seen before? Shifting the weight of the bag on her shoulder, she turned to scrutinize the house.

A sweep of gravel driveway cut between manicured lawns and led to a triple garage and extra parking spaces. A footpath paved in stone curved from the driveway toward a single-story house in the same cream-colored stucco as the perimeter walls. She could see a double front door in varnished honey-colored wood surrounded by windows. It was hard for her to gauge the size of the house, because much of it seemed to be hidden behind towering trees and vines dripping purple blossoms.

She stood mesmerized by the foreignness until her aunt called, "Kagiso, this way."

Mike and Tiny ran ahead of Kagiso, following Ellen around the side of the house to a courtyard paved in cracked concrete where they ducked under sagging clothes lines in order to enter their aunt's room. Ellen showed Kagiso where to set down the plaid bag on the second mattress, the one on the floor.

"Let's go greet the family," Ellen told her three charges.

Kagiso cringed as she watched her aunt go not to the front door but to the kitchen door, open it and call out, "Ooowooo, Mrs. Seibert?" The four of them waited in the kitchen for an answer. Kagiso assessed the long narrow room with its break-fast table, electric stove, double oven, double sink, side-by-side refrigerator, separate freezer, long countertops and velvety African violets lined up in pots along the window sills. These foreigners could enjoy the wealth of her country, though her own family could not, she thought. But it did look like a good place to cook.

Ann Seibert popped into the kitchen wearing a beach robe and flip-flips. Her wet hair was pulled back in a ponytail.

"I'm delighted to see all you children again," she told them. "Come out and say 'hello' to everyone." They followed her through a room full of sofas and a large television set and out sliding glass doors to a poolside terrace where the rest of the Seiberts were lounging on towels and beach chairs.

Ann introduced the Mafolo children to her husband.

Peter quickly scrambled up off his towel and wrapped it around his bare shoulders and wet swim trunks. "Hi," he said to Kagiso..

"Hello." She had forgotten that he would be there. At least there was someone her age, although she didn't imagine they would have much in common. She gave him a quick look: a dusting of freckles across his face, a hunk of wavy blond hair and strange eyes of gray-blue, as if they were part of the sky. She looked away, not wanting to be caught showing interest.

"Would you like to play tennis later?" he asked her.

She didn't know what to say.

"Children, let's go settle your things," Ellen interrupted, shepherding her nieces and nephew back toward her quarters.

"Mrs. Dlamini, I put some extra sheets, blankets and pillows on the family-room sofa for all of you. I hope you'll be comfortable," Ann called out as they left.

Ellen and the three Mafolos walked back through the house, collecting the bedding as they went. Kagiso spied down the long hallway with its many bedroom doors and then thought of the four of them crammed into her aunt's little cell. She said nothing so as not to make her aunt feel bad. It was not Ellen's fault that they had been sent here. Instead, Kagiso helped organize their belongings in the space under her aunt's bed so that they wouldn't be in her way.

Once she had their clothes arranged, Kagiso took a book from her bag and sat on the step outside her aunt's room to immerse herself in a biography of Nelson Mandela. At least she could do something useful in exile: read about the leader she admired most. She ignored her sister and brother who ducked under the clotheslines as they kicked a dead soccer ball around in the courtyard.

"Do you want to play tennis?" a voice asked Kagiso.

She jumped, startled because she hadn't heard Peter coming. She still didn't know how to answer that.

He changed the subject. "What are you reading?"

"*Higher Than Hope.*"

"Isn't that banned?"

"The censors missed this one," she explained, folding down a corner of the page to mark her place.

"When you're done, can I borrow it?"

"OK." With a sideways glance, she tried to check on whether he was mocking her.

"Great. He's not in the history we have to learn at school," Peter said. "But my mom talks about how big a deal he is."

Unwilling to reveal her politics, Kagiso changed the subject. "Very sharp," she said, indicating his white tennis shorts and baby blue polo shirt.

He looked at his outfit and laughed. "Yeah, if only I could hit the ball. Want to come and beat me? Not my best sport."

"I don't know how to play."

"Can I teach you?"

She hesitated, trying to figure out why he was so keen to drag her out on a tennis court. This was not a question she had had to face with the boys she knew. She looked him over – a hopeful grin on a face that still had just a bit of baby fat, but the rest of him lean muscle stretching the freckled skin of his arms, powerful legs swathed in blond hair. Not at all the look she was used to. She saw few white people, and she had never sized them up that way.

"I could get my sister's racket for you."

She wrestled with herself.

"Only if you want," he said, seeming to give up.

She decided it wouldn't hurt to try something new, if she was going to have to spend a whole week there. "OK," she announced.

She went into her aunt's room to change from jeans into faded black shorts. While she was tying her gym shoes on the step, Ann came to the kitchen door to look for Ellen.

"I think she's talking to Huntington, Mrs. Seibert."

"Well, I don't need to bother her. I just wanted her to know that you children don't have to stay in this courtyard. There's a whole big yard to play in. And have you got enough bedding?"

"Yes, thank you," Kagiso said, conscious of all the gaps between the Seiberts and her family but trying to be polite because her aunt's job depended on it. She finished tying her laces and went to the backyard to look for Peter. She spotted the green fence of the tennis court across a lawn beyond the pool.

"Is this OK?" he asked, handing Kagiso his sister's racket.

"For sure."

"Are you right handed or left?"

"Right."

"So, you hold it like this." He showed her how to make a V between her thumb and palm on top of the grip. "Let's see you swing."

She swung hard, twisting her hand until the racket sliced sideways through the air and the force of it spun her in a circle.

He ducked quickly to avoid getting hit. "Try it like this," he said, demonstrating how to keep the racket face vertical and to plant her feet.

She imitated his swing, more or less.

"Good. All right, you stand here and I'll hit to you from the other side." He scurried around the net and hit a soft shot toward her.

She lunged to return it and whacked the ball into the net. She sent the next one straight up in the air off the frame of her racket and missed the third altogether. They collected the balls and tried again. After several rounds, she began to get the hang of it, hitting a few of her shots vaguely in his direction and feeling proud.

Mike and Tiny came running down through the garden, giggling and elbowing to get in front of one another in some unofficial race around the flowerbeds. They distracted Kagiso so much that she hit the next ball over the tennis court fence and close to Mike's path. He grabbed it and ran away with his treasure.

"Bring that back," Kagiso commanded, as she set down the racket and opened the court gate. Embarrassed to have him interrupt the lesson, she chased him. He squealed with delight at the new challenge and dashed back and forth across the lawn. Kagiso kept after him, finally catching him at the edge of the swimming pool. She grabbed his hand and struggled to get the ball out of it, pulling with all her strength. The ball popped loose so suddenly that she lost her balance and fell into the pool.

Kagiso plunged halfway to the bottom of the deep end before she could right herself. Her gym shoes weighed down her desperate, awkward efforts to get back to the surface. Unable to catch her breath before falling in, she reached the surface gasping for air. Just as she was starting to collect herself, someone dived into the pool and sent a wave washing over her. When she surfaced again, she began to paw her way toward the lip.

Someone popped up behind her in the water, flung an arm across her chest and turned her around. As they turned, Kagiso saw the edge grow farther away. She panicked, trying to pull the arm away, flailing, kicking. But the arm was too strong and the grip tightened.

"Let me go. I can swim," she screamed as she fought to free herself.

The swimmer grabbed her right hand and put it firmly on the lip of the pool before releasing her. Coughing and trying to pull herself out of the water, Kagiso clung to the edge. Suddenly, strong hands lifted her onto the terrace. She lay with her chest and face on the warm stones to catch her breath before rolling over, her feet still dangling in the water. She realized that it was Peter who had dived in after her.

"I'm sorry. I didn't know," he said, then easily heaved himself out of the water, twisting to sit on the edge a short distance away.

Kagiso sat up, coughing.

Peter's father came running from the house. "Everyone OK?" he asked them, looking from the wet teen-agers to the two younger children.

"Just fooling around," Peter answered.

"Not near the pool," his father ordered. "You know the rules. Especially when we have guests."

"An accident. Won't happen again," Peter promised.

"Make sure." Richard went back inside.

"They would need you," Kagiso panted, pointing at her sister and brother who stared silently from the far side of the water. "They can't swim yet."

"Where did *you* learn?"

"Soweto."

"Really?"

She nodded. "There *is* a pool. My father is crazy about safety. He made us take lessons," she puffed, stopping after each phrase.

He waited for her to finish.

"But I am not good. I thought the shoes were going to drown me." She tried to laugh but coughed instead.

Peter looked at their feet dangling in the water. "Those are small," he said, pointing at her navy blue and white running shoes. "Look at these boats." He lifted his white tennis shoes for her inspection.

Smiling, she shook her head to send the water flying off her hair. She noticed that his hair was plastered across his brow, his shirt clung to his chest. Then she began to shiver as the shock and fear and wet clothes gave her a chill.

"Guess we can't play any more tennis 'til we bail 'em out," he said. "Want to try again tomorrow?"

"Peter, dinner in ten minutes. Better change," his mother called from the sliding glass doors.

"Yep," he answered. Peter got up and offered Kagiso a hand. Still feeling shaky, she took it and stood up next to him, not even measuring to his shoulder. He handed her a towel.

"Shoes feel great don't they?" he asked as they squished their way through the yard toward the house.

"OK, bye," she said as they neared the door, then she ducked around the outside to her aunt's room as if she were escaping.

What an awful thing to do, Peter kept telling himself as he shifted again and again in bed, unable to sleep. He just couldn't believe that he had grabbed Kagiso in the pool and dragged her to the edge. What was he thinking putting his hands on a beautiful girl he hardly knew? She must have thought he was a monster attacking her. And all he did afterward was make lame jokes about soggy shoes. He tried not to suppress the thrill of holding her. After beating himself up about his error for most of the night, he focused on how to apologize to her in the morning. Even if it didn't do any good.

While her aunt was clearing the breakfast table, he went looking for Kagiso in the kitchen courtyard. No sign of her. He wandered through the property and finally spotted her reading under a mimosa tree in the front yard. He made sure to step on some twigs so he wouldn't startle her again.

"I just wanted to say I'm sorry," he said from about twenty feet away as she looked up from her book.

She seemed surprised.

"About yesterday."

"For?"

"Grabbing you in the pool."

"OK."

"I just had all this life saving training in my head 'cause I just took the course in Nairobi before we left…" he forged onward through the lines he had rehearsed.

"It's very much OK," she interrupted. "You tried to save me."

Suddenly he realized that she wasn't offended. "Yeah?"

"For sure."

"Thanks. Sorry to disturb you." Job done, he turned to go.

"Tell me about Nairobi?"

"Yeah?" He faced her again.

She nodded.

Still getting used to the idea that she wasn't upset with him, he tried to think where to start. He edged a little closer to her in the dappled light.

"There's room that side," she said, indicating a place for him to sit on the bench that encircled the tree.

"What do you want to know?" He sat down, not too close, hands beneath his thighs as if to demonstrate that he wasn't a threat.

"African villages. Wild animals."

"Don't you have those things here?"

"Maybe. I never see them."

Peter described going on safari to the big game reserves in Kenya, seeing cheetahs and elephants and zebras ranging over the grasslands, and Maasai warriors wrapped in red cloth tending their cattle with lions in the distance. He had to set his hands free to demonstrate the scope. He said he thought South Africa had a big park, too, but he couldn't remember the name.

"Why were you in Kenya?" she asked.

"My dad does charity work and my mom's a journalist, so they came for the Ethiopian famine four years ago. Nairobi was their base."

He thought he might be blabbing on too long. He couldn't believe she actually wanted to talk with him. He got all caught up in the telling, then felt self-conscious and tried to say something amusing to cover up his awkwardness.

"Ever eaten zebra?" he asked.

"We do not eat bush meat here," she assured him.

"Well, somebody does. I've seen it on the menu at restaurants."

"I've never been to a restaurant."

He paused, realizing how far apart their experiences were, and reminded himself to think a little more carefully before he spoke. But he couldn't help being a tease because he didn't know how else to impress her. "People in Kenya eat flying termites."

She grimaced.

"The termites build towers of mud and dirt. When the rainy season comes, a whole lot of flying termites hatch. They swarm you," he said, his hands swirling around to demonstrate as she recoiled. "You have to close the windows or they invade the house. Then people collect them and toast them and eat them. Supposed to be nutritious."

"Did you try them?"

"Well, no," he admitted, his bravado challenged. "But our housekeeper ate them. And then my mom tried to gross her out by telling her what we eat."

"Like what?"

"The housekeeper's tribe thinks fish are snakes. So my mom told her about caviar."

"What's that?"

"Fish eggs."

Her eyes widened in horror.

"Very fancy and very expensive," he informed her, "especially if you get the kind from a big fish called, I think, a sturgeon, from someplace in the Soviet Union."

"Nasty."

"They're like little salty beads of jelly. I'll get some for you next time you visit."

"I won't come back," she declared. "Or only to bring you my father's very favorite – *phane*."

Peter was about to ask what *phane* was, but Mike ran out of the house and flopped across his big sister's lap. Christina had thrown him out of the game she was playing with Megan and Tiny because he messed up their dolls and stuffed animals. He had no one to play with. Peter decided that he and Mike needed a little soccer practice. He went off to find a ball.

Tan dust swirled up from the tires and trailed plumes across the open grassland. Kagiso peered out the window trying to be the first to spot a wild animal. She could hardly believe that she was here, on a sort of safari to see the famous wildlife of South Africa.

Tiny slipped an arm around her big sister's neck and whispered, "I'm scared of lions."

"Me, too," Kagiso whispered back. "But they can't get us inside the car."

Ann Seibert drove her husband's minivan slowly around the private game reserve. Tiny was buckled into the middle row between Kagiso and Peter, with Christina, Megan and Mike on the rear seat.

"Warthogs," Christina announced as a pair of scruffy-haired little hogs ran across the road behind the van. "My favorite."

"I can't see," Tiny complained.

"You can take off your seatbelts while we're in the park," Ann said.

As Kagiso reached across her sister to unbuckle the seatbelt, Peter pointed at her wrist and asked, "You never take it off?"

She looked at the string of red-and-white beads. "Not anymore. I made one just like this. My mother was teaching me. Then I lost it that side."

Kagiso pulled her sister up onto her lap. They giggled together about the funny little creatures with their tails aloft as they scurried away. Dusty bushes in the distance began to shimmy.

"Look there!" Kagiso showed Tiny as she pointed to a small group of antelopes leaping gracefully among the leaves. The golden-brown animals jumped easily, as if gravity had no hold on them, their white bellies briefly flashing before they touched down.

"Impalas," Peter said.

This small taste of wilderness, half an hour from Johannesburg, thrilled Kagiso. All those wild animals were right there, close to them, free to roam. She had never seen them except in picture books. One more of the country's treasures that were off-limits to blacks, and she had to rely on foreigners to show her. Deciding to set aside her resentment, just for a day, she focused instead on the beauty of Africa that finally was hers to see.

She studied an impala that paused a short distance away, on alert; its horns spread and curved like a lyre above its delicate face. The warthogs with their curled tusks had to go down on their knees to get a mouthful of grass. Kagiso felt she was in a sort of wonderland.

Ann stopped the van at a set of high chain-link fences that surrounded an island of trees in the middle of the park.

"Now we have to roll up the windows and keep them closed," she told her passengers. "We're going into the lions' den."

Kagiso hugged Tiny, who buried her face in her sister's T-shirt as they passed slowly through one set of gates and then another. Park employees locked the gates behind them.

"There they are," Peter said quietly to Kagiso, pointing out three lionesses sprawled in the shade of a bush near his side of the car.

Kagiso leaned across the seat for a better view. She admired how perfectly the lionesses blended with the golden grass, how they lay against or across one another, how even the two cubs seemed drowsy as they batted at flies in the buzzing afternoon heat. A male lion dozed alone under a separate bush. Kagiso whispered to Tiny that it was OK to look because the lions were sleeping.

Tiny peeked out the window and they watched together as a lioness lazily extended a paw and then rolled onto her other side.

"They're doing nothing," Mike griped from the back seat.

"When it's hot like this, they just sleep," Peter explained.

"That's boring."

"They hunt at night. Want to come back then?"

"Yeah," Mike bragged, standing up and positioning his arms as if he were about to shoot a lion.

"I know it's hot, kids," Ann said. "Can't put the air conditioning on or we'll all breathe the dust. So, let me know when you're ready to go."

"Where are the gorillas?" Mike asked, beating his chest like King Kong.

"Not in South Africa," Ann explained. "They're in the forests in Central Africa."

Mike seemed disappointed. Then the male lion stretched and let out a brief roar – a dark sound as if from the depths of a cave. Mike ducked behind the seat. Peter laughed and reached back to poke him.

The roar shook Kagiso; she could feel the savagery behind it, see the animal's golden eyes staring at her, or through her. Yet the lion seemed to her more desperate than dangerous. All that power, but no freedom. It could not prowl the countryside like its ancestors; it lived in a cage – a large one, but still a cage. She gazed at the lion in sympathy.

Christina and Megan began to argue in the back seat. Ann decided it was time to exit from the lion pen and get some fresh air. Once they were safely locked out, they all opened their windows and enjoyed a slight breeze while the car meandered through the rest of the reserve.

Peter was the first to spot a pair of ostriches, backlit by the powerful December sun as they strutted through the grass. Ann let the van slowly approach the giant birds and then stopped as the pair crossed the road. One walked around the vehicle to inspect the passengers.

Suddenly, the ostrich bent its long neck and lowered its pale head into the van through an open back window. The children screamed and leaned as far away from it as they could. Kagiso shielded Tiny as the head swiveled and the huge eyes scrutinized all of them. Ann honked the horn to divert the bird. Finally, at its own pace, it pulled its head out of the car and moved on, peacefully lifting its feet high one after the other until it caught up to its partner.

Once the scare was over, they all laughed out their fears.

Kagiso shook her head slightly, as if to reassert her self-control. She jiggled Tiny on her lap and said, "Have you ever seen eyes so big?" Tiny shook her head.

Peter sat on the terrace watching heat lightning flash occasionally in the distance. A whiff of chlorine rose from the pool into the warm evening air. He heard someone walking in the garden; the night watchman, he assumed. The voice surprised him.

"Thank you for the lion park," Kagiso said.

He jumped up, thrilled that she had come out. With an extravagant gesture, he offered her his seat. "Yeah, the animals are pretty great, huh?"

"For sure."

He pulled up another chair and they sat in silence for a few minutes. The lights in the pool glowed turquoise as the shadows deepened. He caught the scent of the coconut oil in her hair, earthy and real, not fake flowers from a shampoo bottle. He waited for her to speak in that soft voice that seemed a touch too low for a short girl, but she sat quietly.

"Nice having you here," he said at last, more to himself than aloud.

"I never wanted to come."

"Why not?" he asked, curious rather than offended. He let his eyes slide over her, hoping she wouldn't notice in the darkness. He realized he was staring and reminded himself to listen.

"It's everything that's wrong with this country."

"The house? Tennis court? Pool?"

"Not just the things. The system."

"But my parents are here to help."

"Look from our side," she urged.

Invited, he turned to look at her, noticing how the last light in the sky filtered through her Afro, how the turquoise reflection from the pool curved over her.

"Mike and Tiny and I are guests; my aunt is still a servant," she said. "But at least your mother doesn't call her a 'girl' when she's a grandmother."

"I know that apartheid keeps the races apart so whites can have all the power," he said. "But what does it feel like…?" He hesitated to finish the sentence 'to be black here.'

Kagiso looked at him sideways, leaned forward on the chair, did not speak for a long moment.

"Sorry," he offered, fearing that he had overstepped.

"It's OK to ask. I've just never had to explain."

He nodded in understanding.

"Come back to Soweto sometime and I'll show you what it does to my family and friends."

"Yes," Peter agreed, thrilled by the prospect of more time with her. They sat quietly for a few moments, facing the evening sky.

"But what does it do to *you*?" he asked, sensing it was an intimate question.

After a few minutes, she began a tale. "When I was ten, my father brought Tiny and Mike and me into Johannesburg. They were little, three and five. It was supposed to be a treat." She paused.

"It was 1983. Government promised changes. But they were only for colored people and Indians. For blacks, the same as always – nothing. So, there were big protests.

"We took the bus from Soweto into downtown. For a treat," she repeated. "To buy new shoes and get ice cream.

"The streets were very much filled with protesters outside John Vorster – police headquarters," she explained, her voice going flat, emotionless.

Kagiso stared out over the pool. Peter couldn't help eying her.

"My father picked Tiny up and made Mike and me hold onto him. He said we would be fine together. We got down. Then the police attacked, beating the protesters, firing guns, hauling the men away. Police dogs barking. People screaming, running through the bus station.

"My father held onto us and we hid behind the bus. But the police came around from both sides. They tore us away from him, then they hit him and dragged him off," she said, almost to herself.

Peter suddenly blushed to realize that he was looking her over while she was telling a terrifying tale. He sat up straight and turned to face her, waiting, afraid for her.

"They took him for doing nothing, just caring for his children. They put him in jail."

Peter waited patiently, respecting her pain, but he did want to know what happened next. Finally, he asked, "What did you do?"

She turned to look at him. He was afraid he should not have spoken. Her answer came in a flat tone, without emotion. "I turned my sister and brother around so they would not see the police beating our father. We stood in the bus station for some time until I could think what to do. Then I put Tiny on my back and took Mike's hand. I asked a black taxi driver to take us to Soweto. I had no money, but he took us."

Peter was amazed at how calmly she described the events. How had she found the wisdom, at ten? He could see that she was much more grown up than he had ever had to be. He wanted very much to put his arms around her, to shield her from the past, or maybe to share in that strength. He didn't dare.

At last she spoke again, in a combative tone. "This is why we struggle. The parents are afraid. Only the youth can free us now."

Peter wished that his life, like hers, had a purpose more profound than the next sports competition. He was swept up in her, whether by her courage or her curves or both. He didn't want to figure that out. He only wanted to be carried with the tide.

"Is there anything I can do?" he asked.

"I don't know."

Sandile packed his sports gear – tennis racket, swimsuit, soccer cleats and more – for the visit to Peter's house. They did best together on the sports field, he reasoned; worth building on that. It wasn't like he had other close friends at school. He preferred to keep his distance. Everyone was judging him – at school, in Soweto. He was tired of it. Time to play a little.

Not that Sandile considered Peter the most relaxing person. Peter was so blunt, always asking something awkward. But without an edge or a political agenda. Just out of curiosity. It would be all right for a couple of days of fine summer weather before Sandile went off to his father's village in the Transkei for Christmas.

When he and Peter's father pulled into the driveway of the Seiberts' house, Sandile noticed two small black children he hadn't seen before running around in the garden. The maid's children, he assumed. He lifted his bulging sports bag and followed Richard to the door.

"Hey, it's great to see you," Peter greeted him, showing him to the guest bedroom. Once Sandile had settled in, Peter said there was time for tennis before dinner, if he felt like playing. They headed out for long rallies as the sun began to set. With no lights for the court, they decided to wait until the next day to play a match.

Sandile woke up early in the morning and went out to practice his serve. He had loved tennis since he learned it in middle school, but he had little chance to play because of soccer and cricket practice. He enjoyed the rhythm of tossing one ball after another high in front of his right shoulder and then bringing his racket down and through it as hard as he could. There was a therapeutic feel to walloping the ball repeatedly.

He came in when called for a breakfast of pancakes, bacon and fresh fruit with the whole Seibert family.

Peter seemed drowsy at the table but Sandile saw him perk up when they took their cups of hot, milky tea to the terrace after the meal. While they were discussing plans for the day, Peter suddenly excused himself and ran off. Sandile waited while his host dashed around the end of the house and came back accompanied by a black teen-age girl in shorts and a white T-shirt.

"Kagiso, I want you to meet Sandile, who helps me not flunk out of school," Peter told her as they approached.

By the time they reached the terrace, Sandile began to think that he had seen her before. He wasn't sure where, but it was definitely a face he knew – a small chin, a graceful curve of a mouth between rounded cheeks, tightly curled eyelashes, a soft Afro, a hard look.

Sandile stood up and said, "Good morning."

"Pleasure to meet you," she said, but he thought she didn't mean it, that she glanced up at him as if to size him up and find him wanting.

The three stood awkwardly for a moment before Peter said, "Listen, why don't we all play tennis in a little while?"

"Can you play with three?" she asked.

"Course. Canadian doubles," Peter assured her.

"What's that?"

"Meet us at the court in half an hour and I'll teach you."

Sandile felt he'd been dragooned. On the court, the whole thing seemed awkward to him. Kagiso didn't know how to play tennis. Peter explained about rotating partners. She started paired with him. They lost that game. When she moved to join Sandile, she asked him bluntly where he had learned to play.

"At school," Sandile replied, as if that were obvious. Where did she think?

She sniffed in disapproval and lunged at the ball, missing it completely.

He tried to show her how to swing with the racket face vertical.

"I don't want lessons from you," she shot back at him in Setswana. Then she whacked ball after ball out over the fence.

Sandile thought she did it on purpose so she could waste time looking for them in the flower beds. He waited on the court, trying to remain patient, watching as she bent over to search among the flame colored amaryllis blossoms and the green stems. Then Peter went out to help her, as if it were a difficult task. No way for Sandile to get back into the rhythm of the game.

Worse, each time Kagiso returned to the court, she glared at him, as if he had done something wrong. Finally, she excused herself and said she needed to go look after her brother and sister. What a relief.

After she left, Sandile just stood there shaking his head for a moment before suggesting that he and Peter play a real match. They slugged it out through hard-fought points. Somehow, Sandile prevailed. He assumed it was because he was so frustrated at being judged, yet again, by a girl he didn't know, even up here in this white preserve where he thought he would be shielded.

"Something wrong?" Peter asked as he congratulated Sandile on his victory.

"Tough match."

"I'll say."

Looking for a way to include all the kids, Peter decided soccer was the best answer. He talked Christina, Megan, Mike and Tiny into meeting him and Sandile on the lawn to pick sides.

"Wait just a minute," he told them as he ran to the kitchen courtyard to speak to Kagiso.

"Hi," he said, interrupting her reading again. "Want to play soccer with us? All the kids are in."

"No, thank you," she answered, using her finger as a bookmark. "I've got a lot of reading to do."

He looked at the book and saw that she had just a few pages left. Hard to figure why she fibbed about it, but he gave it one more try. "You sure?"

"I am not keen on sports," she admitted.

"Oh. OK," he conceded. It wasn't like his tennis lessons had been a success. He'd have to let her be. Nodding acceptance, he headed back to the group on the lawn.

Mike had his foot on the soccer ball but was looking the other way. Peter dashed in and tapped it out from under him. The little boy tried to steal it back, but Peter dodged him as he announced, "OK, everybody. Sandile and I are captains. Let me introduce you so he can pick."

He dribbled the ball away from Mike as he added, "Tiny is seven and Mike is nine…"

"Ten," Mike corrected, puffing his chest in pride.

"Your mother said nine."

"Tomorrow I am ten," he insisted.

"OK, ten. Megan is eight and Christina is twelve."

"What about the captains?" Christina asked, demanding strict equality.

"Fifteen years," Sandile said, placing his hand on his chest.

"Me, too," Peter added. "OK, Sandile, you're the visiting team so you pick first."

"You know the players. You must choose."

"All right, you take Christina and Tiny and I'll take Mike and Megan." That seemed pretty fair to him: Christina was big for her age, strong and disciplined, though kind of a fuss-budget about rules. She would make up for Tiny's hesitancy. Mike and Megan were small and unpredictable but fierce.

He set up orange cones at each end for goals and stuck garden stakes in the ground to mark the corners. The six of them played in a mad scramble for an hour or so, with Peter and Sandile trying to set up the smaller ones to shoot on the unguarded goals. Christina kept score with a pad and pencil, but Peter overruled her on giving out yellow cards for infractions.

"You scrape it smooth like this," Ellen demonstrated as she leveled off a cup of sifted flour.

Kagiso followed her aunt's example, eager for the chance to learn how to bake a birthday cake, and to do it in the Seiberts' well-equipped kitchen.

Ellen turned on the electric oven to preheat.

"Our stove can do this?" Kagiso asked, intrigued by the idea of setting a precise temperature.

"Difficult with coal. But you can learn to tell how hot it is and adjust the time."

They moved on to measuring sugar and salt. Ellen explained that all measurements had to be just so or the cake would not rise. It would become a dense lump in the bottom of the pan. They melted chocolate squares and butter, then let them cool. They greased two round cake pans and dusted them with flour so the batter would not stick.

"That smells good, Auntie. What is it?"

"Vanilla flavoring. Tastes bitter but smells sweet. Here," Ellen put a dab on each side of Kagiso's neck. Kagiso breathed in the peaceful aroma.

They added a teaspoonful of vanilla to the batter before turning on the electric mixer to blend the flour, chocolate, eggs and other ingredients into a uniform color. Next, they poured it evenly into the two pans.

Peter came into the kitchen. "Want to do something outside?" he asked Kagiso.

At least it wasn't another sport he was asking about, Kagiso thought. His interests seemed so limited, although at least he appeared to care about politics.

"Maybe later," she replied, but she didn't mean it. If she went into the garden, she would have to see Sandile again, and she didn't know if she could hold her tongue.

"OK." He headed out.

Kagiso thought about when she had first seen Sandile as he was lecturing a shop assistant. How arrogant. As if his private school and his family's money made him superior. He was a puppet of the apartheid government who needed to be told off, or stopped.

Licking the chocolate batter off the beaters and the rubber spatula and her fingers, she made herself stop thinking about Sandile and enjoy the luxury of all this space in which to cook something delicious.

"What's going on with you and him?"

Startled by her aunt's question, Kagiso leaned away from Ellen and looked at her crossways. "Nothing." It wasn't as if there was anything to hide.

"Hmph," Ellen responded, but she said no more.

Suddenly, Kagiso felt less comfortable in the kitchen. No place for her to relax around there either with her aunt scrutinizing her every move.

"It must bake thirty to thirty-five minutes," Ellen said as she slid the pans into the oven and turned the dial on a timer. "When it rings, come and I'll show you how to test for 'done.'"

"For sure," Kagiso agreed. She washed up the cooking utensils before heading to the kitchen courtyard. Having finished her only book and unable to think of anything else to occupy her time, she opened to the first page and started again. This time she decided to concentrate on how Mandela had become a lawyer without completing university. Maybe that would be a better path for her than teaching history; she could defend the people.

The jarring brrrinnnggg of the timer brought her back to the kitchen, where Ellen showed her how to use a cake tester.

"Done," Ellen declared, sniffing the chocolaty steam and smiling at her apprentice. "Good work."

Kagiso beamed at the two pans full of smooth, dark cake cooling on a rack. This was special. Her first cake, and Mike's, too. He was a fussy eater, but she was sure he would like it, if it tasted anywhere near as good as the batter. The dessert would celebrate his birthday, and count for hers, too, though that was four months off.

Mike ran in. "Smells good, Auntie. What is it?"

"Out, both of you," Ellen said to him and Kagiso, shooing him away from the dessert surprise. "I've got cleaning to do."

As they went out the back door, Tiny dashed up and grabbed her sister's hand. "Come see," she said tugging Kagiso toward the back lawn, where Peter and Sandile were hunched over doing something that Kagiso couldn't decipher.

Tiny picked up a wooden mallet that was two-thirds her height and painted white with a red stripe. She tried to show her sister how to play croquet.

Peter came over to explain the game. It sounded pointless to Kagiso – tapping wooden balls through bent wires and then across the lawn to other bent wires. Just like tennis, she thought. Back and forth for no reason, getting nowhere. But she didn't want to be rude and say she wouldn't play. He seemed like a nice boy, just clueless. Then again, there was his friend Sandile, who scowled at her across the lawn. How did she get stuck spending her holidays with a do-gooder and a sell-out?

"Like this," Mike demonstrated, swinging a mallet hard and missing so badly that he fell over. Everyone laughed. He got up in a huff.

"You be my teammate," Peter told him. "We'll show them. Laughing at the birthday boy…"

"Can I be your team?" Tiny pleaded with Kagiso.

"For sure."

Tiny hugged her and added, "You smell nice."

"Vanilla," Kagiso explained.

"Two teams and three individual players, right?" Peter clarified. "Christina, you start."

So, that was it, Kagiso thought. Trapped. How could she join and still have nothing to do with Sandile? That might require concentrating on the foolish game itself. She listened as Peter advised Mike on technique and strategy. Trying to apply the lessons, she alternated shots with Tiny, sometimes sending their ball way off track or hitting the wickets and bouncing back. Eventually, they got through some of the hoops. Keeping her emotions fully in check, she didn't even gloat when Sandile hit a disastrous shot into the bushes.

The scent of a charcoal fire gave Kagiso the first clue on how to escape. Seeing that Peter's father had just lighted the barbeque on the terrace, she excused herself to go help her aunt get the dinner ready. Peter's parents had insisted that everyone join them for a *braai* for Mike's birthday.

Peter's mother acted as lifeguard. Mike splashed the little girls in the shallow end of the pool. Sandile played one-on-one water polo with Peter in the deep end, but checked out Kagiso, too, as she propped herself up on a towel to keep an eye on her brother and sister. Or was she staring at him from behind her sunglasses? He could see why Peter was taken with her. A high-cut bikini with diagonal red and white stripes accentuated her figure.

When the younger children got out of the water, Kagiso walked down the steps and took a few cautious strokes across the middle of the pool. Not a good swimmer, Sandile noted, but she managed. Peter quit the water polo game to swim beside her.

Sandile was still trying to remember where he had seen her. Must have been at his parents' store, where so many people passed through. What gave her the right judge him? What a stupid situation Peter had unwittingly created, he thought. Diving to the bottom, he pretended to explore the floor of the pool rather than face her accusing eyes. He blew out long streams of bubbles, coming to the surface only when he had to, until she got out of the water.

Ann announced that they all had to get out and come inside so that she and Peter's father could go out to dinner. All the children would be under Ellen's care, she said. Sandile did not relish another evening with Kagiso, but he told himself to rise above whatever was bothering her.

For dinner, the seven young people took their seats at a big kitchen table topped with steaming platters of spaghetti and meatballs.

"What is that, Auntie?" Mike asked Ellen, pointing at the meal.

"Spaghetti and meatballs, child. Don't be scared of the food."

"Haven't you ever had it before?" Christina marveled.

Mike shook his head and refused to try it.

"People in Soweto don't cook expensive foreign foods," Kagiso explained to Christina. "We eat mealie meal and pumpkin."

Against his own advice, Sandile waded in to contradict her: "Many township people buy spaghetti."

She switched into Zulu, charging, "Maybe the rich people at your store."

"Our customers are not rich and our food is not expensive," he rebutted in Xhosa.

"And your clerks are not 'boys'."

Suddenly he knew when he had seen her – that day she had stared hard at him as he was teaching the shop assistant how to read. Typical of the comrades, he thought, to accuse him when really he was trying to help.

"He asked me to teach him to...," Sandile flashed into defensive mode.

"*Haw!*" she replied in disbelief.

"Who are you...?

"We very much appreciate your superior education..."

"This is not expensive," Peter interrupted them.

Sandile knew that Peter could not have understood their words. It must have been the tone. He burned with anger when he saw Kagiso silently mouth the word 'sell-out.'

"It's what poor people in Italy live on," Peter continued. "And here, at the Seibert residence, the proper eating technique is to fling it by the spoonful into someone else's mouth. Ready, Mike?" he said, arming a spoon with a meatball.

The little boy ducked and ran for cover behind his aunt, who shared her own dinner of mealie porridge and stew with him.

Sandile finished eating without another word. This was not fun, despite Peter's clowning. He had not come to this white neighborhood to be attacked by radicals. He was glad he would be going home the next morning. Luckily, she shut up for the rest of the dinner, too.

Later, as he and Peter sat in the family room watching an old "Star Wars" video, Peter asked Sandile if there was some problem between him and Kagiso.

Sandile hesitated to reply. He didn't think Peter would get it. And he was too polite to insult his host.

"I was hoping we could all be friends," Peter said.

"I wouldn't mind, but I think she does."

"What do you mean?"

"Ask her," Sandile suggested, trying to sound ingenuous. Peter was naïve, harmless. She was neither. He felt sure Peter was getting in over his head – politically and personally. Better to keep his distance from whatever was going on there.

"You're a guest here," Ellen scolded Kagiso after they had put the younger children to bed. "What right do you have to judge that boy?"

Kagiso was shocked by the reprimand from the aunt who had always supported her. Why couldn't she see that Sandile was a sell-out? "Peter?" she asked, pretending not to know who her aunt was talking about.

"Don't get smart with me."

Caught, Kagiso didn't dare reply.

"You're a brave girl to join the protests," Ellen said. "But wrong to judge others."

Kagiso sat on the steps of her aunt's quarters with her arms folded across her chest and her lips pressing hard against each other to hold back angry words.

"A leader does not get followers by insults and threats," Ellen advised. "A leader invites them, shows the way."

Kagiso wasn't buying it. What had Ellen ever led? What did she really know about the struggle? About the student movement? Kagiso sighed in frustration, still too annoyed to speak.

"Now let's go to bed," Ellen instructed.

"Yes, Auntie."

But Kagiso couldn't go to sleep for a long time. She kept coming back to her aunt's advice, looking for ways to argue her point of view, to show her aunt how out of touch she was, living up in this white area, being too old to protest. She went 'round and 'round until she began to hear in Ellen's words a few of the things that she herself had said at student meetings. She didn't like Sandile one bit, but she let herself imagine the triumph of converting him from a strikebreaker into a protester.

"Merry Christmas," Peter wished Sandile as they stood on the doorstep of Sandile's house. Sandile thanked him for the weekend in Houghton but didn't invite him in. They shook hands and parted.

Why couldn't his two friends be friends? Peter wondered as he walked back to his mother's car. What had they said to each other in some African language? He understood that their lives were different from each other; that was obvious from seeing their houses. But he liked both of them, so why wouldn't they at least try to be friends with each other? At least be polite? He blamed himself for not having mentioned Kagiso to Sandile before the visit. But what would he have called her? The maid's niece? She was much more to him than that, though he didn't try to define it.

Climbing in, he looked quickly at Kagiso and smiled. She had promised to introduce him to some of her friends. He couldn't wait to get to know her better through them.

His mother pulled the car up outside the Mafolos' house. She and Ellen and all the younger children went inside. Kagiso poked her head in to greet her mother, then led Peter off to meet Palesa.

"Where you going with your boyfriend?" a woman's voice mocked.

"Ignore her," Kagiso advised Peter. "She runs the shebeen next door."

"What's that?"

"A nightclub. She makes traditional beer. Drinks it, too, for sure."

That explained the drunken man he had seen on his first visit. Didn't bother Peter, though. Kagiso hurried him onward.

"Mind where you step," she said as they picked their way down the rough path through the squatter camp toward Palesa's place.

He stepped over trash and puddles with unknown contents, afraid to touch the shacks crowding the path for fear they would collapse. With no solid buildings to lean against, they seemed even more fragile than the ones he had seen in Alexandra township.

"*Umlungu*," a small boy called out before running away among the shacks. It sounded to Peter like the Swahili word for a white person, '*mzungu*' that he had heard in Kenya. He ignored the comment and kept his eyes on the path.

Kagiso slowed on a treacherous part. Peter looked up and saw five boys about his age who stared at him from beside a shanty. Their faces were unreadable. He waited a beat to assess their mood, then decided to take the initiative.

"Good morning, guys," he said.

They burst out laughing. One thrust a hand up to give him a high-five. Another called out, "*Yebo, baas,*" but grinned to show it was a joke.

"This is Peter," Kagiso told Palesa's neighbors. No further explanation.

High-fives all around before Peter and Kagiso moved on.

Kagiso knocked on a crooked door. The door popped open as a woman came out and gave Kagiso a hug; then she noticed Peter.

"Oh, a visitor. We are in a mess. Quick," she said to her son, "fetch Palesa."

"Sorry to trouble you, Mama Mhlongo," Kagiso told her. "This is Peter. I wanted him to meet my friends."

"You are very much welcome," she said, ushering them into her one-room shack. "I clean the Madam's house all week. Some days I have no time for mine. Sorry for that."

"Very pleased to meet you, Mrs. Umlongo," Peter replied. "I hope we're not intruding?" He took a seat on a rough bench.

Every item Peter could see was neatly folded, stacked or stowed. The walls were covered with pages from fashion magazines folded into neat squares.

"So cool," he said, pointing at the kaleidoscope of fur coats and evening gowns and lipstick ads.

"Thank you, thank you. Palesa makes them from Madam's magazines," Mrs. Mhlongo said. "There you are, Palesa. We have guests."

The girl's smile put Peter at ease. Her mother fluttered around mumbling to herself about the condition of her home and insisting on making tea, although Kagiso begged her not to go to the trouble. Peter was embarrassed when she served his tea in a china cup but everyone else's in chipped enameled mugs.

When they finished their drinks, they thanked Mrs. Mhlongo, and Kagiso said they must be going. Palesa accompanied them out into the glare of mid-summer sun.

"Kagiso, we must go to Sonny Boy's," Palesa said. "About his father."

"His father?"

"You didn't know? But you've been away. Two fingers on his right hand."

"Ayeee." Kagiso grimaced. "How?"

"Accident where he works. Last week. And they fired him."

Peter saw the tall slender girl wiped tears from her eyes.

"Let's go," Kagiso suggested. The three of them started toward Sonny Boy's house, but their progress was slow because friends and acquaintances stopped to greet them.

"You are welcome in Soweto," an older woman told Peter when Kagiso introduced him to one of her mother's best friends.

"Thank you, ma'am."

"From U.K.?" she asked.

"U.S.," he corrected as four children, maybe her grandchildren, clustered around her.

"Very nice," she said. "First time I meet an American."

The three teen-agers finally reached Sonny Boy's house. Peter spotted a man whose clean white bandage stood out against the background of drab concrete-block houses and scrubby lawns. The man was sitting outside on a chair, squinting into the sun.

"Hello, *Baba*," Kagiso addressed him, bowing slightly. He looked around, focused on Kagiso, seemed to recognize her.

"Hello," he replied distantly, then noticed Peter. "Who is this?"

"Mr. Gumede, this is Peter. He brings you greetings."

"Hello, sir," Peter said. He couldn't offer to shake hands. He didn't know what else to do so he bowed slightly. It hurt just to look at the man.

"Kagiso," a big teen-ager called out as he and another boy came from behind the house.

"*Sanibona*," she shouted as she dashed over to get a hug and to pat the other boy very lightly. "Lawrence and Sonny Boy, my friend Peter," she said, signaling for Peter to join them.

He was honored that she would introduce him that way.

"You are welcome," Sonny Boy said.

"Thanks," Peter said. "It's great to meet Kagiso's friends."

Lawrence acknowledged the visitor with a slight nod of the head, no words.

After small talk among the five, Kagiso said she and Peter were expected at her house.

"OK. See you tomorrow," Sonny Boy replied.

"Sorry for that," she countered. "My parents are sending me to Bop with my aunt for the holidays. They don't trust me to stay out of trouble here."

Sonny Boy's face fell.

Peter felt a flash of jealousy as he witnessed the reaction.

As Peter and Kagiso walked back toward her house, he tried to make sense of the glimpses she had shared of Soweto life.

"How can they fire Mr. Gumede?" he asked. "Isn't there some kind of worker's insurance?"

"Not for blacks in South Africa."

"What will he do?"

"Try to live off his wife's pay; she works at Dion's. Maybe find some place he can work with one hand. He built such beautiful things – cabinets, tables, chairs, everything." Her voice trailed off, and Peter waited before asking more questions.

"And Palesa's family?"

"Squatters with no permit to live in the township. Government threatens to evict them."

Peter wished he could help somehow. But the thought of Sonny Boy's obvious affection for Kagiso crossed his mind, too. He dared another question, hoping his own stake in the matter didn't show. "Is Sonny Boy your boyfriend?"

"No," she laughed. "I don't have one. He's a good friend."

Peter took some comfort.

"Lawrence," she continued, "almost never speaks now. Sonny Boy watches out for him."

"What's wrong with him?"

"The police took him."

"Why?"

"We don't know. He was just one of us protesters."

It sent a chill through Peter. What if she was in danger, too?

The ten-hour bus trip down through the cliffs and canyons of Natal province gave Sandile time, too much time, to think. He nibbled at his sack lunch. Sports magazines lay on his lap unread. The image of Kagiso's accusing face kept crowding into his mind. She had called him a sell-out. What right did she have to pass judgment without asking why he did what he did? He resented having to justify himself. But militants had been easier to dismiss when he didn't know them personally.

Fine for them to protest if they liked. How would it help the cause if he, too, boycotted school? The authorities would be unmoved by his absence from a private academy; he would merely fail to get the education his family had worked hard to provide for him.

Sandile tried to shove his internal debate aside and absorb the beauty around him. Rugged cliffs and canyons gave way to the rolling green hills of the Transkei perched just above the Indian Ocean. Round turquoise huts with tidy thatched roofs stood in clusters along dirt lanes. He saw old women smoking long clay pipes and balancing heavy parcels on their heads as they strode along the paths. He was glad to return to the serenity of his father's and his grandfather's village.

He got down from the bus and walked the last mile. His half-sister's twin boys met him along the way and helped carry his bags. As they neared the family compound. Sandile looked for his grandfather and quickly spotted him just where he would have expected – on a stool in the shade in front of his home, both hands resting on top of the walking stick that signified his rank as a sub-chief.

"*Molweni, Utatomkhulu,*" Sandile called out. The white-haired man turned toward him and smiled. Sandile bowed respectfully and sat for a moment on the ground next to the old man.

"*Unjani,* Sandile?"

"*Ndiphilile. Ninjani?*" Sandile assured him he was well and asked about his grandfather's health.

"*Ndiphilile.* How are your father and mother?" his grandfather continued in Xhosa.

"Well." Sandile chose not to worry his grandfather by mentioning his mother's mother's slow recovery.

"How are you doing in school?"

"I am near the top."

Sandile decided to ask his grandfather for his views on school boycotts. Not right away, but later in the week. He would look for a moment. He wanted to know that the choice he had made lived up to the revered man's expectations.

When they finished their formal exchange, Sandile went to look for his father's senior wife, Nontsikelelo, an energetic woman several years older than his own mother. He found her organizing the women and girls who were preparing dinner for a big gathering.

"*Molweni, Umama,*" he said.

She smiled, stepped away from her work and embraced him. "We are very much happy to see you."

Her powerful hug made him feel at home immediately. It was good to be surrounded by the larger family, not alone in the house in Soweto. Sandile handed her the packet of money from his father that supplemented the corn and vegetables she grew.

"Is your father coming later?"

"Sorry for that. He says not this year. Too much work."

He saw the disappointment in her face, even as she assured him that his hut was ready.

Setting off on the obligatory round of greetings, he called on his uncles and aunts, his half-brother and half-sister, their spouses and children, and a whole array of other relatives. Going through the age-old ritual seemed to peel off layers of his uncertainty and defensiveness.

Next, he went back to the turquoise rondavel he shared with the twins. He knew they would have dropped his bags there and that Nontsikelelo would have swept the dirt floor and folded the blankets across the end of his bed. He unzipped a bag, took out a deflated soccer ball and a pump, and inflated the ball until it was quite firm. Then he rounded up the twins and some cousins so they could play a short game of soccer before supper. After hours on the bus, he really needed to stretch his legs.

With nine boys in tow, Sandile headed to a worn soccer pitch to choose sides. They were thrilled to have a new ball.

"We're on Sandile's team," the twins insisted in chorus.

Sandile made the sides as even as he could, for the sake of family peace. They launched into a game of mad dashes and debates about what was outside the unmarked boundaries and fanciful displays of dribbling, and a disputed score that almost came to blows. Evening suddenly took over their field, calling an end to the game. As they headed back to the compound, Sandile could smell the beef stew and the *umngqusho*, made of dried corn and beans, cooking in large cauldrons over an outdoor fire. He was eager to join the family for a favorite meal, tall tales, firelight and a sky full of stars that he never took the time to contemplate in the township. A perfect way to turn sixteen, he thought.

A bustle of activity woke Sandile early on Christmas morning. He lay in bed listening as girls went off with buckets to fetch water and women started fires to begin cooking the feast. These were not his duties; he kept out of the way. But he got up and dressed so that he would be ready to join the family as they walked together over the next hill to the church.

Many groups converged on the white stucco building with its name, Christ the Redeemer, painted in black over the door. The church was too small to hold all the families swelled with visiting city dwellers. Instead, the minister asked the congregants to carry the long wooden benches and the simple table used as an altar out into the shade of a large acacia tree, so that all could hear the service. Sandile's grandfather and other elders took their seats in front, while the younger people stood in clusters behind the pews.

The choir filled the warm air with joyous hymns in Xhosa. Sandile clapped and swayed to the rhythm as they sang. But a teen-age girl in the choir distracted his thoughts from worship. Much as he tried to listen to the minister during the two-hour service, he kept angling for a better glimpse of her long, dark neck rising from the stiff white choir robe and her wide lips forming the sounds. The girl never quite looked his way. Undaunted, fascinated, he resolved to find out who she was.

After church, Sandile and his extended family returned to their compound, reprising the hymns and shuffling in small dance steps to celebrate as they moved along the dirt path that ran between green fields. Cows stared at them as they passed. The family gathered around fires where the feast was bubbling in black cauldrons. They served out plates for the older members, who sat on stools. The younger ones pushed in line to fill their own dishes with meat stew, corn, beans and squash. Sandile sat with his cousins, mostly boys, and ate more than he usually allowed himself. They were too full for a soccer match, agreeing to play the next day, instead.

When Nontsikelelo finished her duties as head of the cooking and washing team, Sandile sidled up to ask her about the girl in the choir.

"Who were the new singers?" he asked, describing two others before he mentioned the girl. He hoped she wouldn't notice his real interest.

Nontsikelelo turned and looked him squarely in the face. "Not her," she warned. "Her father has accepted the cows."

Sandile's heart sank: she was engaged to be married. "She's too young."

"As old as I was when your father and I married," Nontsikelelo explained plainly.

"And the others?" he continued, pretending to be interested in who they were but not listening to her answer. He wandered back to the group of cousins.

By the end of the week of festivities, Sandile realized he had nearly forgotten to consult his grandfather about protests. The day before he had to return to Soweto, he made a point to ask.

"Grandfather," he said in Xhosa, "Soweto students strike because their schools are bad. They pressure all of us in private schools to boycott, too. Tell me what's right to do."

"Sandile, my grandson, our people rely on you to go to university, to make us proud and strong."

That issue settled, Sandile slept peacefully in the round house with its thick thatched roof. The scent of dried grass and the whiff of wood smoke from a dying fire filtered into his dreams. He knew what to do with his life.

But doubt leaked into his thoughts during the trek back to Soweto. He could see burned out buildings in Natal province, where supporters of the African National Congress and Zulu traditionalists had clashed. Did his grandfather's advice, granted in the countryside on the basis of tradition, apply to the urban areas? And "our" people, was that his family, or all Xhosas, or all the blacks of South Africa? He struggled to banish subversive thoughts. He hoped his grandmother would be well enough soon for a long talk. He needed advice from an elder who knew the township, too.

"How close are we?" Richard Seibert asked.

Ellen Dlamini leaned forward and replied, "You go with this road for some time. Then you come to a little dorp with some few houses. After that, we are taking a right turn."

Peter wished he could sit next to Kagiso, but Ellen was wedged between them on the middle seat of the van for the two-hour drive. His parents were dropping them at Kagiso's grandmother's home near Rustenburg. Not likely he would have a chance to say goodbye to Kagiso in private. And when would he see her again? Would he see her again?

They drove through dry scrubland until Ellen called out, "There. You go with that one," as she directed Richard to a rough dirt road that seemed to head nowhere. Several miles from the main highway, they crossed over a small ridge and saw rows and rows of small houses, hundreds of them clustered together on the high plains.

"We are reaching now," Ellen assured the driver.

Peter wondered what on earth people could be doing out here in the middle of nowhere. He didn't see any farms or factories or towns. How did they live? Kagiso would be able to explain, if he got the chance to ask her.

Richard pulled up in front of a two-room cinderblock house with a porch.

"We are very much thanking you," Ellen said to Richard and Ann as they all climbed out of the car. "By bus, the trip is too long."

"We're happy to do it, and it's on the way," Ann said.

Kagiso went to the back of the van to get their luggage and Peter moved to help her.

"Let me carry those," he said as she pulled out two large plaid bags.

"It's OK."

"At least one," he insisted as he grabbed the straps of a bag.

She lifted the other onto her head and started toward the house. He walked behind her, studying the way she swayed under the load, as if she were a village girl, although this was clearly an apartheid place, not a traditional African community. Up the two steps to the porch, then she set down the bag.

"*Dumela, Nkuku.*" Kagiso bowed and addressed an old woman who sat hunched on a wooden chair.

The woman blinked repeatedly and then answered, "*Ahe.*"

Kagiso spoke to her in Setswana and then turned to Peter. "This is my grandmother, *Nkuku* Mary. I gave her your greetings."

Ellen and the rest of the Seiberts crowded onto the porch and exchanged greetings. Mary invited them inside.

Peter perched on the porch railing. His time with Kagiso was coming to an end, and he didn't want it to, even though he wasn't sure what to make of it. She came back out and sat on the railing, too. He had to ask, even if he might be overstepping.

"Can I call you when you get back to Soweto?"

"Too expensive."

"I don't think you pay to get calls."

"My father doesn't allow."

"Then why'd he get a phone?"

"For emergency. Because he works nights."

"I see."

After a pause, she added, "He threatens to make me live with his family up here and says I'm getting too much into danger."

"Are you?"

"We are suffering. I only want to do my part."

They sat quietly for a moment.

"What can I do to help?" he asked.

"For sure, it's not your struggle."

"I meant help you."

"You can't stop the police. Or my father."

Chastened by her frankness, he did not reply.

"There is one thing," she said at last.

"Yes?"

"Bring that Sandile sometime. I'll take him to a student meeting."

Peter agreed to rope Sandile in. Eager to please her, he dismissed any thought of whether Sandile would appreciate that.

Richard and Ann and the girls came out of the house, calling out 'thank you' and 'goodbye.'

Peter hopped down from the rail to say goodbye to Ellen and Mary. To Kagiso, he whispered, "See you sometime?"

Before she could answer, Megan dragged him away, insisting, "Let's go. I wanna swim."

Back out the dirt road to the main highway, and then another twenty miles to Sun City resort and casino complex. Peter had thought the vacation sounded cool when his parents first booked it. Now he saw it through Kagiso's eyes – as a place the local people couldn't afford to visit. After miles of parched fields, an oasis with sprinklers running constantly to keep the lawns and exotic flowers lush.

On top of that, he was arriving at a casino for the first time in his life – but not like James Bond in a tuxedo driving an Aston Martin. Instead, in a white van with the words International Child Aid in primary colors on the side. Like a Mission Impossible truck. He slunk down in his seat, as if he might be seen making this embarrassing entrance.

The Seiberts checked in, took their bags upstairs, changed into swimsuits and went to an outdoor café for lunch. Peter surveyed the multiple swimming pools with islands and water slides, and the brilliantly-colored birds in vast netted aviaries. He could not live in this fantasy world without second thoughts. He kept thinking back to the hardships of her life, her reasons for protesting, her coquettish eyes.

After lunch, Peter stretched out on a lounge chair near the pool while his family splashed in the water. Ignoring them, and the heat, he concentrated on reading *Higher Than Hope*, the biography of Nelson Mandela that Kagiso had entrusted to him. This was his solemn commitment to understanding the plight of black South Africans. Maybe he would find in it a clue to how he could help. Touching the pages that she had touched, made him feel almost as if he were holding her hand. That kept him going even as sweat coated his brow and ran down his bare chest.

Suddenly a sprinkle of cold water hit him from the side.

"Help me do somersaults," Megan demanded.

"Stop splashing. You'll ruin the book."

"Come swimming or I'll get it all wet."

Telling himself he was just protecting Kagiso's property, he placed the book in a beach bag and ran headlong into the pool to tackle his little sister.

January 1989

"It's bad, for sure," Palesa warned Kagiso, who was just back from her stay in Bophuthatswana.

"How bad?"

"Almost half the school."

"I must see. Come that side?"

They headed to their high school, still closed for the holidays, to read the results from the December final exams that were posted outside. Kagiso ran her finger down the notice until she found her own numbers. They were good, even in history. Then she went through the list line by line. If anything, Palesa had understated the problem. Well over half the students had failed. Most of her friends had made it, Lawrence just barely. But T.S., Zwele and other radicals, and hundreds of other students, had failed and would have to repeat the grade or drop out.

"They are just punishing us," Kagiso fumed, blaming the Department of Education and Training. "What's the plan?"

"Stay-away on the first day."

Kagiso nodded. It made sense to her. A student strike alone would not be enough. They needed all the adults to stay home from work in solidarity. It was a lot to ask; people could lose their jobs. But anything less would show weakness.

"Will your mother strike?"

Palesa shook her head.

"My parents the same. If I say anything, they'll send me back to Bop." She set her lips tight together, trying to turn anger into answers. She changed the subject, cocking her head as she asked, "How's Lawrence?"

Palesa smiled and fidgeted and finally said, "Fine."

"For sure?"

"Sonny Boy goes with him everywhere."

"And you?"

Palesa didn't answer. She just smiled again.

On what was supposed to have been the first day of the new academic year, Kagiso and Palesa hurried to meet up with friends outside their high school. They talked little, trying to hide how nervous and excited they felt as more and more students gathered to chant and stamp and demand change. They had no intention of studying; this would be their biggest protest yet.

Surprised to see Lawrence at the demonstration, Kagiso thought he seemed scared. "You OK?" she asked.

He nodded, looked at Sonny Boy for reassurance, then said softly, "I must be seen here."

"We'll stay together," Sonny Boy declared.

The four of them joined the crowd. Kagiso felt the anger surging through every protest song, every chant of *"Amandla, awetu"* and *"Viva,* Mandela, *viva."* Frustration shot up through her, through all of them, like a volcano about to blow. Convinced that the failure rate was a plot to crush the student movement, Kagiso flung herself into that revolt, belting out *"Nkosi Sikelel iAfrika,"* shouting along with the mob at the few students who came to school expecting to study.

Action gave her courage. She looked around for better targets, for police enforcing the government crackdown. As if on cue, a pair of armored vehicles appeared on the crest of a low hill, making straight for the school gate.

"Almal van julle huis toe gaa," a policeman shouted in Afrikaans through a bullhorn for them to depart.

But the protesters didn't go home. This time, they didn't falter. Kagiso felt a chill of excitement run up her spine as the big beast with many legs raised its hackles and prepared for a fight. The police stayed in the protective cover of their vehicles. She and her classmates swarmed the front of the vehicles, shouting out their rage. Then she heard pings and clanks as other students threw rocks at the back of the armored vehicles.

The police whirled their rolling fortresses around and followed the rock throwers as far as they could, demolishing chicken coops, fences and outhouses as they drove through the narrow spaces between homes. The Casspirs did not circle back to the school but kept going across the township.

The protesters roared in triumph. Kagiso pumped her fist in the air as she joined the celebration. They believed that they had made the police flee. They were free to raise their voices as long and loud as they liked. She stayed on for hours, thrilled by the sense of power the confrontation gave them.

Sandile returned from the tranquility of the Transkei to a township seething with rage. Customers at his parents' store talked of little except the widening protests. Civic associations, women's groups, youth committees – all the anti-apartheid organizations, legal and outlawed – backed up the school boycott with calls for a general strike. No one was to go to work or school.

The afternoon before the start of the new academic session at Saint Andrew's, Sandile fixed a pot of tea and took it up to his grandmother's room, hoping she would feel strong enough for a serious conversation about school and boycotts and what he should do. A traditional healer living in the township, she would know best, better than his grandfather in the Transkei.

Dorah Sizani stirred as he set down the tray. She opened her eyes and looked at her grandson.

"Would you like some tea and biscuits?" he asked.

She nodded and tried to sit up a bit. He placed more pillows behind her head and shoulders to support her. She smiled at him, but he thought she looked weak, vague, as if she could not summon her spirit. He poured the tea, adding sugar and milk, and placed the cup on a small table next to her bed. By then, she had fallen back to sleep.

Her fatigue sapped Sandile's energy. He slumped onto a chair, wishing he could make her well. Her gunshot wounds had closed, but still she struggled with exhaustion from the pneumonia she had contracted in the hospital and with pain in her left shoulder and right biceps where bullets had torn through her flesh.

The tea grew cold. Sandile put it back on the tray, took all the tea things down to the kitchen and washed them. With nothing better than his own judgment to go on, he prepared his things for the first day of classes.

In the morning, fearful but determined not to give up his goals, Sandile planned a way to get to the bus depot along back streets. No sign of comrades until he approached the bus loading area and heard shouts. Five boys were forcing commuters out of the line. Two middle-aged women, as angry as they were scared, cursed the boys, shouting that the strike would cost them their jobs, that their children would go hungry. The comrades chased away the flapping, hollering women and several men along with them, whacking them with long sticks, flashing knives. Then the comrades stood guard over the depot. Buses and mini-vans sat idle and empty.

Dismayed, Sandile wished he hadn't been too proud to take Peter up on the offer to stay at the Seiberts' house when boycotts were called. He slouched home.

When he reached his house, its view of the highway inspired a new plan. He decided to walk the four miles from Diepkloof to the modest white suburb of Evans Park and see if he could get a bus from there to central Johannesburg. He could still get to some of his classes. He packed an extra set of clothes, hoping to stay with Peter that night, and left his mother a note before setting out on foot along the highway.

Because he had never ventured into Evans Park before, he wasn't sure of bus service for blacks or of how he would be viewed. He put on his striped blazer. Maybe that would help white people see him as a school boy, not a radical or a thief.

"Nice you could come," Peter whispered across the desks when Sandile reached Saint Andrew's Academy two hours late.

Sandile just heaved a sigh of relief and exhaustion. Under the circumstances, he welcomed Peter's little attempt at levity.

"We're glad you've arrived safely, Sandile," their new teacher, Mrs. Fielding, assured him. "Come to me after class for the details of what you missed."

"Not fair, you pitching up late," the rugby player Andre Malan scolded Sandile from the row behind him.

Afraid he would explode at his ignorant classmate, Sandile stared straight ahead and gripped the desk leg as if to crush it.

"Are you crazy? What about the strikes in Soweto?" Peter demanded, turning toward Andre.

"Staged for you foreigners," Andre declared.

"Quiet now, boys," Mrs. Fielding commanded, leaning on her desk with both hands as she surveyed the room. No one dared speak. She turned to the chalk board to continue outlining the biology course they were just beginning, starting with the structure of cells.

Sandile felt as if Andre's eyes were burning holes in the back of his head. But he didn't turn around. Sitting up very straight in his wooden chair, he focused on writing down every word the teacher said. Glances out the tall windows to the sun-filled sports field lifted his spirits. At the end of what seemed an endless introduction to the animal kingdom, he went straight up to the teacher while the other students filed out for the break.

"Thanks for trying," Sandile said to Peter, who waited for him outside the classroom door. He let his breath out in a strident sigh.

"What an idiot," Peter remarked.

Sandile said no more. He knew that Andre's father, an Afrikaner mining magnate, had chosen to send his son to a multiracial school. So why was he being judgmental? If white people like him were so hard on blacks, what chance was there for change? He couldn't let himself dwell on the implications. He had enough problems already.

"And he has yet to explain rugby," Peter complained.

Sandile appreciated his friend's jest, but he could not make room for that either.

"Don't you think you better stay at my house tonight?" Peter asked.

"Would that be OK?" The one thing Sandile wanted, offered without prompting.

"Of course."

Heavy machines snorted as they rumbled past Kagiso's house before dawn. Their caterpillar treads clunked along the street, waking her early. A sound like that could not be good, she knew. Instantly on alert, she slid out of bed and into jeans and a T-shirt. No one else in her house was up. She slipped out the back door so that she could observe unseen.

Once outside in the beginnings of daylight, she saw a line of bulldozers followed by empty dump trucks and police vans. Keeping hidden, she watched until they all passed, then followed their trail. It suddenly hit her that their destination might be the squatter camp where Palesa and T.S. and their families lived. She hurried along, reaching the camp just as the destruction got under way.

A bullhorn blasted an announcement in Afrikaans: "This is an illegal settlement. Lorries are waiting to drive you to your homelands. Get out now."

People rushed from the shanties toward the top of the gulch, pulling on clothes, grabbing their children and whatever belongings they could. They scrambled up to the crest, fleeing as the bulldozers destroyed their few possessions.

Some older women planted themselves in front of their shacks, defying the authorities to run them over. Policemen dragged the women away. But young men and women darted back into the squatter camp, playing a dangerous game of cat-and-mouse with the bulldozers, looking for missing family and friends or hoping to salvage property.

Kagiso waded in and shouted for Palesa over the din.

"Come now, now, now," Palesa called back from somewhere in the rubble.

Kagiso followed the sound and found her friend – hair poking out in all directions, forest green sweater half covering her nightgown – as she searched frantically through the remains of her shack. The wooden walls, with their wallpaper cut from magazines, lay splintered across the shelves and bedframes. Palesa was bent over trying to lift a large board. Kagiso grabbed it and helped her shove it out of the way. Palesa's brother, Paul, hauled metal roof panels up the slope, to rebuild somewhere, if they could. He came back repeatedly for metal and boards and bricks as the girls searched for crucial belongings.

"What are you looking for?" Kagiso asked Palesa.

"Grandmother's beads."

"What are they in?"

Palesa didn't look up. "Silver biscuit tin."

They dug through scattered clothing, shoes and a sack of cornmeal, all tumbled onto the dirt floor of what had been a home, making a pile of other necessities as they worked. Palesa tried to lift the table. Pieces of the corrugated metal roof weighed it down. Kagiso joined her and together they pried up the tabletop long enough for Palesa to reach under and grab the silver tin.

"Hold this?" she asked, handing the tin to Kagiso. Palesa picked through the rest of their possessions, found the one china teacup, broken in half, dropped it, pulled out school uniforms and a maid's dress, and handed those to Kagiso, too.

Screams rose from below them. Kagiso looked out and saw the bulldozers coming back.

"Let's move," she shouted.

The two girls rushed up the slope to where Palesa's mother stood by the road, tears streaking her tired face.

"Found it," Palesa assured her mother.

Kagiso handed over the tin. Mrs. Mhlongo peeked inside to be sure that the beaded necklaces her mother had made for her wedding had somehow survived, then she closed it quickly to protect them.

Mrs. Mhlongo moaned to herself as she held onto what the girls had saved.

Kagiso watched with Palesa and her family and neighbors as bulldozers passed through the camp again. But the steepness of the ravine made it hard for the police to get everywhere. Kagiso, Palesa and Paul waited for the right moment to plunge back in.

The three young people stepped carefully among splintered boards, broken glass, blankets and unseen dangers hidden beneath them. They were only partway down to the remains of the Mhlongo's shack when they heard a swarm of police shouting at the people, hitting them with sticks and trying to drive them toward a row of open trucks to deport them to the tribal homelands.

Retreating temporarily, waiting for a chance to run in again, they heard a terrible wail pierce the early morning air.

"My grandson," a woman cried out to her neighbors.

The three teen-agers and others leapt over obstacles to come to her aid. She pointed to the small boy's hand sticking out from under a corrugated metal panel. The rescue team surrounded the panel and lifted it carefully to free the child. The woman gingerly embraced the little boy in blue shorts, gathering him into her arms. He whimpered. She sighed in relief that he was still alive. Paul and Kagiso each grasped her elbows to steady her as she carried the ashen faced boy up the ravine to the road.

The bulldozers returned for two more passages to complete their devastation, bending and breaking and smashing people's homes, and then drove briskly away as if proud of their accomplishment. In the melee, Kagiso spied T.S.'s parents and his little brother and sisters scurrying to salvage belongings from their flattened shack. He would be furious that he couldn't be there to help them, she thought.

The three young people dashed back up the slope to escape the police. Mrs. Mhlongo stood motionless at the top, too traumatized to move.

"Come to my house, Mama," Kagiso urged her. They hustled to her home, where she made tea for all of them. Her father wasn't back yet, but she didn't fear his disapproval. She was confident he would see that this wasn't politics, it was friends in need.

Palesa wrapped long arms around her mother, as if to hold her together like the bands of a wooden barrel.

Slowly, Mrs. Mhlongo dried her own tears, pulled herself up straight and began to face the loss of her home. She asked Kagiso to guard the tin of beads for her.

"I need to go to Madam's," the woman said, "or she will fire me." She went out back to wash and put on her pink maid's uniform and apron. She returned to hug each of her children before heading to the bus depot, holding her head high.

Kagiso went to wake her sister and brother. When she put the tin of beads in her bureau drawer, she noticed the oversized green shirt her mother had given her. The big shirt would look good on her tall slender friend, who was still in pajamas and a sweater. She unwrapped it from around her sister's Hello, Kitty T-shirt and brought it to the kitchen.

"On you, very sharp," she told Palesa.

Palesa smiled, biting her lip.

Kagiso gave her best friend a hug, and then the flood started as tears washed over both their faces and Palesa shook with sobs. Without a word, Kagiso held on as long as Palesa needed her.

When Palesa relaxed her hold, they stood back and caught their breath. Then they turned to the daily task of preparing for school. They inspected the pile of rescued clothing and found enough pieces of Palesa's and Paul's uniforms to get dressed. The girls folded the remaining clothes and set them in a neat pile on an armchair.

Peter could not believe that Sandile had invited him to the Miss Soweto beauty contest. Actually, he could hardly believe that there was such a thing in a community convulsed by protest. But Sandile said his brother, George, had tickets because his girlfriend was a contestant and wanted supporters in the audience.

Peter's mother said she might go, too, to write a feature story. He hoped not.

"Better dress your best," Ann Seibert recommended. "Could be very swish."

He had seen enough of Soweto not to expect glamour. When the day came, he put on what he considered dress-up clothes – khaki trousers, a navy blazer, a tie with stripes, not the one with Saint Andrew's lions, and battered boat shoes.

The event was at Share World nightclub just outside Soweto; a real nightclub, he was told. He was glad when his mother said she couldn't go because of a news story in Port Elizabeth.

"No drinking," his father warned.

Peter didn't commit. He fidgeted in his dress clothes and only put on the tie just before they reached Sandile's that Saturday evening. As soon as he walked in the Malindis' door, he felt distinctly underdressed. There was Sandile, resplendent in a golden-tan suit and a silky black shirt and tie. George bounded down the stairs in his cream-colored suit and crimson shirt.

"Let's move," George told the boys. They climbed into the backseat of his BMW, polished like a candied apple. George gunned the engine and sped off to pick up his girlfriend at her home a few blocks away. She hesitated at the rutted path in her four-inch black heels and her skin-tight evening gown of canary yellow ruffles. George came to her rescue.

On the short drive to Share World amusement park and disco, Peter sat behind her and studied her elaborate hairdo of many slender braids swept to the left side and dotted with yellow plastic flowers. She looked like a movie star – sexy and sophisticated, more dressed up than any girl he'd ever seen. George escorted her into a special entrance for contestants and kissed her at the door. Then he drove to the main entrance.

Inside, Peter stared up at the spinning ball covered in small mirrors that threw slivers of light across the darkened room. The nightclub was a cavern sheltering them from the outside world, focusing their attention on a broad stage. George claimed a table, gathered his friends and flagged down a waiter.

"A round on me."

One group after another made an entrance, greeting legions of friends. The women wore evening gowns of red or turquoise or lime or gold or silver, most of the dresses tightly fitted and draping down to their high-heeled sandals. A few older women wrapped their heads in scarves of vibrant colors, but the younger ones wore their hair in intricate cornrows or smoothed and curved into stiff sculptures.

The beers arrived, a whole tray full of chilled glass mugs.

"To Precious," George toasted, lifting his mug.

Peter followed suit. It took him a moment to realize that Precious must be George's girlfriend's name. He glanced at Sandile, who took a small sip. Whew, Peter thought, not sure that he could down a whole mug as George had just done.

Loud pop music made conversation difficult. Peter watched the couples who strutted and swirled across the dance floor to "Let Me Be Free" and he studied the men who circulated through the crowd as if they owned the place.

"See that man?" Peter asked Sandile, pointing toward a stocky man in a huge white dinner jacket.

Sandile nodded.

"Is he the organizer?"

"Not sure. But he owns one of the big taxi companies."

"Yeah?"

"And that one," Sandile said, glancing at a tall man in a cream-colored tuxedo with a gold shirt, "is his arch rival."

Sandile spoke of others in the crowd, but without pointing at them. A man in blue ran a string of auto repair shops. One in black and gold, several shebeens. One in a red-and-black striped jacket, construction. A woman in a purple head scarf employed a dozen seamstresses. Another in a silver-and-gold gown owned hair salons.

Peter wondered how there could be so many businesses in Soweto. He hadn't seen any except the Malindi's store and a gas station. He took a sip of beer and waited for the show to begin.

But the start was a long time coming. The crowd mingled, danced, drank, laughed and showed no signs of impatience. A

second beer, spinning lights and smoke-filled darkness began
to make Peter feel dizzy. The last thing he wanted to do was
embarrass Sandile by keeling over or throwing up, so he made
himself sit in an awkward position to keep alert.

"And those two," Sandile said as he stood up, "run the
biggest grocery store in Soweto."

Following Sandile's gaze, Peter saw Stephen Malindi in a
black tuxedo with a ruffled magenta shirt. Grace's gown was a
swirl of tangerine and purple. The Malindis worked their way
across the room, greeting people at every table before reaching
their sons. Peter wondered if Sandile's mother carried her pistol
in this swanky place.

Way past the appointed hour, the master of ceremonies
took the stage. He began with long introductions for dignitaries and contest judges, praising their contributions to the
black community, including donations for the squatters forced
from their homes the week before.

Peter was struggling to focus. Finally, the contestants
strutted one-by-one across the stage to whoops and cheers
from family, friends and admirers. That woke him up. He
tried not to gawk at the girls whose slithery dresses showed
off their figures. Then he imagined Kagiso in a dress like that.
Red, like her earrings, and curving everywhere that she curved.
Suddenly, he didn't feel drowsy at all.

When the emcee called out "Precious Luthuli," George
and his friends jumped up and hollered for her. She smiled
magnificently, turned around slowly to admiring whistles and
took her place in the line of beauties.

With much fanfare, the emcee announced the three win-
ners. Precious came in third. Her fans paid no attention to the
winner and runner-up. Then all the contestants paraded across
the stage, down the steps and into the crowd.

Peter plunked back into his seat, woozy again. He tried to keep his head up straight.

"You OK?" Sandile asked him.

Peter nodded as if he were fine. His focus was on staying vertical and still.

"I'll ask my cousin to take us home."

In the morning, Peter lay in bed in the guestroom at Sandile's house, half under a blue-and-green plaid quilt. His ears still rang with "Izolabudd." His head hurt a little. Was that the beer? Was that why he had woken up unusually early? Or was it because he was pondering the ruse he had devised to get Sandile over to Kagiso's house? He didn't think it was a good plan.

"George has not pitched up," Sandile said as he and Peter ate cold cereal for breakfast. "Mind if we walk?"

"No problem," Peter said. "Uh, Sandile, my mom wanted me to take some papers to Mrs. Dlamini's. Can we stop on the way?"

Seemed odd, but Sandile read the directions Peter handed him. Not too far off their route. He went upstairs to let his grandmother know they were going.

The two boys walked a mile or so west, from Diepkloof into Soweto proper. Peter pointed out Kagiso's house. Her mother answered the door when they knocked. Kagiso was standing right behind her.

Sandile said a formal good morning. No interest in seeing Kagiso, but he couldn't be rude to her mother.

He grew suspicious when Kagiso welcomed them in, chatted politely, offered them tea. She asked how their school year had begun. They knew the turmoil that surrounded hers.

"Sorry but we need to go now," Sandile said. He had had enough of the reunion.

"We can start out together," Kagiso said.

Trapped, Sandile held his tongue. He wasn't sure if Peter was mesmerized by Kagiso and had forgotten his errand, or if maybe there was something else going on.

Peter suddenly piped up. "My mom wanted me to deliver this," he said as he pulled an envelope out of a back pocket and handed it to Kagiso. She put it on the kitchen table.

The three of them started out in silence. Then Kagiso said to Peter, "Palesa lost her home."

"What happened?"

"Bulldozers wrecked the squatter camp."

"No."

"For sure."

"My mom wrote a news story on it. I didn't know it was Palesa's place."

"We're meeting at Sonny Boy's to try to help her. You must come."

Peter nodded.

Sandile definitely didn't want to join them, but what could he say – that Palesa, whoever she was, losing her home didn't matter?

They walked into the workshop behind Sonny Boy's house. As they entered, Sandile heard a skinny boy haranguing a small group of students. The speaker stopped and turned his anger on them, demanding in Zulu, "Who are these people?"

"It's good to see you, T.S.," Kagiso answered.

"Who are they?" he insisted.

"Friends of mine."

"Who authorized you to bring them?"

"They're here to help."

"Spies," he spat the word

Palesa turned to say hello to Peter.

"Palesa, this is Sandile Malindi," Peter introduced them.

Before Sandile had time to speak to her, T.S. jumped on that information. "Malindi? Owns that big shop? And a Diepkloof palace? What are you doing with the likes of us?"

"He's come to help," Kagiso repeated.

"No he hasn't. Get out, you sell-out. And take your white friend, too."

As Sandile turned squarely toward T.S., he narrowed his eyes. "I am not a sell-out," he responded low and steady in Zulu.

"What do you do for the struggle?"

"I support our liberation as much as you ..."

"Prove it."

"I do not have to prove myself to you." Sandile turned his back on T.S. and stepped out of the workshop. He wanted no more of this. He would have walked away completely, except that he felt he had to protect Peter, who could not have understood the argument in Zulu or the risks he faced, being white in that band of radicals. "Time to go," he said emphatically as both Peter and Kagiso followed him outside.

Palesa ran after Sandile and said, "Please don't mind T.S. He's been in hiding for months."

Sandile said he was sorry about her home. Then he strode away.

Peter and Kagiso caught up with him. "If something's wrong, it's my fault," Peter apologized. "I just wanted my two best friends to be friends, too."

Neither answered.

Sandile fumed. He planned to cut ties with both of them.

As she struggled to keep up with Sandile's race-walk, Kagiso huffed in English, "The government succeeds by dividing blacks against each other."

He whirled to face her, brushing Peter out of the way.

"You and your friends divide us, claiming there's only one way to freedom," he shouted at her. "I work for it every day."

"You work to make your parents rich."

"That's a lie they tell in your little meetings. Without my family, you would have to go to Jo'burg for every sack of mealie meal. We create jobs. We give a lot to those in need."

"Then join us openly. Not me and my friends, if you don't like us, but the freedom struggle. For the sake of all who suffer."

"Suffer?" he demanded. "Let me show you suffering." Sandile clamped his long fingers around her upper arm and steered her toward his house.

"Let me go," she shouted, struggling to wrench her arm free.

Peter stepped up protectively. Sandile released her. Palesa came running over.

"I will come if I choose. Not like that," Kagiso declared, rubbing her arm.

Sandile marched onward, indifferent to whether they joined him or not. Peter and Palesa matched his pace but Kagiso had to trot to keep up. They pushed on in silence until they reached the upstairs hall outside Sandile's grandmother's room. Then Sandile swept the anger from his face and approached the old woman with nothing but compassion.

"Grandmother," he said in Xhosa. "We're back. May I introduce Kagiso and Palesa?"

The girls greeted her respectfully. Dorah Sizani turned in bed and smiled at the friends her grandson had brought home.

"Is there anything we can get you?" Sandile asked.

"A cup of tea," she whispered.

The four young people went downstairs where Sandile filled the electric kettle and set out the tea tray. Speaking in a low voice through clenched teeth, he informed Kagiso that his grandmother had not recovered fully from being shot by burglars who had attacked the shop months before.

"Don't tell me about suffering," Sandile warned Kagiso.

"Until we topple this racist government, police will chase students instead of the *tsotsis* who shot her," she insisted in turn.

"You think a school boycott will bring down the government? That your 'comrades' have a right to beat me if I don't strike?"

"Why should you alone get a fine school?"

"What kind of future if everyone is ignorant?" he answered in a shout reined in just enough so that his grandmother would not hear it.

"If the future is you, we will be suffering."

"You would go to private school if you had the chance," Sandile charged, trying to cut her down to size.

"I had the chance and turned it down."

"What?"

"Redhill offered me a bursary. I didn't take it."

"Your parents are fools."

"I didn't tell them."

Stunned by her admission and by her commitment, however misguided he believed it to be, Sandile couldn't come up with a reply. The kettle whistled and he took the tea to his grandmother, trying to compose his thoughts.

By the time he returned, Kagiso and Palesa had left.

"I'm sorry, Sandile," Peter said.

Sandile was too unsettled to reply. He thought Peter was an idiot and Kagiso was a dangerous radical. When at last he spoke, it was only to warn, "You don't know what you're getting into with her."

I get why they clash, Peter thought, but is there any way to bring them together? He kept rolling it over in his mind and getting nowhere. Restless, he began to look for concrete ways to respond.

First, he organized his household to help out Palesa's family. He dug into his own drawers for pants and shirts he had outgrown that might fit her younger brother. He explained to his mother that Palesa was about her size; she gave him hand-me-downs. His father found a camp stove and camping cookware. His sisters gathered towels and pillows and soap and some toys that weren't appropriate, so Peter secretly put them back. Even Mrs. Dlamini came up with a dress for Mrs. Mhlongo. Peter packed it all in one of the mover's cartons that lingered in his bedroom and put it in the back of the van. His father promised to deliver it Monday after work.

Peter had one more project, for his mother. He asked her to buy a jar of caviar.

"You're not going to do that to her, are you?"

He feigned innocence. Ann said she wouldn't waste expensive caviar on people who might hate it but agreed to buy a little jar of salmon roe.

At school on Monday, Peter tried to repair the other part of his friendship.

"My dad says he can get us tickets to the big match," he told Sandile. "Want to come?"

Sandile ignored the question.

Peter casually pulled on a bright yellow cap with the logo of the Kaizer Chiefs – archrival to Sandile's beloved Orlando Pirates soccer team.

"Want to see the Chiefs whip the Pirates?"

Sandile did not respond.

Peter tried another tactic, hoping to revive their friendship where it had begun, on the fields at Saint Andrew's. "What should we go out for this season? There's the tennis team, swimming and what else?"

"I'm playing cricket," Sandile said.

"Cool. I like cricket," he said.

"I thought you Americans played baseball."

"When are the try-outs?"

"Tomorrow."

"Better stay with me tonight 'cause of the strike."

"I have made other arrangements."

Kagiso listened with dread as T.S. dominated the clandestine meeting in Sonny Boy's shed on the eve of the whites-only elections. With his moderate rivals detained by police, he gave his extreme ideas free rein.

"No school, no work, no shops," T.S. insisted, as had all the major anti-apartheid organizations. "The government must see unity against these racist elections. It must feel the power of the freedom movement. *Amandla*."

"*Awetu*," twelve classmates answered, pumping their fists in the air.

All agreed up to that point. Then he went through the orders for places to attack.

"Zwele, councilor Luthuli's house. Burn it."

"*Yebo*," Zwele confirmed.

"Thabo, house of the policeman Mahlangu."

"Me, I'm ready."

T.S. pointed to the next boy. "Ezekiel, Malindi grocery. Put the fire."

Ezekiel saluted.

The list went on, but for Kagiso, it was muffled as if she had gone partly deaf. She knew that some students at the meeting had doubts about targeting homes and black-owned businesses. But none of them dared to speak. T.S. drove them onward into battle, leaving no chance for second thoughts.

She feared that if she argued one more time against violence, T.S. might label her a sell-out and even target her family. Still, she would not let freedom founder on his personal vendettas. She determined to do what she could.

Kagiso left the meeting waving a clenched fist, repeating "*Amandla, awetu.*" Then she took a tortuous route, careful not to be followed.

"What do you want?" Sandile demanded when she knocked on his door.

"Let me in."

"To denounce me again?"

She ducked under his arm and in the door.

"How dare you."

She pushed the door shut and warned, "Comrades will attack your family's shop tomorrow, even if it's closed for the strike."

"Why would you care?"

"Maybe I don't." She spun around and went out the door, leaving it open.

Kagiso made her way to Palesa's new shelter, a backyard shack next to the bus depot. As she neared the transportation center, she saw five strike enforcers deployed around the taxi rank, ready to stop the few adults who were trying to go to work. Familiar faces, Zwele and other followers of T.S. Then she heard a voice that surprised her. Could it really be T.S. himself, venturing out of hiding in the daytime? She peered into the shadows behind a van and picked out a lean figure shouting orders to the others. She knew that voice. She kept her distance.

A truck screeched to a halt not far from the taxi rank and half a dozen Soweto police hopped out. Kagiso ducked behind a shack. The comrades retreated, trying to act innocent. She could hear the undercurrent of T.S.'s voice urging them to confront the police. She peeked out and saw him edging between the parked vans, trying to stay hidden.

"Ha," a policeman shouted as he came around the back of a van and spotted T.S. The boy ran, weaving in and out among the vehicles, eluding his pursuers, slipping underneath a taxi.

Kagiso breathed a sigh of relief.

Suddenly, all the police converged on the vans, picking their way among them systematically until they were down to two. Seemed they had been fooled, Kagiso thought. But one dropped to his knees, looked underneath and then shouted for his companions.

Kagiso trembled as she saw the policemen pull T.S. out by his left foot, kicking him as soon as they had him in the open, shouting in triumph. He struggled with all his strength, but they were too many, and the other comrades had disappeared.

"*EMA!*" she shouted. The police looked toward the sound, searching for her, until T.S. kicked and they turned their attention back to him. Quickly, Kagiso stepped back behind the shack, grabbing a door frame to steady herself. Knowing what they had done to Lawrence, she could not bear to watch them take T.S. But what could she do to stop them? Six against one.

Trembling, she crawled past another shack to a flimsy fence where she forced herself to do the only thing possible – to spy through a hole so that she could bear witness to his capture. Four of the policemen, each grabbing a foot or a hand of their writhing prisoner, carried T.S. to their truck, heaved him into the back compartment and shut it. She could hear him shout and pound on the insides of the truck as they drove away with their catch.

Kagiso slumped to the ground behind the fence, hiding her face in her arms as she wept in anger and fear and shame. How could she have abandoned T.S.? What had he ever done to her? She could feel the warmth of his skinny arm across her shoulders. It crushed the breath out of her.

Letting herself sob for a few minutes, she tried to gather what was left of her courage. Slowly, Kagiso lifted her head and forced her arms to push her up, her legs to come underneath and enable her to rise, her feet to step forward. In robotic motion, she made her way toward Palesa's place.

"What happened?" Palesa asked, at the sight of Kagiso's face streaked with tears and dirt.

Kagiso fell into her friend's arms, sobbing for minutes before she could catch her breath enough to say, "They took T.S."

Palesa held her, lifted her, stroked her hair.

When she closed her eyes, Kagiso could see T.S.'s eyes, fierce and eager as he led the comrades against the police. Palesa told her it was not her fault. Six against one. The odds had never been in his favor or in hers. But the whole school would know before morning. His followers would blame her, although they had run away to save themselves.

Palesa broke into her dark thoughts. "We must find his parents."

Sandile distrusted Kagiso's motives, but he took no chances with his family's safety. He went directly to the shop to alert his father, who called on the extended family to come with guns or machetes or clubs and stay until the danger was over. Sandile's mother grabbed an extra clip of bullets and returned to the house to protect her mother.

The men of the family, Sandile proud to be among them, took turns standing beside the store windows and peeking out periodically, weapons in hand. They kept watch throughout the night before and the day of the strike. All was quiet.

By the second evening, the men guarding the store were tired and tense. They had slept little, stood guard, listened intently. They faced another long night on alert.

Sandile took over from his brother George on guard duty in the office, listening carefully for anything strange. He thought he heard noises in the dark, somebody walking outside, but when he looked, all he saw was the silhouette of a nearby house. Maybe the sounds were from inside it.

But, no, he heard something again. He peered out the window and barely made out two youths crouching near the neighboring house. A dim light from the shop reflected on something as it moved. Suddenly, one of the crouching forms lit a match and touched it to something that burst into flame. The other rose quickly and threw an object that broke a window. Sandile ducked behind the wall. Another bang as a second object hit the building. A whoosh as flames leapt up outside.

Sandile's father immediately joined him, crouching below the broken window. They peeked out just as the second boy, highlighted by the flames, rose to light the gas-soaked rag in another bottle. Sandile recognized Ezekiel, the neighbor whose family they had helped. His father fired a warning shot aimed well above the young man, who flopped instantly to the ground.

"Ezekiel Dube," Stephen called out in a booming voice that immobilized the youth, "if you burn my shop, who will give your sisters food to eat?"

Ezekiel rose to a crouch, lit the bottle and gave it an awkward sideways toss that landed well short of the shop. Then he crawled backward, jumped to his feet and ran away.

Sandile picked up a fire extinguisher. His father and brother kept watch, guns in hand, as he slipped out quickly to douse the flames.

"Thanks for speaking up for me at cricket yesterday," Sandile greeted Peter in the morning.

"Only a pleasure," Peter replied, borrowing the South African expression. He was delighted but mystified by Sandile's cheerful tone.

After cricket practice, and the welcome news that there was a position for each of them on the team, Sandile and Peter again sat near the gate waiting for rides home.

"You were right about her after all," Sandile began.

Peter knew Sandile was referring to Kagiso, but he was surprised. He chose to wait and see where this was going.

"She saved us."

"Saved you?" Peter asked. Very strange, he thought.

"Came to my house to warn us they would burn our shop. Thanks to her, we were ready."

Peter didn't know what to say.

"Risked her life," Sandile added. "T.S. could target her if he finds out."

February 1989

Although there was no boycott that morning, Sandile followed another circuitous path through Diepkloof and into Soweto to catch the bus; it had become a habitual precaution. As he walked beside a set of abandoned workers' hostels, he heard a motor being gunned and tires squealing. He hid in a doorway. A police truck skidded as it sped from behind the building, onto the street and away.

Quiet returned. Sandile emerged from the doorway and started onward in the expanding light of early morning. Then he heard a long moan, someone in great pain. He looked for the source. In back of the hostels, he saw a man lying on the ground, heard him utter that unearthly sound again.

Gingerly he approached. It wasn't a man but a skinny youth, his face purple with bruises, his eyes swollen shut from a beating, blood dripping from his mouth, nose and ears. Sandile realized quickly that the mangled figure before him was T.S. He knelt beside the boy, struggling to think what to do, wishing he knew something about medicine, or at least knew someone in the neighborhood who could help. His brain seemed to freeze. Then he thought of Kagiso. Her home was not far away, and she knew T.S. well. Wiping away his anger at T.S.'s insults, he placed a finger lightly on the boy's hand.

"I'll get help," he promised, leaning close.

The groans emerged again but the eyes did not open to recognize Sandile, the imagined enemy.

Sandile dropped his book sack and ran top speed for Kagiso's house, the fastest mile he had ever run. Her father answered, tired after a long night at work.

"Sorry for troubling…," Sandile said as he fought to regain his breath. "Speak with Kagiso?"

Her father scrutinized him for a moment, then called to his daughter.

Kagiso came to the front door, did a double take to see Sandile, then stepped outside to speak with him.

"T.S.," Sandile whispered, voice and body shaking. "Behind the hostel. Dying."

"Where you going?" Kagiso's father bellowed after her as she raced away with Sandile.

Sandile's heart pounded, especially when he had to slow down for Kagiso. But he couldn't face this alone. He had to bring her to her classmate. They dashed across the open field and cut in between two buildings in the hostel complex to reach the spot where T.S. lay. Kagiso cried out when she saw him.

Sandile knelt beside T.S. and asked, "Can you hear me?" He listened for breathing, put his hand lightly on the boy's chest, picked up a limp wrist.

They were too late. T.S. had uttered his last sound alone. He had rolled onto his back, arms slightly spread on each side. His clothes were dirty and blood-spattered. Blood dripped from his wounds and formed tiny puddles in the dust.

Kagiso flung herself across T.S.'s body as if to shield him from death. Sandile got out of her way and waited in silence. When she sat up, he could see blood smeared across her face. He offered her a tissue.

"Do you know his parents?" The words barely came out of Sandile's throat. He felt as if they were choking him.

Kagiso nodded.

Sandile crouched next to the body, sliding his right arm under T.S.'s back and shoulders and his left arm under the knees. He could feel the warmth still in the body. The weight of such a wiry boy startled him. He struggled to stand up. Kagiso helped him to his feet. Sandile shifted the weight in his arms. Blood smeared his shirt. He nodded to Kagiso that they should start.

The body was so heavy that Sandile could barely think beyond the effort of getting all the way to T.S.'s family, wherever they might be. He had to look ahead at where his feet were going, not down into the battered face. Maybe it was better not to think, he told himself. He staggered forward, this time with Kagiso waiting for him and carrying his backpack.

Because the day was just starting, they saw few people as they trudged through Soweto. Some recoiled in horror or ran as if misfortune were contagious. Others came to see who was being carried and why and to offer sympathy. A couple of children followed them silently.

"He is not well," Kagiso told those who asked, as if that explained the matter. "We are taking him to his parents."

Sandile didn't speak to anyone; he reserved his strength for the journey, which seemed to take forever. His arms and back ached. Kagiso assured him it was not much farther, less than half a mile, to the place where T.S.'s parents and their three remaining children crowded in with relatives. They rested for a moment, Sandile leaning his back against a fence post but afraid to put the body down because he wasn't sure he could lift it again.

"This side," Kagiso told him as they moved along a secondary street. They stopped in front of a typical Soweto bungalow where she knocked on the door. They waited a few minutes, Sandile slumping against the outside wall of the house, with T.S. still in his arms.

Finally, the door opened.

"Mama Mkondo," Kagiso said, pointing toward T.S.

A woman's head poked around the doorframe. A wail pierced the air, nearly knocking Sandile down it was so loud, so sudden, so filled with agony.

The woman rushed out and wrapped her arms around T.S., tugging and sobbing and wailing as she and Sandile brought him into the house and stretched him out on a couch.

Sandile fell into an armchair. He was drenched in sweat, stained with blood, exhausted in every fiber. He barely heard what T.S.'s mother said. Someone brought him a glass of water. With terror trying to strangle him, he struggled to swallow, then sprawled across the upholstery as he gasped for air.

"How could they do this to him?" T.S.'s mother asked over and over, addressing no one and everyone – her sister, Kagiso, Sandile, God. Kagiso did not try to explain anything about T.S.'s life as a radical. She knew that there was no answer that could ease his mother's grief. She sat on a wooden chair and rocked slowly back and forth, trying to think, trying not to think. Bringing her knees to her chest, she curled into a ball. Streams of tears dripped down her face. She made no attempt to wipe them.

"Kagiso, you must have some tea," T.S.'s aunt urged, breaking into the girl's thoughts.

Accepting the mug, Kagiso put her feet on the concrete floor and inched her chair backward, trying to disappear into a corner of the room. She could not stand to look at T.S.'s body lying limp along the sofa cushions, yet she could not look away. The bruises and cuts on his face, the ring of chafed skin at his neck all looked much as Lawrence's wounds had looked. The stillness of a boy who had been so agitated, so in command, weighed on her, weighed on time itself, emptying it of all meaning.

People began to flood into the house – neighbors, relatives, busybodies. The noise became a roar of intermingled wails and moans and sobs and prayers, as if the room itself were crying out for a son lost. Kagiso had no idea who most of them were. T.S.'s father had not come back from work yet. Dreading the sight of his face, she wondered what it had been like for her parents when they lost their first child. Her only memories of it came from her father's words.

Mrs. Mkondo's sister eased her way among those who had come to mourn. They stepped away from the body. A hush descended on the room. She signaled to Sandile and Kagiso to help her.

"He must be washed," the woman informed them as she indicated that Sandile should grab T.S.'s feet while she and Kagiso each held a shoulder. The crowd parted to let them pass into the kitchen, where they placed T.S.'s body on the table.

Kagiso could feel his arm cold against her. The fire in him had gone out. As she set him down, the sleeve of his sweatshirt pulled up. She gasped as she looked at his wrist: he wore a single strand of red and white beads with alternating triplets of each color. Placing her bracelet next to his, she saw that they were exactly alike. She could not breathe. She looked at his aunt in panic.

"Yes, go," the woman nodded.

Kagiso fled the house, her hand over her mouth.

"I'll have another funeral to cover this Saturday," Ann Seibert told her husband as their children got up to clear their places after dinner. "Can you take the girls to their riding lesson?"

"Of course. Who is it this time?" Richard asked.

"Another student leader. Anti-apartheid groups say the police killed him."

"I'm so sorry," Richard said.

"He was just a kid," Ann replied, turning toward Peter. "About your age."

Peter stared at her wondering what connection she saw.

"You're not going alone, are you?" his father asked.

"With Jim and Stanley. We'll be OK at Regina Mundi and the graveside, and stick together if it gets rough back at his house."

Peter cleared his place, but the conversation made him sad. Could be someone Kagiso knew. He tried to concentrate on his homework and the math questions he would need to talk to Sandile about in the morning.

Neck, shoulders, lower back, even his fingers. Sandile ached in muscles he hadn't known he had. The strain of carrying T.S. for a mile had cost him. He could see how bad he looked by the expression on Peter's face when he arrived in class. Telling Peter what happened to T.S. made him relive all the horror of the day before.

"I'll be OK," Sandile tried to convince them both. "It's Kagiso I'm worried about."

"Me, too."

"Do you think you can come to the funeral with us?"

Peter promised to try.

All that day, Sandile writhed on his wooden chair.

"I am hurting," he told Peter late in the day. "Tell Coach Haverford I'm sorry?"

"'Course. You got aspirin or something?"

"For sure."

It wasn't just the aches that made Sandile skip cricket practice. Everything seemed off to him. Walking out the school gate, he carried his book bag in his hand, to avoid putting it on his sore back. The street lined with mansions appeared changed. Pairs and threesomes of maids and gardeners headed to the bus stop. There seemed to be more than usual, maybe because he had left early.

Holding onto a bar on the bus, he felt the strain in his shoulder whenever the vehicle swerved. To keep his mind off that discomfort, he studied the other riders. Women in maid's uniforms of pink, yellow, baby blue, white. Young women with babies tied to their backs, the tiny feet sticking out on either side of the mothers' hips. The men, some of them young and others gray-haired, wore pants and jackets caked with garden soil and, from the smell in the crowded bus, with sweat. Sandile suddenly felt uncomfortable in his jacket and tie, as if he were pretending to be better than they were.

Some seated passengers slumped against one another, nodding their heads as they tried to sleep. But others, standing and sitting, chatted, laughed, told jokes in most of South Africa's languages – Zulu, for sure, but also Xhosa, Pedi, Tswana, Sotho. He listened to the men standing next to him, regaling one another in Ndebele about some foolish instructions from their bosses.

How many times had he rung up men and women like them at the cash register in his parents' shop? But now he asked himself if he had he ever really looked at them, ever wondered if they had dreams. Had he ever done anything for their freedom? Sell them groceries at fair prices, and give some away, yes, but was that enough? Gotten himself a fancy education. Was that enough? He could almost hear T.S. demanding answers. His record was hardly heroic compared with a boy who risked, and lost, his life for everyone's freedom. A boy from the shacks. A boy with courage. Sandile held himself up to that example and felt the gap.

Walking slowly from the bus and taxi rank in Soweto, he returned to the site of T.S.'s death. Aside from small dried-up puddles that only he would recognize as blood, there were no signs that T.S. had ever been there. T.S. was gone. His home was gone. His family was itinerant. But, Sandile reminded himself, his work remained unfinished. The only question was what to do about it. That was not a question for his grandfather or his grandmother. It was a question for him. He was certain of that.

The Malindis' grocery was crowded when Kagiso reached it after dark on Friday. She waited in the check-out line for a chance to speak with Sandile. While paying for a chicken leg for her father and pumpkin and beans for the rest of the family, she asked to speak with him for a moment.

"Coming just now," he resoded.

She waited outside the entrance, sliding the beaded string around and around her wrist. The situation was not good, she fretted. T.S.'s funeral was set for the next day. Why had she urged Sandile to bring Peter? Neither boy had any idea what they were getting into. And she would be responsible. Sandile could blend in, but Peter would stick out, become a target.

"What is it?" Sandile asked when he stepped outside.

"You coming?" She knew he would know that she meant to T.S.'s funeral.

"For sure."

"And Peter?" She prayed that the answer was no.

"Yes. Coming to my house in the morning."

Kagiso closed her eyes for a moment. "Meet me at Palesa's?" she asked.

"Not your place?"

"My father is already asking who you are. He'll try to keep me from going."

"Where does she stay?"

Kagiso explained which shack near the bus depot.

"Ten?"

"For sure." Kagiso nodded, then hurried home because she didn't like to be out alone in the dark. The sack of groceries weighed little, but she felt a burden on her shoulders. Tossing her head repeatedly, she tried to regain her confidence. But she ended up shaking her head slowly. It would be up to her to get these two boys through it safely, just as she had shepherded Tiny and Mike home from the bus station years before. But this time the problem was *her* fault.

Peter hopped out of his mother's car at the Malindis' home. Then she and two other journalists headed to Regina Mundi Church. Peter watched them drive away before he and Sandile set out on foot for Palesa's place. They walked in step, in silence, until they saw Kagiso and Palesa leaning against the shack, heads down.

Kagiso looked up as they approached, then stepped forward and hugged Peter.

Astonished, Peter felt guilty for the thrill her welcome gave him. Then she broke free to shake hands with Sandile. Palesa quietly greeted both boys. They set out on their long walk to the church.

Noticing that Kagiso had trouble keeping up, Peter slowed down for her.

"It's OK. We need to move," she told him, doing her best to keep the pace.

Peter walked along street after street of small houses ringed by rusting fences and makeshift outbuildings. They must have walked a couple of miles, he thought. But, without street signs, he had no idea where they were or how to get back to Sandile's house. He just had to trust the girls.

The four of them drew near the church. Peter had expected a big stone building, or maybe concrete like some of the churches in rural Kenya. He was surprised by the modern brick and wood structure with stained glass windows under its eaves.

Security forces stood several deep in a ring around the church. Kagiso identified them for Peter: black Soweto Police in their jumpsuits, white soldiers of the South African Defense Force in khaki and white South African Police in pale gray-blue. Armored vehicles and trucks full of reinforcements backed up the men on foot. The white police bellowed orders at the crowd.

"What did they say?" Peter whispered to Kagiso, wishing for the first time that he had learned some Afrikaans.

"'Move inside,'" she said. "Always yelling, even at a funeral."

As the four made their way through the security cordon, Kagiso pointed out to Peter different types of mourners in the huge crowd. Women's groups carried long banners with hand-painted slogans. White diplomats in expensive, somber suits talked with leaders of the anti-apartheid movement.

In the distance, he spotted a group of news reporters and photographers – his mother and her two colleagues among them. Watching her snap photos and jot down comments, he suddenly realized how hard it might be to avoid catching her attention.

Kagiso, Peter, Sandile and Palesa waded into a throng of young mourners. The two girls greeted schoolmates and shared their grief and their anger over the killing.

Peter felt the eyes of all those grieving students on him, the only young white person in the crowd, and tall and blond at that. Would they take their anger out on him? His self-mocking style would be inappropriate here. And Kagiso and Sandile probably wouldn't realize his position. What could he do?

He took a deep breath to collect himself, and then he put his hand out to shake hands with whoever would accept him.

"I'm so sorry," he said to the black student closest to him.

The young man seemed surprised, but he grabbed Peter's hand, gave it a big shake and said, "You are welcome here."

Quickly, others moved to shake Peter's hand, many others, a steady flow of students. He felt a flush of pride at being accepted.

Kagiso wedged herself in among them and said to Peter, "We need to move inside."

He tried to disentangle himself, shaking several more hands that were thrust at him as he followed her. He and his friends made their way into the back of the church, finding some of the last seats.

Police guards watched at every open door, their guns at the ready. They did not enter the sanctuary, but Peter thought they looked prepared to do so on the slightest excuse.

For half an hour before the service began, hundreds of students sang freedom songs and danced the *toyi-toyi*. Each time a group finished the many verses of an anthem, someone from the other side of the church struck up a different tune and fired up another faction.

Peter was swept up in the huge sound that filled the church. He could not pick up the words in various African languages, but he began to copy the movements, punching the air with his fist, trying to get the hang of the *toyi-toyi*. Hearing the click of a camera as a photographer began snapping images nearby, Peter dropped quickly out of sight. Crouched down, he looked around for his mother. She was speaking with other journalists, some he recognized from his parents' dinner parties. But her back was turned to him. He was in the clear for now.

The crowd hushed as a procession of priests and ministers entered the church and walked to the altar to open the service. Kagiso whispered to Peter that many of them were great men in the anti-apartheid movement who spoke out when other leaders were in prison or banned from public gatherings. She pointed out Anglican Archbishop Desmond Tutu among them.

"I know. My mother writes about him all the time," he whispered.

When all those who had seats sat down, Sandile showed Peter where T.S.'s parents were seated near the altar facing the sea of mourners. The black coffin topped with yellow roses rested front and center. Diplomats and other dignitaries filled the first rows; anti-apartheid activists sat behind them.

"Brothers and sisters, we are gathered here today for the somber task of burying our beloved Thomas. We ask the Lord's blessing so that all His children might one day be free," a minister intoned from behind the communion rail.

Peter stopped to think whether he had ever been to a funeral before, but everyone else seemed to know exactly how it would unfold. He listened intently to all the speeches and eulogies, the hymns, the prayers that poured out for an hour and a half in a pattern he did not foresee. The service ended with the churchmen and the coffin bearers and the family recessing down the main aisle and out into the bright day.

Dignitaries and leaders slowly followed the ministers. The young people waited their turn, but they did not wait in silence. They filled the church with freedom songs. Not knowing the words, Peter could only hum along, but still he felt carried by the sound, embraced, included.

The students began to flood out of the church, defiantly dancing and chanting in front of the police as they waited to board buses to the graveyard.

"Stay close to me, no matter what," Kagiso told Peter and Sandile. They moved with the crowd toward a fleet of buses and then boarded one where jumping youths kept the floor shaking for the short ride to the cemetery.

The crowd gathered again at the graveside, standing on the mounds of other graves, among the headstones and the artificial flowers and the wrought-iron fences. The ministers said more prayers. The pall bearers lowered the casket into the earth.

Peter saw the dignitaries leave in large, black Mercedes cars while the young people got back on the buses.

"Where we going?" he asked Kagiso as the four of them waited in line to board.

"Where T.S.'s parents stay. For the funeral meal. It's tradition."

"OK."

"But it's dangerous. The police attack after the diplomats leave." She fished in her pocket and pulled out three bandanas. "Which color do you want?"

"I don't know. Blue?"

She handed him a light blue bandana, gave the green one to Sandile and kept the yellow one. "Tie it around your neck," she told them both.

"Why?" Peter asked as he tied. It reminded him of playing cowboy as a child.

"Tear gas."

Peter was alarmed but excited, his blood pumping fast like at the start of a soccer match. This was the real thing. He had heard about township protests from his mother. He had wondered what it would be like to see one but never thought he would be in one.

The bus carried them through Soweto streets to the end of a block where Peter could see large white tents stretched across three front yards to shelter dozens of tables and more than a hundred plastic chairs. They got down and entered a street so crowded with mourners that no traffic could pass. A long line formed on the edge of a drainage ditch.

"First, we greet his parents," Kagiso explained as they joined the line. "Then we eat."

"How can they feed...?" Peter began to ask.

Suddenly shouts rose from the crowd behind them. The four friends whirled around to see young people and old scattering as an armored vehicle barged through. The police barked orders to disperse through their bullhorns and fired tear gas canisters. The people panicked.

"Pull up your bandanas," Kagiso told Peter and Sandile. "Let's move." She grabbed Peter by the hand and tugged as the whole crowd around them began to rush along the street, desperate to keep ahead of the Casspirs. Peter looked back and saw Palesa take Sandile's hand and follow Kagiso.

A tear gas canister whizzed past them and landed on the roof of a nearby house, spewing its noxious fumes. Peter began to choke, then pulled the bandana over his nose with his left hand. He did not let go of Kagiso's small hand. He knew he needed her. She was his guide, his lifeline.

"For sure they'll make trouble," Kagiso warned.

Shots rang out through the street and cries told of some violence the four friends could not see through the haze. Kagiso shepherded them along the side of the road, careful not to let the fleeing crowd separate them. She led them on a detour through side yards and out onto another street. They saw an armored vehicle looming in the unbreathable atmosphere and shooting off another tear gas canister. She turned their party around and led them through a series of twisting alleys.

They ran along a narrow passage until a wall of corrugated metal, stacks of wooden boxes and other discarded items blocked their way. Kagiso stopped and tried to get over it. She did not ask for help, but Peter saw her struggle and gave her a boost. He checked to see that Palesa and Sandile made it over. Then he took a few steps back and vaulted over the heap. He knew that he was not the rescuer here; he was completely dependent on Kagiso to get them through this maze. There was no time to be scared, only time to act.

They ran through a yard on the other side until Kagiso suddenly stopped and knocked urgently on a door.

"Auntie Noma, it's Kagiso. Please, let us in," she called.

They heard the latch turn and slipped in quickly as a woman opened the door a crack. Aunt Noma locked up behind them, then shooed them behind furniture, reminding them to keep low and out of sight, as they were already doing.

Screams in the street just outside. The rumble of an armored vehicle. Shots fired. Footsteps running. No one dared peek out a window. Peter stayed crouched down, tightly packed in with his three friends.

The sounds of confrontation gradually subsided. Aunt Noma signaled that they could emerge from hiding and sit in the chairs.

"Thank you, Auntie Noma," Kagiso whispered. "These are my friends – Palesa, Peter and Sandile." And to her friends, "My father's older sister."

Suddenly there was a tap at the door. They all jumped in their seats but no one rose to answer it.

"Hello. I'm a journalist. Please let me in," a man's voice said quietly in an American accent.

"Who are you?" Aunt Noma demanded from behind the door.

"Michael Nesbitt, *Washington Post*."

Peter remembered seeing him at the church. One of his mother's friends. He told Kagiso, who asked her aunt to let him in.

"I can't thank you enough," the reporter said as the woman opened just wide enough for him to enter. "Do you have a phone I could use for a few minutes?"

She nodded.

"Sorry to disturb you," he said. Then, to Peter, "I think we've met."

"Yes," Peter confirmed, aware that he would have to face the consequences if his mother found out. "Ann Seibert's son. *Dallas Morning News*." He offered the journalist his hand, man to man.

"I thought so. Saw you in the street. Seemed like you knew where to go, so I followed."

Peter wanted to say it was his friends who knew the way, but he didn't want to expose them so he let it drop.

"Sorry. I better call this in," the reporter said as he began to write in his notebook. In fifteen minutes, he asked Kagiso's aunt if he could use the phone, for a local call.

"Michael Nesbitt, Staff Writer, Soweto, South Africa," he began reciting slowly. "Dozens of people were injured Saturday as police fired tear gas and buckshot into peaceable crowds of mourners after the funeral of one of South Africa's most charismatic student leaders...."

Sandile listened intently as the journalist dictated his story. He wondered how the man could describe the terror they had just survived in a dispassionate manner. But it tore at him to hear a journalist repeat the lie the police were telling – that T.S. had jumped from a building to evade capture. If he spoke out against it, would the police target him?

Bad enough that the comrades pressured him. Now to add the police as his enemies? Too much risk. But how could he let the police get away with that lie? Was he really so weak, such a little boy, that he could not speak up?

Churning and churning as the dictation dragged on, Sandile gradually came to the conclusion that there was only one right way – to tell the truth.

"Mr. Nesbitt," Sandile said once the dictation was finished, "the police are lying."

"That's the only way we can cover it," Michael explained. "The police say he was never in their hands. There's no proof."

"There is proof," Sandile said, slowly, deliberately, weighing his fate. "I saw them."

"You saw the police kill Mkondo?" the reporter asked, pen and notebook at the ready.

"No. I saw them speed away after they dumped his body at the hostel. T.S. couldn't open his eyes, they beat him so badly."

"Let me get this straight. You saw the police dump his body at the hostel?"

"No. I saw them drive away, in a hurry, from behind an abandoned hostel. There was no one else around. I heard moaning. I walked behind the building and found T.S. He was dead by the time I came back with help." He decided not mention Kagiso's role and drag her into danger, too.

"Soweto police or South African?"

"Soweto."

Michael wrote down every word, then challenged the speaker, "The police will say you lied."

Peter jumped to his friend's defense. "You ask T.S.'s parents who carried him home."

Michael nodded and turned to Sandile again. "And what's your name?"

"Sandile Malindi."

"Spell it for me?" He wrote it down. "And your position in the student movement?"

"None."

"None? You've never been involved?"

"Not until today."

"You went to that funeral yesterday."

Patrick Mafolo spoke those words to his daughter from the depths of the couch, but Kagiso, just waking, heard them as if they were a shout inside her head. She halted at the bedroom doorway, tempted to make a run for the front door.

"You think I'm a fool? That I don't speak to my own sister?" he demanded, sitting up, leaning his powerful shoulders into the queries, shaking off fatigue from his long night at work.

Kagiso did not breathe.

He waited for her reply, the weight of his silence bearing down on her.

Kagiso knew that voice, the one that said she was still his little girl and he was her protector. But she would never again depend on him, on anyone, to be her shield. She would stand up for herself. She knew he couldn't see that, or didn't want to see that. She had to show him that she was strong, like the anti-apartheid slogan: You strike the woman, you strike the rock.

"I only went to show respect, because he was from my school. The way everyone in a village goes to a funeral," she answered him, trying to twist the facts into a tradition he would recognize, to wring out of them an escape route.

"With that Xhosa boy, smartly dressed – the one who came here early in a hurry," he resumed his review of the case. "And you dragged along that son of your aunt's employer. Perhaps you do not worry that she could lose her job."

"*Baba...*" she started, wanting to protest her innocence, tempted to promise that she would have nothing more to do with politics. She stopped, unwilling to tell that lie even in

self-defense, apprehensive but stalwart in the face of the expected punishment.

There was no argument she could make that she had not
made countless times before. He is like so many parents, she
told herself, too weak to fight for what they know is right,
but clinging to their power over their children. She would
carry on the struggle whether he approved or not, for all of
them.

Kagiso's father stood and looked down on her with the
full authority of the head of household. He waited for her to
beg for mercy. He waited patiently, powerfully.

She did not bow. She saw only a man who did not understand, who dictated.

"I have made my choice," he declared against her silence.
He proceeded to the bedroom.

Kagiso prayed that he would calm down after a rest.

Sandile stopped by Kagiso's house later that Sunday morning,
but she said she would not join him in paying respects to
T.S.'s parents. He walked alone across Soweto back to the scene
of the funeral meal, barely looking at the little girls in frilly
dresses who were bound for church and the men studiously
drinking beer as they watched other men adding rooms to
their small homes.

In his mind, every young black face he saw turned purple
and red with bruises and blood. Murder, he thought, writhing
as the word flashed through his mind. No one – not even a
boy who had threatened him – no one should be killed like
that. He was proud that he had spoken out about the police
role, whatever risk it might involve. Silence did not seem an

adequate response to T.S.'s death. Telling the truth was only the start. But he needed to do much more, take real risks, fight back, only he didn't yet know how.

Sandile found Mr. and Mrs. Mkondo, now honored parents of a community hero, a martyr, talking with relatives and friends at one of the many tables that still filled the front yard. One of the tents had collapsed. The rented plastic chairs were scattered and toppled.

He approached quietly, waiting until the adults paused before he offered his respects and apologized for having left the day before without speaking to them. They did not mention security forces, tear gas, police beatings or speeches. The age-old ritual of mourning provided a small healing gesture in itself.

After the brief, formal exchange, Sandile politely stepped back to allow them to resume their conversation. He was unsure what to do, what move to make toward his new goals.

"The other boys are inside," Mrs. Mkondo said, interrupting her conversation. "You can just be free," she added with a gesture of welcome toward the house.

"Thank you, Mama," he murmured as he started for the half-open door.

Inside, several boys about his own age were huddled in furtive discussion on the sofa where Sandile had laid T.S.'s body. They abruptly ceased talking and turned to scrutinize the intruder.

Sandile had seen a few of their faces before somewhere – whether at T.S.'s meeting or the funeral or the shop, he was not sure.

"What do you want?" one challenged him.

Sandile paused to ask himself the same question, then he realized that these were boys prepared to act. They were ready to take the fight against apartheid all the way. This could be what he was looking for. "To join you," he replied.

"Why should we trust..."

"I know who he is," a short boy interrupted, pointing a finger at him.

Sandile braced to be condemned again because of his parents' wealth or his private school.

"Mama Mkondo said he is the one that tried to save T.S. and carried him home."

With that credential, they took his loyalty for granted, let him sit, did not ask his name. They said that knowing names would be dangerous if the police captured one of them.

The one who had challenged Sandile handed out the assignments: "You," he pointed to the short boy, the house of the councilor Dlamini. And you," he said to the next one on his right, "the house of the policeman Rachidi." Each boy nodded assent as the commander went around the circle of six.

Sandile felt the pull of belonging, the compulsion of vengeance. He did not allow himself to think deeply about the choice to join them. He let himself be tugged into their world. It was better than being alone with the horror of T.S.'s death. Rather than reflect on what they planned, he accepted his assignment:

"You," the commander told Sandile, "house of the policemen Chikane."

"Could be my best story yet," Ann Seibert bragged at breakfast, handing her husband a typed copy.

"Congrats. Think it'll make page one?" Richard asked.

"Don't know yet."

"Gotta run to tennis," he said. "Can I read it later?"

Peter picked up the paper as his mother went to the kitchen for a second cup of coffee.

By Ann Seibert
Special to the Morning News

SOWETO, South Africa – Rachel Mkondo planned the details: The yellow roses and green ferns atop the black coffin – the colors of the African National Congress flag. The eulogy by the minister who had baptized her son.

But she did not plan the police bullets that injured dozens of mourners.

She had not planned to bury her son at age 15. The funeral for student protest leader Thomas Mkondo, known as T.S., filled the biggest church in South Africa's biggest black township with students, diplomats, ministers, journalists and friends.

Anti-apartheid groups say the police beat T.S. to death, and then dumped his body near an abandoned workers' hostel. Police say he was never in their hands and accused rival activists of killing him. T.S. is the third young leader to die this month in connection with nationwide protests against the government's system of racial discrimination.

Police and soldiers ringed Regina Mundi Roman Catholic Church on Saturday. They hovered over the graveside service. But when the mourners moved to the Mkondo's home for the traditional funeral meal, security forces launched tear gas to disperse the crowds, then opened fire with live ammunition...

Peter put the paper down. The story was surreal, as if the terror he had seen and felt were scripted. How could his mother be objective about this? Had she not been afraid? Had she not cried, like a normal person?

Richard Seibert burst into the kitchen still sweaty from a tennis match at a friend's house and said, "We must talk immediately."

Peter looked up from making himself three tuna fish sandwiches. He gulped hard and followed his father to the door of his mother's office.

She was on the phone but quickly ended the conversation. Richard shut the door behind them. He took a deep breath.

"John Nelson couldn't make it for our doubles match today," he began. "So Mike Nesbitt filled in." He paused and looked at Peter.

All the blood drained from Peter's face. He stood slightly taller than his father but suddenly weak, defenseless, awaiting the storm.

Richard went on, still watching his son. "He told me how much he admired us for taking our son to political funerals...."

Ann swiveled to glare at Peter. "You were supposed to be at Sandile's."

Peter couldn't speak.

Ann turned to her husband for an explanation.

"Let him tell you," he said.

"Peter?"

"We went to the funeral with Kagiso," Peter replied in a voice far too small for his size.

"You lied to me."

"No, I didn't," he shouted, trying to generate some courage. He knew that being technically right would not get him out of this fix. But it could buy him a little time to think.

"This is not about lies," his father bellowed. "This is about the risk of getting killed."

The burst of anger, so rare in his pacifist father, sent Peter stumbling backward as if from a blow.

"Did it not occur to you," his father continued, "that you stick out in Soweto, a lone white face in the crowd – a target? Mike saw you. He followed you."

"There were other white people. Mom was there."

"Your mother was there to report. What purpose did you serve?"

"To support Kagiso and Sandile. They were the ones who found T.S.," Peter explained, hoping the truth would show them he had been right to go. When he had promised his friends he would join them, the choice had seemed obviously good.

"They what?" his mother asked.

"Sandile found him. He saw the police drive away, then he heard this moaning and he found T.S. almost dead," Peter spewed out the story in a rush to defend himself. "So he went to Kagiso, 'cause she knew him from school, and...'"

"That's not the point," his father roared directly into Peter's face. "You could have been killed. Don't you see?"

"So you want me to not help my friends?"

"You've lost your mind," his mother replied. "This country is in civil war and you think you can go around taking up causes?"

"At least I care about these people," he told her, angry now over her news story. "I don't try to make a career out of other people's suffering."

"How dare you?" she fumed at him.

"Peter, stop your insults this minute," his father ordered. "There's no comparison with your mother's work. You did something very dangerous, and stupid."

"You're grounded from going to Soweto," his mother declared.

Obviously, since he had no way to get there on his own. He would see Sandile at school, but he would miss Kagiso more than he could say. Muttering "you hypocrites" under his breath, he marched off to whack balls around the tennis court until he was exhausted and starving.

When Sandile arrived at his parents' grocery after cricket practice on Monday, his mother was keeping two reporters at bay.

"I tell you my son knows nothing about student protests. He does not go to a township school," Grace Malindi declared. "Sandile, tell them you know nothing and then I'll chase them away," she said, pulling up the butt of her pistol so the journalists could see it at the neckline of her dress.

The two reporters peppered him with questions: "Did you see the police beat him?" "Was he still alive when you found him?" "What did he say before he died?" "Soweto police? In a dark blue truck?"

"No. Yes. Nothing. Yes and yes."

"Any other witnesses?"

"No," Sandile answered. Kagiso had only seen T.S.'s body after the police had gone. No reason to drag her in, he decided.

They wanted to go on with the questions, but Grace recovered from her surprise enough to force them to leave.

"Sandile," his mother's voice trembled after they left.

"I didn't want to worry you."

Her eyes brimmed with tears as she took a long look at him. Sandile hoped she could finally see that he was growing up, one of the men in the family.

"Oh, my baby."

"I'm not a baby, Mama."

"No," she allowed, "but even a grown man can be killed. The police…"

"I had to speak. They beat this boy to death. And lied about it."

"They will target you now," she moaned.

"I am only a witness, not a radical." He knew he would have to plan carefully to carry out his assignment without blowing his cover as a private school boy.

"Talk to your father when he comes back." She wiped at the tears that had started to fall. "About protecting yourself. From them."

Kagiso fingered the beaded string around her wrist as she lay awake in the half-light of dawn. T.S. was really gone. She had failed to talk him out of violence. Her duty now was to try to stop others from being killed. But how could one girl make a difference?

Rolling onto her side, she nestled in with Tiny. Maybe she should give the little girl's Hello, Kitty T-shirt back, she thought. OK, but too soon to get up for school.

School. Her school. Tiny's school. The nursery school. Suddenly Kagiso had a plan. The crèche was next door to the clinic where Albertina Sisulu, one of the most important leaders of the struggle against apartheid, worked. What about talking with her? Maybe she wasn't back to work yet after the murder of Doctor Asvat who ran the clinic. But when she came back. She would know what to do. But it couldn't just be Kagiso asking; she would need a delegation. It would be risky, she knew, if the radicals heard about it. Best to keep it among trusted friends.

Kagiso jumped out of bed, forgetting about her sister's pink T-shirt, and started getting ready for the day. She hardly paid attention to the lessons in class, instead thinking of what to say to her friends at the end of the day.

"We are very much suffering," she whispered to Palesa and Sonny Boy. "We need to stop the killing." Her friends murmured approval. "Attacks on police and councilmen are black-on-black violence. Just what the government wants."

"An excuse to murder and torture," Sonny Boy said, glancing at Lawrence, who waited for him outside the fence.

"But they'll target *us*," Palesa warned. They all understood that she meant radicals would call them collaborators.

"Those ones are hiding," Kagiso answered her. "Now is the time. I want to ask for a meeting – just us and a few we really can trust – with the Soweto Civic Organization."

"No one can call them sell-outs," Palesa concurred.

"I'm in," Sonny Boy agreed, "but I better go. Lawrence is getting nervous. Tell me later what I can do."

"OK, bye," Kagiso replied, then went on explaining her plan. "When I see Ma Sisulu at the clinic, I can ask her if she'll…"

"Kagiso," Palesa interrupted, "what about Sandile?"

"Sandile? He can join us if you like," Kagiso replied with a sly smile as if her best friend had just revealed her affections. "Nice looking, isn't he? Tall and strong and…"

"I'm worried about him," Palesa said.

"Why?"

"He's running with T.S.'s friends."

"What?"

"Saw him talking with them at T.S.'s parents' home. The handshake. Everything."

"We have to stop him, them."

"How?"

Kagiso tried to think: she didn't know his family or friends.

"Peter?" Palesa suggested.

"Have to try," Kagiso agreed.

March 1989

His father was more flexible than his mother, Peter figured. Try him first. Try not to get sucked into one of those serious father-son talks. Just ask the question.

Peter peered into the living room and saw his father reading the newspaper, alone. Good timing.

"Hey, Dad. Can Sandile come visit this weekend?"

Richard set the newspaper on his lap and replied, "First we need to talk."

Peter swallowed hard but gave his father an innocent look. "About what?"

"You know very well," his father insisted.

"Well… I guess…"

His father folded up the newspaper and set it on the coffee table. "What lesson have you learned?" He waited for an answer.

"It was dangerous," Peter allowed, mumbling the words.

"Un-huh. And?"

"And?"

"And you have to check with us. Always."

"OK."

"Very violent situation here. You know that, but you have to think about it much more clearly. All the time."

"Yeah."

"What else?"

Peter hated this way his father had of making him prosecute himself. What was he supposed to have learned? Obviously it was dangerous; otherwise T.S. would not have been dead. That didn't mean he had been wrong to go. He needed to make his father understand that.

"You need to show your mother, and me, respect – not lie to us, not denigrate our work here."

"I didn't lie," Peter muttered.

"What's that?"

"I didn't lie," he repeated aloud, quickly adding, "and I do respect both your work."

"You need to show her that."

Peter nodded acknowledgement. He waited, hoping the interrogation was finished, before asking, "But Sandile can come here, right?"

"I'll talk with your mother about it." His father picked up the newspaper.

"Thanks, Dad." That was about enough of a confessional for Peter. But, as he stood up to go, he realized that he hadn't made his other point. He had just fallen back into being a little boy. But this wasn't little boy stuff. He needed to show his parents that he had not been irresponsible, that he was old enough to make the right decisions.

"You know," he started, "it wasn't stupid."

His father looked up.

"Dangerous, OK. Not stupid. My friends needed me. That's why I went," Peter continued, his voice quiet but his determination clear.

His father's face betrayed no emotion, but he nodded his head slightly.

Peter took a second to absorb that gesture, to be sure he really had seen it. Then he turned to go.

Kagiso waited until she heard her mother say goodbye to her aunt and leave for work on Monday morning. Then she went to the living room, where she found Ellen already up and folding the blanket she had used while sleeping on the couch.

"*Dumela*, Auntie," Kagiso said as she slipped into an armchair.

"*Ahe*," Ellen replied. "You're up early."

"A little."

"How're things with your father?"

"Not good, Auntie. So I very much wanted to talk to you."

Ellen turned to face her.

"Can I stay with you on the weekend?"

"Hmmm."

"I want to show I am out of politics."

Ellen scrutinized Kagiso as if she doubted the girl's claim, but she also agreed to ask the Seiberts. She finished packing her things, took the last sip of tea from her mug and left for the bus station.

Kagiso sat for a moment longer, her knees folded up to her chest, her bare heels on the edge of the cushion. She was pleased with her plan. She would talk to Peter, and he would talk Sandile out of radical politics. Peter could do it. He seemed to be catching on about the struggle.

Asking her aunt to take him a note would have been quicker, but riskier. Not a good idea to put her fears about Sandile in writing, she thought. And then she had to admit, though only to herself, that she liked the idea of seeing Peter again.

She remembered that, after the funeral and the tear gas and the news reporter, Peter had turned to her as if to say something personal. He had looked down at her with those strange eyes, unlike the eyes of anyone else she knew – the color of a hazy summer sky – that seemed to look deep inside her. More intimate than touch would have been. Then he had looked away and said that he needed to go, and he and Sandile had sprinted off, matching each other stride for stride. She liked his smile, his height, his speed and grace as he dashed through Soweto.

Kagiso shook her hair as if to break a spell. Back to the plan, and to a weekend with no chores, maybe a chance to swim. That was a bit of guilty pleasure, a sort of holiday while the township was in turmoil. But she would be there on a mission to save Sandile, so it was OK. In her room, she tucked a few things into her plaid bag before making breakfast for Tiny and Mike.

When he returned from school on Friday afternoon, Peter dumped his book bag in the middle of his bedroom and stripped off his blazer and tie. The envelope on his bureau seemed to mock him. His hopes of cheering Sandile up with coveted tickets to the Pirates-Chiefs soccer match in a few weeks seemed misplaced. Sandile had seemed so distant, tense when he declined repeatedly to visit Peter for the weekend. Just gave an excuse: "There are some things I must do in the township this weekend."

Wheels crunched on the gravel driveway. Peter looked out the window to see his father's van stop in front of the garage.

And Kagiso get out.

Barbara Borst

His heart raced to see her step across the gravel in her tight white jeans and red shirt, red-and-white earrings bobbing beneath her Afro. No one had told him she was coming. He watched until she moved out of sight, heading to her aunt's quarters. Then he scurried to make himself presentable. Dashing into the bathroom, he showered, shaved twice, nicked himself, blotted it with tissue, tried to wash out the blood that had dripped onto his polo shirt, gave up on that shirt, tried three others before he found an acceptable color, royal blue, then fussed over his unruly hair.

Ready. But ready for what? She wasn't there as his guest. But she was there. That was what mattered. No idea what to say to her. But hard to hold back from going to see her. He made himself wait, sitting on the edge of the couch, pretending to watch cartoons with Megan. Paying no attention to whatever was on TV. His mind flying all over the place.

Then he heard Kagiso in the kitchen with Auntie Ellen. He poked his head out of the family room and looked down the hall, hoping to catch another glimpse of her. There she was, but he pulled back quickly as she turned toward him.

"Stop bouncing the couch," Megan complained next to him.

Peter turned and bounced it on purpose.

"Go. I'm watching," she insisted, pushing him with both hands.

He got up, not remotely interested in a battle with his little sister, and moved to an armchair where he could think about what he might say to Kagiso, if he got the chance. That he wanted to thank her? Well, he couldn't say that in front of her aunt or his parents. What? What was it that was bursting out of him? His thoughts just got more confused the more he contemplated the prospect. Better just to act.

Peter got up and walked toward the kitchen, trying to look casual but feeling wound up. He was all set to ask Auntie Ellen what was for dinner, but when he entered the kitchen, only Kagiso was in the room, washing carrots in the sink at the far end.

"Oh. Hi," he said, surprised and completely off balance.

"Peter…" she began. He thought she sounded as if she had something urgent to say, but her aunt walked into the room.

He blushed and asked his earlier question, "Hi, uh, Auntie Ellen. What's for dinner?" He didn't listen to the answer. He was looking at Kagiso, who seemed to gesture toward the back-door.

"Sorry to bother you," he said, and went back into the front hall. He peeked behind him and saw Kagiso go out the kitchen door. He dashed around the front of the house, hoping to meet her outside, and found her at the big tree in the front yard where she had sat to read the Mandela biography in December.

"Hi," he said again, out of breath, out of words, knowing he sounded stupid repeating himself.

"We must talk. Later," she said, then hurried back to the kitchen.

Falling backward onto the bench, unsure what any of it meant, he watched her scurry back to the kitchen entrance. The sun set without his noticing. He was still sitting on the bench trying to harness his heart when his mother called him in for dinner.

They must have eaten something, but Peter didn't taste it. His thoughts were racing into the darkness. He finished his dinner and took his plate to the kitchen, stealing only a sideways glance at Kagiso as she scrubbed the cooking pots. Back in the family room, he paid no attention to the show on the television as he waited until Kagiso and her aunt finished washing up.

"Goodnight," Auntie Ellen called as she closed the kitchen door.

"Thanks for the great curry," Peter heard his mother answer. Was that what they had eaten for dinner? He waited as long as he could make himself sit still. Then he stepped out the sliding glass door to the back terrace, in case anyone was watching, and made his way around to the big tree in front of the house to wait for Kagiso.

The security lights glared across much of the yard but left deep shadows toward the kitchen courtyard. Peter tried to peer into the darkness there, to see her, if she was coming out. He heard a soft rustle of feet in the grass, then saw Kagiso emerge from the shadow, split like the moon, with half of her in brilliant light and the other half in darkness. A dream walker, she seemed to him.

She moved toward the other side of the bench, where it was encased in shadow. He slid around to join her there. Neither of them spoke. Then they started at the same time.

"We must talk…"

"I never thanked you…"

They stopped.

"You first," Peter said.

"I am very much worried about Sandile."

Peter felt his heart plummet into his running shoes. He had hoped she cared for him a little. But he bucked up his courage to say, "I'm kinda worried about him, too."

"That's why I came. To tell you. Can you help?"

"Sure," he agreed, though he doubted he had much influence.

Kagiso took a deep breath and delivered the news. "He is running with T.S.'s friends."

Peter wasn't sure how bad that was. He realized that he knew little about T.S. and his followers. "What's that mean?"

She turned to face him, but he couldn't see her expression clearly in the shadows. She seemed very serious.

"T.S. was one of the radicals, for sure. A leader. I'm telling you he was very much violent."

Peter sat in silence, trying to absorb that news.

"His followers, you find them there, plotting revenge."

"On who?"

"Soweto police."

Peter sucked in his breath.

"Talk to him?" she pleaded.

"Think he'll listen?"

"You must try."

He nodded assurance, as if she could see him clearly.

"For sure?"

"Yes. Yes, of course." Troubled, Peter shook his head in the darkness. Her fear added to his own worries about Sandile. He would have to find a way to talk with him.

They sat for a while in silence.

"You're that worried?" Peter asked. He wondered whether she had fallen for Sandile – a strange turn if she had gone straight from fighting him to this. How had he lost out when he hadn't even known there was competition?

"For sure."

The sounds of a car in the street and a chorus of dogs howling as it passed their turf interrupted the talk. When the night quieted down, Peter promised to find out what he could from Sandile, but said he didn't expect to hear much because Sandile had clammed up again.

"I think finding T.S. twisted him all up inside," he said.

"All of us," she said.

Peter hung his head as he thought about that, wondered what it had done to her. She was the one who knew T.S. But what was their relationship? Did she like him? Hadn't he shouted at her when they all arrived at the meeting? And yet she was there with Sandile, helping to carry T.S. home.

"You OK?" she asked, touching the top of his hand as he gripped the bench between them.

"Me? Yeah, fine," he perked up. "But I never thanked you."

"For what?"

"You saved me. And Sandile."

After a long pause, she replied, "My fault you were in danger."

"I'm glad I went. You shouldn't have to face that alone," he said. Then he wished to take the words back. How dumb was that to say "alone" when she was surrounded by hundreds of friends?

"I'd still be trying to get over that fence," she laughed at herself.

"And I'd still be shaking hands outside the church." He stood up and imitated himself, stiffly pumping his hand in thin air again and again.

She chuckled softly.

"And playing reporter." He imitated a journalist taking notes, sticking a microphone in her face. "Young lady, what did you see at the riot today?"

She laughed out loud, then clamped a hand across her mouth. "My father," she said, standing up and spreading her arms away from her sides as if she were a bodybuilder. "'You went to that funeral. You think I don't talk to my own sister?'" she repeated in a deep voice, shaking a fist to reinforce the point

Peter mimicked his own father, leaning toward her face and interrogating her, "'Did it not occur to you that you stick out in Soweto?'" Both of them laughed, and tried to stifle their laughs.

"How did your parents know?"

"Nesbitt."

"Who?"

"The journalist. He played tennis with my dad the next day."

"What will they do?"

"'You won't be going to Soweto, you know,'" he answered in his father's voice.

"Oh. Sorry for that. For my side, 'I will send you to Mmabatho,'" she said gruffly.

"No," he protested. That was too far. Then he would never see her. He thought of urging her to stay with her aunt, come to Saint Andrew's with him and Sandile. Not exactly realistic.

They stood facing each other in the half-dark. With the security light behind her, he could make out only her silhouette. Her hair was a luminous halo around her head, with two small tails at her earrings.

"I'm glad you came." Were those his words? Had he found the courage to say them or had he just imagined them unleashing themselves, building a bridge across that chasm.

She took a step closer. Maybe he *had* spoken. He took a step toward her, close enough to reach out. He touched a finger to her left hand.

"Kagiso," he started, then he stopped because he didn't know how to channel the flood of feeling inside him into words. Somehow, her small hands were in his, yet he was unsure how that had happened. It just felt right. He let his thoughts carry through the touch of their fingers. He looked over her head as if the distant stars and scraps of clouds would hold a message he could share with her.

Kagiso waited.

He didn't have any particular words he wanted to say. He just wanted to savor a moment when nothing had been specified and all was possible, hoped for. To be with her, just to be with her.

"I wish I could see you more," he said at last, so much from the heart that it was as if he had said it to himself.

"Yes."

He was surprised to hear her reply, as though he had been dreaming her presence. Looking down into her face, hidden in shadow, he thought of kissing her, wanted to kiss her.

Kagiso wriggled her right hand free. She reached up to his neck to pull his face down toward her. He bent to her touch. She kissed him lightly on the lips.

Peter tasted a hint of curry on her lips. Still bent over her as she relaxed her hold, he kissed her again, then slipped his arms around her and nearly lifted her off her feet in the surge of joy to think, to know, that he meant something to her. Eyes shut, face stretched into the widest smile.

Hoping not to wake her aunt, Kagiso slid under the blanket on the mattress on the floor. Ellen snuffled and rolled over in her bed but then lay quietly. Kagiso listened to a night so silent that all she could hear was the pounding of her blood.

What had she done? Had she kissed him first? Was that OK? Why would she do a thing like that? Did she have any idea how a white boy thought, what he would think of her, what she thought of herself? How could she allow herself such a distraction with all these crises?

How could she not.

She could see him again standing in front of her, the light flooding his ghostly eyes. He was not guarded and domineering, but almost vulnerable. Studying that pale face, with the freckles washed out by the glare and the unruly hair framing it and the thin lips slightly parted, she felt him waiting for her.

The light had played across his shirt, stretched over the muscles of his shoulders and chest, and down the lean curves of his long arms. His height thrilled her as she reached up to touch his neck. Recalling the touch of her dark hand on his light skin sent a shiver of pleasure through her.

Was it just the novelty? The forbidden fruit? He was the first white boy she had had a chance to get to know. Why hadn't T.S. caught her fancy? He was hard and angry, but he must have cared. He had worn her bracelet. Why not Sandile? He was handsome, too, in a distant, regal way. She cared enough to try to save him.

Was it something about Peter? That he made her laugh? That in a world filled with pain, he made her dream of being happy?

She thought of the other times that Peter had touched her. That first time in the pool when he believed he was saving her life, his powerful arm stretched across her chest, his hand placing hers on the edge of the pool. As they escaped the police, he had lifted her over the barricade. He had been constant, strong, sure. Never reining her in, not claiming to protect her, not telling her what to do nor talking down to her. Instead, lending his strength to hers.

It had felt good when he had lifted her again in the dark that very night. Like she was tall, like she was floating, like they could do anything together. She felt his arms as they encircled her. She wrapped her arms around herself to get the feeling again.

Lingering over his cup of tea long after it had turned cold, Peter wondered how to handle the new situation. Everyone else had finished breakfast and gone on to other tasks. How could he clear his place when she was in the kitchen, washing his family's dishes? He didn't want her to think he thought of her as a servant. But, honestly, he wasn't awake enough to handle it yet.

He waited until she slipped out for a moment and then began to wash his own dishes, inexpertly. Kagiso reentered the kitchen and watched him. He felt his technique was not up to scrutiny.

"Not my best sport," he admitted at the same moment that she reached for the dish and said, "You must let me wash."

They both stopped short, their hands touching on the edge of a plate in the soapy water. Surprised, embarrassed, thrilled, he started a gentle tug-of-war.

"Mine," he declared.

"Careful or you'll break it." But she was laughing as he pulled her arm into the suds up to the elbow.

Megan ran into the kitchen calling out, "Kagiso, want to go for a swim?"

"For sure, but we must ask your parents first," Kagiso replied, releasing the plate and wiping her arm with a dishtowel.

Peter caught her sideways glance that said she liked the game before he went off to look for his parents. The door to Ann's office was slightly ajar. He heard bits of a heated conversation between his parents that made him think he shouldn't interrupt.

"… stop me writing," Ann insisted.

"Not what the letter said," Richard replied.

"How can I live here and not work?"

Startled by her tone, Peter decided to keep it to himself until he found out more. All he said to Kagiso and Megan was, "I think we'd better ask them later."

The three of them retreated to the family room, where Christina was watching Japanese space cartoons on television. Peter and Kagiso sat near one another, but not touching. They looked at each other, then Peter quickly looked away, as if the cartoons were his real interest. This was way too hard, he thought, trying to figure it out in front of his family.

"I have to go on some errands," Ann announced as she emerged from her office.

Peter glanced up and saw that his mother was upset; he hoped it wasn't about him, again.

"Kagiso wants to swim. Can we?" Megan begged.

"I'll supervise," her father volunteered.

The water in the pool was chilly on a morning in March, almost fall. All the children jumped in. Kagiso played with Megan and Christina, lunging with eyes closed and calling out "Marco" as she tried to locate the answering call of "Polo." Richard watched from a lawn chair.

Peter was unsure how to behave around Kagiso. She looked so sexy in her red-and-white bikini. But his father was watching. Action became his solution to nervousness. Repeatedly, he dived deep into the pool, grabbing her feet or popping up right behind her back with a splash. She laughed and jumped to get away. Disappointed when she got out because she was shivering, he turned on his sisters and harassed them. Kagiso watched from the terrace, wrapped in several towels.

When Christina and Megan climbed out, too, Peter had to admit that he was chilled through. He heaved himself up onto the lip of the pool. All the towels had been taken. Kagiso offered him one of hers. He loved the warmth of it as he stretched it across his shoulders, her warmth surrounding him. Still, it was cool enough that they all ran inside to change into dry clothes.

Kagiso set the outdoor table as Richard lighted the charcoal grill to make lunch. Peter brought out a platter of canapés to pass around.

"Guests first," he said as he offered them to Kagiso.

She turned a suspicious eye on the crackers topped with translucent red pearls. They brought back a vague memory of some food Peter had described. What was it called? Definitely time to be wary. She took a cracker, but deftly slid the beads off into her hand before tasting it.

"Delicious," she exclaimed. Whatever his game was, she was not going to fall prey.

Peter looked disappointed when she asked for another.

Before the sausages and hamburgers were ready, Kagiso quickly stepped away to use her aunt's bathroom, where she washed the caviar off her hands, and then took a can of *phane* worms from her luggage and placed it on Peter's bed.

She was especially proud to play the trickster, not her usual role.

After lunch, she and Peter stretched out on lounge chairs by the pool in the afternoon sun that warmed the terrace. She watched as he squirted blobs of white sunscreen into his hands and spread it all over his face and shoulders and arms and then started on his legs.

"I know," he said, looking up from trying to coat his calves, "I'm the wrong color for Africa."

She just laughed at another little piece of his world that she had never thought about before.

He stood up to try to spread the cream on his back.

She couldn't help studying him, lean and well-muscled, strong legs covered in blond hair and sprinkled with freckles, muscles rippling across his back as he spread the cream. He turned toward her. She felt embarrassed to be caught staring and quickly asked a question to cover up.

"How tall are you?"

"Six-one," he said.

"What's that mean?"

"Oh, yeah. In centimeters that's about one eighty-six."

"Way taller than my father."

"And you?"

"Guess."

"Perfect," he replied immediately.

She gave a second look to see if he was making fun of her.

He grinned, thrust the sunscreen at her and said, "Did you know that this stuff is what makes you white?" He stepped forward and added, "Sit still so I can spread it all over you."

Before he could strike, she snatched the sunscreen tube and held it aloft in triumph.

"What color would you be without it?" she asked.

"Sunburn red."

"Let's see that."

"You won't like it; I'll be mean." He sat with his back to her.

She felt bad, until he turned quickly and grabbed the sunscreen back. She lost her grip on the tube and fell off the other side of the low chair.

"Ha," he said in triumph, though he did hop up to offer his hand.

She took it and got back onto her chair.

"Gotcha," he said, pointing at her hand, now covered with sunscreen. "Better wash that off before it bleaches you."

She wiped her hand on the towel and pushed her sunglasses back into place as if nothing had happened. Too silly, she thought, but so novel to be able to joke about their differences here in South Africa where everyone was divided by race. Feeling uncertain of herself in this new world, she was glad to hide her thoughts behind the sunglasses.

"Oh, Auntie Ellen, we had spaghetti and meatballs the night before," Christina pleaded at the kitchen door as Kagiso prepared to set the dinner table. "Can't we have something else?"

"Of course. Chicken?" Ellen asked.

"Mmmm."

"Chicken it is."

Kagiso was glad when she heard that Peter's parents were going to a dinner for journalists and had asked Ellen to take over for the evening. She hoped to catch a few more minutes alone with him. She didn't mind helping her aunt make dinner, and Peter offered to work in the kitchen, too. Kagiso put him in charge of chopping vegetables, and held back from commenting on the mismatched results.

After dinner, Ellen watched a video of "The Princess Bride" with the younger girls while Peter and Kagiso sat on the terrace studying distant thunder clouds that stabbed the sky with lightning. They talked, they laughed. They did not touch. Kagiso kept glancing at the house to see if her aunt was spying on them.

"Want to go for a walk?" Peter asked her.

"In the dark?" A night stroll in Soweto was risky, so she had never developed that habit.

"Well, just in the yard."

"My aunt is watching us," she warned.

"Really?"

Kagiso nodded. Maybe Ellen was stuck in the old laws of a few years before when it was a crime, under apartheid, for blacks and whites to kiss. But how had she known about her and Peter?

"The movie's just about over. I know 'cause they watch it all the time," Peter whispered. "Let me know when Auntie Ellen puts my sisters to bed."

Kagiso shivered slightly at the thrill of doing something forbidden. They didn't speak. She kept an eye on the family room window.

"Now," she said.

Peter grabbed her hand and they slipped into the shadow of a flowering shrub that engulfed them in perfume. He enfolded her in his arms. She slipped her arms around his waist. They kissed quickly before they heard Ellen's call.

"Kagiso, Peter, time to come in."

They stole a final embrace, caught their breath and emerged from the shadow, trying to look as if nothing had happened.

"We were just looking at the stars," Peter told Ellen as they reached the terrace door.

Kagiso glanced at the cloud-filled sky and smiled at his silly excuse for something that felt wonderful.

Sandile worked the cash register at this parents' shop, stepping lightly from one foot to the other, nervous to the tips of his toes as he made small talk with customers.

"Where you keep pilchards?" a customer asked behind him.

"Center aisle, on the left," he answered without looking around.

"On my tab?" the woman who was checking out asked.

"For sure." He wrote her name and the amount in the ledger for those buying on credit. He tried not to let himself think about anything. Stick to the work, he told himself. Steady on.

Sandile left the shop shortly before sunset and headed toward home. Trying to make his journey look normal, he called out to Josephat Dube as he passed that family's shack. When he was well beyond the store, he changed course. Orlando East, then Orlando West, not too close to the homes of the anti-apartheid leadership – the Mandelas and Sisulus, the Motlanas and Tutus – whose houses he assumed were always under surveillance.

Nearing the spot at Moema and Vilikazi streets where police had shot student protesters to death, launching the Soweto Uprising in 1976, he veered away. Too heavy a thought. He had to keep his mind focused on his assignment. Watch for the smallest sign of trouble. Go over the plan. Do not fail on this, no matter how nervous.

As the light faded, he reached the policeman's home, the one he was assigned to burn, on the western edge of Orlando. The man had two young children, Sandile had heard. Didn't look like anyone was home, but he circled around the house at a distance, keeping behind other houses, shacks or fences as he listened for any activity and peeked in the windows. The house, three small concrete rooms with small windows, matched the other bungalows the government rented to blacks, except for a couple of new corrugated metal roof panels that reflected the last light of day.

Satisfied that the house was empty, Sandile hunted silently for the bottle, rag and gasoline he had stashed behind a trash bin on a neighboring lot. Hiding behind the bin as the night settled, Sandile thought of his half dozen new acquaintances, all followers of T.S., who crouched as he did at houses across Soweto, ready to throw homemade bombs that would light up the night and take the fight directly to T.S.'s enemies.

Calm as ever on the outside, Sandile shivered inside with bitterness over T.S.'s death, with passion for revenge, with suspicion that something was wrong. He closed off his doubts and prepared his bomb. His hands shook slightly as he poured gasoline from the plastic jug into the glass bottle. Some spilled on his fingers. Could he burn himself that way? What did he know about bomb-making? Sandile set both down, trying to steady himself. He poured again, more cautiously, then wiped his hands with the rag and stuffed it into the top of the bottle. Waiting for the gasoline to soak into the rag and make a fuse, he felt for the matches in his pocket. The odor of gasoline stuck in his nostrils as he crawled through the dirt to the wire fence that surrounded the policeman's home, hoping to get within throwing distance of the house. All was ready.

Still he hesitated, held back by an uncertainty he could not identify. Though he told himself he was just waiting for the right moment, he suspected it was more than that and hoped it wasn't cowardice. Ezekiel had run away after throwing a gasoline bomb at his family's store, he remembered. A coward, and with no reason to attack them in the first place. But this was different. Soweto policemen had killed T.S. Sandile made himself see T.S.'s bleeding face again. That memory strengthened his resolve.

Suddenly a light appeared in a window of the policeman's home. Caught in the glare, Sandile quickly slid back from the fence on his belly. When he peeked through the weeds entangled with the fence, he saw an old woman, stooped like his grandmother, who was carrying a lantern as she shuffled into the kitchen. The sight paralyzed him. The thought of his grandmother lying on the shop floor, wounded and suffering, erased the image of T.S., erased the anger, replaced it with remorse.

Sandile waited while the woman finished in the kitchen. As soon as she went to another room, he crept back to the neighboring lot, poured the gasoline in a ditch, rubbed his hands in the dirt to reduce the odor of it and walked away.

He was no longer bewitched by violence. No matter whether T.S.'s comrades would seek revenge on him, he would face their threats knowing that he was not weak. To have harmed an innocent person – that would have been cowardice. He was ashamed of what he had almost done.

"Yours?" Ellen asked Kagiso as they took their seats on the public bus heading back to Soweto on Sunday afternoon.

Kagiso feigned surprise when her aunt handed her a can of *phane*. She smirked to think of how Peter must have reacted. But she did wonder how her aunt had gotten possession of it. She admitted nothing.

"He's a nice boy," Ellen said.

Kagiso wasn't sure where the conversation was headed.

"But be careful. You have got too much trouble with your father."

Kagiso contemplated the issue, then decided that Ellen was the one potential ally among the adults in her life.

"Would you talk to him for me, Auntie? I don't want him to send me to Bop. Please?"

"You know, I am a guest in your father's house. There is little I can do."

"Please?" Kagiso begged.

"I will try. But don't hope for much."

"Give him the *phane*," Kagiso recommended, not really thinking it would do much good but desperate for some way to appease her father. She relaxed and listened to the music of Brenda and the Big Dudes coming from another passenger's radio.

The song stopped and the news began: "The South African Police are investigating arson attacks on the homes of six Soweto policemen. 'The attacks on Saturday are the work of terrorists,' police detective Johan Smuts told SABC radio."

Kagiso sucked in her breath and held it. Afraid that she would explode with worry, she kept her mouth shut the rest of the way into Soweto and pretended to listen to the next song.

"Excuse me, Auntie, I just have to run an errand," she explained to Ellen as they dismounted the bus. Walking calmly until she was out of sight, Kagiso then ran all the way to the Malindis' shop, terror and regret pounding in her head like a drumbeat.

"We must talk," she told Sandile when she found him at the cash register.

He asked his brother to take his place briefly and stepped outside to a spot not visible through the store windows.

"Please," she begged, "don't get sucked in by them."

"It's OK," he steadied her with a hand on her arm.

"But Palesa said..."

"It's OK. I went to do what they asked and I saw it was wrong. I didn't."

"Thank God."

"I have to go back to work," he broke off. "Don't worry. It's OK."

She nodded assent and let relief flood over her as she walked home. When she reached her house, she could hear voices through the open windows.

"Patrick, my dear brother, she will not make trouble," Ellen declared

"She doesn't need to make it. Trouble will find her," Kagiso's father answered.

Kagiso quickly unlocked the door and burst in.

"Sit down, child," her father instructed her as Ellen retreated to the kitchen.

Kagiso closed the door and sat only halfway onto the dining chair closest to it. She shook her head to slough off any fear.

"I have spoken with my brother," he began. "Amos will come for you on Sunday."

"NO!" she protested. She bolted for the door. But her father was quicker than she thought and blocked her way. She pounded his solid chest with her small fists, trying to barge through. He let her flail away until she realized it was futile, then held her loosely in his massive arms.

"No, *Baba*," she begged.

"You will be with family. Schools are better in Mmabatho," he consoled her. "You'll make new friends."

"NO!" she cried, breaking loose. "It's not just about my friends. It's about the freedom struggle. I must do my part," she insisted, her mind thrusting forward to the meeting with the Soweto Civic Organization.

"Do you think I don't understand politics, just because I'm a poor man, working night after night?" he demanded, peering fiercely into her eyes.

"*Baba*, I..."

"Do you think this *thing*, this apartheid does not hurt me, too? That I do not want to stand up to all the insults?"

She hoped she heard a new voice speaking to her as an adult for the first time, granting a glimpse of his feelings, maybe leaving her a way to convince him that she needed to stay. She opened her mouth to say so, but he started again.

"Do you think I want to see you tortured and beaten and thrown into prison like the leaders of the struggle? Do you think I want to go to your funeral?

"Your friends, the 'comrades,' they know everything," he continued the lecture, his voice growing louder with each sentence. "They are going to win the fight that generations of elders were not clever enough to win. They will be heroes.

"But they will be dead."

He let the words hang heavy in the suddenly silent house.

"And you will not be among them," he declared.

"No, I won't be," Kagiso agreed, regaining her voice. "My friends and I are trying to end the violence. We don't believe..."

"The police do not care what you believe. They shoot you just the same."

"That's why we must change ..."

"I will not let you take that risk," he said, standing squarely in front of her, extending his arms to make himself look even more formidable. "That much of a man I can still be, apartheid or no. I can protect my family. If not here, then in our homeland."

Kagiso felt as if a prison door had slammed shut; she heard the key in the lock, saw the end of her life in Soweto. Her father spoke with a finality that showed her the matter had never been open to debate. He dwelt in ancient traditions and spoke to her not as an adult, but as a woman – old enough to be told the reason, powerless to change the decision.

Her father sat down heavily in the chair at the head of the table. "Is there nothing to eat?" he demanded of his wife, who cowered in the kitchen.

Kagiso glanced at her mother and aunt on her way to the new bedroom her father had recently finished building, then lay across her new bed, too angry to cry. She thought of every argument she could have raised and dismissed them one by one. She had made them all before. They had never altered her father's views.

Once her father left for work, Kagiso came back out to the main room. "Why didn't you help me?" she accused her mother.

"There was nothing I could do.".

"You could have argued for me."

"That would make me his enemy."

"He's my enemy," Kagiso declared, shaking her head in defiance.

"No, Kagiso," her mother said quietly. "He loves you and he wants to protect you."

"He can't even protect himself." Kagiso was far too angry to give him any leeway. Disgusted at how little her mother and her aunt had said in her defense, she was determined not to be weak like them.

Kagiso slammed the front door on her way out, but only went as far as the front steps. Sitting in the first shadows of evening, she set her mind on doing what she could with the civic organization before her father sent her away, and she forbade her thoughts to wander into the darkness of exile.

Sitting alone on the terrace gazing at the turquoise light from the swimming pool, Peter tried to think of what he was supposed to say to Sandile on Monday. Something that would persuade him not to get involved in radical activity. How could he counsel someone on things he knew little about?

He wished Kagiso would do it. She was good at political arguments – why all black South Africans needed to unite to fight apartheid, why it had to be a non-violent struggle – and he admitted that he was not. He could try parroting her arguments, but he was pretty sure it would sound staged.

OK, something else, the sort of thing Sandile had said about getting an education, becoming a leader of his people. But what if Sandile said that stuff didn't matter if the police could just kill anyone they wanted? What would he say to that?

He was halfway through Kagiso's book on Mandela. What about something from that? OK, he'd look through it again before he went to bed. Or what was that thing his mother had talked about, a freedom charter Mandela helped write? He'd have to ask her. Maybe some ideas there.

Really, this was Kagiso's specialty. He wished at least he had asked her for some ideas on how to talk to Sandile. But that hadn't been on his mind. When she was there, he couldn't think of anything but her.

He could almost feel her presence at the table where she had sat with him the night before. The scent of coconut that hovered around her. The glimmers of light on her hair. The feel of her soft form against his chest. The electric charge of a second kiss, one that made the first one real, that dangled the promise of more. How was he supposed to put those thoughts aside and concentrate on politics? How was he supposed to sleep when he had her on his mind?

Peter forced himself to get up, switch off the pool lights and go in to look through Kagiso's book again.

The light was starting to fade as Sandile left his parents' shop, heading home for dinner with his grandmother and a night of schoolwork. He walked along his usual route, keeping away from the workers' hostel where he had found T.S. Too many bad feelings there, but the darkness tugged his thoughts back anyway. T.S. remained a mystery to him, a brief flash across his life – intense, angry, brilliant, gone. Sandile was sorry for T.S., and sorry that he had almost followed his lead. Need to make your own choices about right and wrong, about the struggle for freedom, he counseled himself.

Picking up his pace, he headed through the maze of streets that led to Diepkloof Extension. A few dogs howled in the darkness. Mostly it was quiet. But a small noise behind him put Sandile on alert. What was that? Footsteps? The sound stopped when he stopped to listen. He moved into a race-walk, long strides carrying him onward. The sound followed. Was it in his head? Or was it real?

Tsotsis, he concluded. Criminals following him. No time for fear. Must move faster, must escape. Sandile broke into a run, keeping to the middle of the street, away from shadows. He could hear breathing behind him, footsteps of more than one assailant. They seemed to be keeping pace. He looked back quickly, saw little in the darkness, took off at a sprint, began to gain ground, could see that he was nearly to the bigger houses of his neighborhood.

Entering an intersection, he glanced both ways, noticing a truck parked on the far side. He sped past it. Suddenly, he heard the cab open. Men rushed him from behind, threw a blanket over his head and tackled him, bringing him to the ground. Other footsteps caught up. Someone wrenched his hands behind him and tied them together. Someone tied a canvas bag over his head.

"Let me go," Sandile shouted at them in Zulu, Xhosa, English.

"You go with us," one of the men ordered him in Zulu.

"I have a little money. Take it." But the men ignored his offer. "Help me!" he called out into the night. Only a dog howled in reply.

Four men grabbed him and carried him. He heard them open the truck. They tossed him into the back, slammed it.

What kind of robbers were they? Why didn't they just take the money?

"Help me!" Sandile shouted in every language he knew.

"Shut him up," one of the men ordered.

Someone opened the back of the truck and punched him in the jaw. He fell across the truck bed, bumping his head on the wheel well. Struggling against the rope on his wrists, he rubbed his skin raw but did not manage to free himself. The bag over his head kept him blind.

And then he heard a sound that made his heart stop: the squawk of a two-way radio demanding confirmation that they had made the arrest. These were police.

The truck swung around turns, throwing him across the metal ridges of the back compartment before it stopped abruptly. The back opened and the men dragged Sandile out on his stomach. The bag covered his face, so he never saw them, only felt their rough hands on him. They stood him up and pushed him into some sort of building. Although he could not see, he could hear that the voices seemed contained inside a small space. Feeling dizzy, Sandile tried to steady himself.

"Stand up," a voice commanded, bouncing off nearby walls.

"Do not lean on anything," a deeper voice barked into his ear, the warm breath startling him as much as the loud words.

Sandile tried to comply but fear rose to choke him. He wobbled on clumsy feet.

Suddenly something thin and hard whacked him on the back of the legs. A stick, maybe, or a whip. The sharp pain forced him to pull himself up as straight as he could.

The blows did not end, but they came less often. The pattern was clear to him, but as the evening turned into night, exhaustion hollowed out his resolve to stand tall. Losing all sense of time, he did not allow himself to contemplate his fate. He concentrated on staying upright. That was all his mind could handle.

As dim light sneaked through the cloth bag over his head, Sandile roused himself from semi-consciousness to discover that he was still alive, still more or less upright, hands still tied behind his back.

The policemen's voices moved around him. Their conversations with superiors in Zulu and Afrikaans on the two-way radio and on the telephone drilled into his memory.

"We have the terrorist," one confirmed in Afrikaans.

"Get me some tea," another called in Zulu.

The police surrounded Sandile again. They spat his name at him, mocked his school, threatened his family.

He blacked out. When he came to, he felt cold water running down his face inside the bag and rough hands forcing him to stand again. He must have collapsed.

The policemen shouted that he was a terrorist. They demanded answers over and over again to the same questions:

What are the names of the other terrorists? Where are they hiding?

The first time they asked, he replied that he did not know. They whacked him with sticks or whips across the shoulders and the legs. The strikes hurt more than the night before as they landed on tenderized flesh. His shirt and pants offered no protection.

When they asked him who told him to lie about T.S.'s death, he said that he had not lied.

"This time, you will see nothing," one man taunted.

Blows to the tendons behind his knees made his legs crumple involuntarily. Sandile tried blindly to find something to lean against. The sticks found him again. The water splashed his face again, with the dirt of the cloth bag running into his mouth.

After that, he did not try to answer their questions. He realized that the truth offered him no protection; they would beat him whether he answered or not. The memory of T.S.'s bleeding face returned, showing him the fate that awaited him.

Sandile hardly knew whether he was dreaming or blacking out or dying by the time the police dumped him in a stinking cell with no window. They loosened the bag and slammed the door. He lay curled up on the concrete floor, mindless of the stench of urine and the unidentifiable scum on the floor and walls, relieved to be horizontal. There was a bucket of water. Not clean. Smelled of dirty dishwater. He drank anyway, then collapsed into tormented sleep.

In the patches of time when he was awake, he tried to focus his mind beyond this world of pain and fear. He thought of his family, of the shock and tears in his mother's eyes when she learned he had spoken to the journalist. He tried to hear his father's voice, deep and warm, guiding him thorough challenges, solid, not stern. Then he worried that thinking about them might lead him to reveal something that would put them in danger, too. He decided not to think about anyone in Soweto. He was grateful he did not know the names of T.S.'s supporters. Violent as they might be, he would not wish this on them.

He chose at last to concentrate on Peter; that seemed safe. He tried to remember life outside this cell – every word of their conversations during the trip to Zimbabwe, even the explanation about his mother's green car, "You got a fast car. Is it fast enough so we can fly away?" and the lyrics to other songs from the concert, having to teach Peter about his own ancestors' defeat, and every move of every soccer game and cricket test and tennis match they had played together, even the profile of a chief in a war bonnet stitched in black on the bright yellow of Peter's Kaizer Chiefs cap – anything to lift his thoughts and keep himself alive.

Four comrades taken. That was the only topic at Kagiso's school on Monday. No mention of Sandile. Except for Palesa, no one else at school would have thought about him. But Kagiso was desperate to know whether he was safe. She could barely sit through classes.

When school finally closed, Kagiso and Palesa headed to the Malindis' store. The neighborhood should have been bustling with customers, but instead it was strangely quiet. The store was closed for the first time that Kagiso could remember, other than Christmas Day.

Fear began to rise into the roots of her hair as she led the way to the Malindi home. She had no idea what she could say to them if Sandile had gone missing. At the gate to his house, cars overflowed the driveway. In the window, she saw a crowd of people standing inside. Her knock on the door went unanswered. She tried again. Finally, a young man who looked much like Sandile came to the door.

"Yes?"

"We are friends of Sandile."

"He is not here."

The voice was somber. The words hit like a blow to the stomach, making it hard for Kagiso to breathe. "Can we help?"

"I'm afraid not."

After Tom's mother dropped Peter at home, he went straight to his mother's office to phone Sandile and find out why he hadn't been at school. He looked in his wallet for the battered paper on which he kept the numbers for the house and the store. Pulling the contents one by one, he became distracted by the official looking seal on the paper where he was spreading things. He knew it wasn't right to read his mother's mail, but he did it anyway:

Binnelandse Sake/ Home Affairs Ministry
Pretoria
1989 March 15

Mrs. Richard Seibert
97 Coronation Straat
Johannesburg

Dear Mrs. Seibert:
Under what authority you are reporting for the American newspaper Dallas News? Our records

doesn't show a work permit. You required to appear before the ministry on 30 March at 10 o'clock of the morning.

Petrus Nel
Assistant to the Minister of Home Affairs
and of Communications

Pretty strange, Peter thought. Wonder what that's all about. And look at all the grammar mistakes, too.

He turned back to the task at hand and dialed the store. No reply, although he let it ring many times. Dialing the home number, he waited through many more rings. Finally, someone picked up.

"Hi. It's Peter Seibert. May I speak with Sandile?"

"Wait," Sandile's brother George said.

After a pause, Sandile's father came on.

"Who is this?" Stephen asked.

"Hi, Mr. Malindi. It's Peter Seibert. Can I speak to Sandile?"

"Sandile has gone missing," he said solemnly.

"What?" The message knocked Peter back in the chair.

"He did not reach home from the shop last night."

The words stunned Peter into silence.

"We checked everywhere, even the hospital," Sandile's father continued.

"You think the police took him, 'cause of the newspaper?" Peter was afraid to hear the answer to that question.

"Very possible, but they refused to say."

Peter nodded. He had nothing to add, but he didn't want to hang up. The phone connection seemed to provide some measure of hope. Eventually he asked, "Is there anything I can do?"

"I don't know yet."

They hung up. There was no one to show Peter how to help, but he knew he had to do something. He sort of had an idea.

Ten minutes later, his mother returned.

"Sorry, Peter, but I need my office. Story on the arson attacks," she said, setting her camera bag on a bookshelf.

"Sandile's missing," he blurted.

"What?"

"I just spoke to his dad. He didn't make it home from the store last night."

"They have any clue?"

"Not really. But could be Nesbitt's story."

Ann covered her face with her hands.

"Think we could call Nesbitt? And other reporters?"

She uncovered her eyes and nodded. "Good idea. Let's check with the Malindis first."

Peter handed her the crumpled paper with the number.

"It'll mean more to them if you call," she said.

Peter gulped and tried to think of what to say. Harder this time because he knew what anguish the Malindis were going through.

"I'm so sorry to bother you, Mr. Malindi. We were wondering if it's OK to tell reporters."

"Yes, yes," Stephen replied. "Tell everyone you know."

"And did he call the Detainees Rights Committee?" Ann coached Peter, who forwarded the question.

"He says he will," Peter relayed back.

They said goodbye. Peter and his mother looked at each other, grim faced, silent. He thought about that chance meeting with Nesbitt at Kagiso's aunt's home and all that had come of that terrible day.

"Maybe I should be the one to call Nesbitt," he said, though the thought of it scared him. He urged himself to do this hard thing and do it right.

Ann handed him her address book. "Call all of them. Much more powerful from you 'cause you know him as a friend, not just a victim."

He nodded. Not that he had any idea what to say.

"Make some notes for yourself so you don't get nervous," she suggested.

Peter outlined the main points. They were a jumble. He tore the top sheet off the yellow legal pad and tried again. Then he dialed Nesbitt's number, half hoping the journalist wouldn't pick up.

"Hi, Mr. Nesbitt. This is Peter Seibert, Ann's son." Peter could feel his voice getting squeaky with nervousness.

"Hi, Peter. Sorry but I'm on deadline."

"It's about Sandile, my friend you interviewed."

"OK."

"He's missing and his family thinks the police took him."

"Oh, no. Tell me what happened."

Peter went to the office at Saint Andrew's on Tuesday morning to ask for an appointment. He was told that the headmaster, Mr. Collins, was not available but that Mr. Smythe-Harris would see him.

"You ought to be in class," the assistant head master told him.

"Please, sir," Peter began, "Sandile needs your help." He summarized the predicament: Sandile had told the truth about the police and T.S., and now Sandile was missing, presumably detained by the police.

"Young men who consort with terrorists have only themselves to blame," Mr. Smythe-Harris lectured. "The Academy will absolutely *not* become embroiled in Soweto politics."

Outraged that Sandile's years as a star student and athlete meant nothing to this cold prig, Peter rehearsed a string of curses in his mind, thought about slamming his fist on the man's desk, decided he could not risk those actions with his friend's life at stake. He glared at Smythe-Harris and left with only one word. "Sir," he flung at the assistant headmaster.

He went to class, but he could not let the issue drop. His mind in a mad dash to keep ahead of his fears, he could barely stay in his chair through the Afrikaans lesson. At lunchtime he spoke with his cricket teammates Tom and Vusi, telling them what had happened to Sandile.

"You must talk with the headmaster," Tom recommended.

"Tried Smythe-Harris. He said no."

"That's just Smythe-Harris for you. Cruel bastard. We should try Collins."

"Come with me?"

"Of course. Who else is in?"

Several hands went up among their teammates, white and black.

"Another terrorist meeting?" Andre Malan sniped as he passed behind them. Peter jumped up, ready to argue with him, but Andre had three of his rugby pals around him, taunting Peter, Tom and Vusi.

"Ignore them," Tom said. "Ignorant brutes."

"How do you put up with that crap?" Peter asked Vusi.

"What choice?" Vusi replied. "We are all on bursary. Except Sandile, of course."

Vusi didn't sound angry, but Peter got the point – that Sandile was the only black student who didn't need a scholarship to attend Saint Andrew's.

"OK, we've got a delegation," Peter said, focusing on the urgent issue. "Now for a petition." He ripped a lined page from his notebook, pulled a stubby pencil from his pocket and paused. He looked at his teammates as if they might suggest the words, but heard nothing. What should it say, he asked himself. Start with the date: March 21, 1989.

"Write it proper," Tom said. "Twenty-first March 1989."

Peter scratched it out and wrote it South African-style. "What about this: We students of Saint Andrew's Academy request...?"

"The undersigned. Hereby request."

"Yeah, that's more official," Peter agreed. "Request that Saint Andrew's officials speak out about..."

"Call upon the authorities to release..."

"You're good, Tom."

"My father's a member of Parliament."

"Really?"

"Always sounds official, even at breakfast."

"Will he get mad about this?"

"No, no, no. He's in the opposition."

The two of them drafted a brief petition. Vusi, seeing Peter's scrawl, volunteered to copy it in pen on a clean sheet of paper. They all signed and set a time to meet after school.

Peter, Vusi and Tom led a delegation of twelve to the headmaster's office at the end of the day. They declined to speak with Mr. Smythe-Harris and waited patiently until the headmaster had time to see them, long after most students had gone home.

Mr. Collins took a careful look at their petition and at the boys in front of him, five of them black. He asked for details of events leading to Sandile's disappearance. He inquired about Sandile's political activities.

Peter told him about Sandile discovering T.S.'s body, the funeral, the newspapers. He did not mention any ties with T.S.'s supporters; he refused to believe that Sandile had become violent just because of them.

"This is grave," Mr. Collins told the delegation. "I shall let you know soon what the academy will do."

The delegation thanked him and left.

That was not an answer, Peter noted. It was better than Smythe-Harris, but not by much. Peter wanted to believe that Mr. Collins would help and that it would make a difference. But he couldn't take that for granted. Whatever the headmaster was going to do would be way too slow or cautious or both, he thought. They needed to organize something more, and he needed a channel for all his fear.

Vusi punched the wall in frustration. He bloodied his knuckles. No one had tissue to wipe up the blood. Peter fished the blue bandana Kagiso had given him out of his pocket and handed it to Vusi.

"We gotta go back and demand action," Peter insisted.

"Confronting him won't help," Tom replied. "But Collins will come 'round."

"You hope," Vusi said.

"We gotta do something more," Peter insisted. "What about a student organization?"

"Malan will fight it," Vusi cautioned.

"Fuck Malan. This is about saving Sandile's life," Peter shouted.

"OK," Vusi said. "Let's do it."

"You writing anything on him?" Peter asked his mother on the drive home.

"Of course. A feature. Want to see it when we get home?"

In her office later, they read through the article that was hanging out of her typewriter.

"Put more about sports, OK?"

"Good instinct. That helps readers see a person instead of just an issue." Ann pulled the pages out of the typewriter and penciled in changes. "Cricket?"

"And soccer and tennis. I'd don't think he plays rugby. He's a huge Pirates fan."

"Who?"

"Orlando Pirates. Soweto professional soccer. Dad got us tickets to a game. Didn't he tell you?"

Ellen came to the office door. "Sorry to interrupt, Mrs. Seibert."

"That's OK. What's up?"

"About the cake for Saturday. What flavor?"

Ann sighed and said, "That was supposed to be a surprise, Auntie." She looked at Peter.

"For what?" he asked.

"Really?"

It dawned on Peter that the cake was for him, but it seemed so trivial to think of celebrating his sixteenth birthday with Sandile missing.

"Sorry for that," Ellen said. "I must leave early that day." She turned and looked directly at Peter even as she spoke to his mother. "My niece Kagiso is moving to Bophuthatswana on Sunday and I want to see her before she goes."

Peter froze. "What?"

He could feel his mother's scrutiny, but he didn't care if she found out his secret. How was he supposed to cope if both his friends were gone? Why hadn't she called? Surely this qualified as an emergency, even by her father's rules. Had she sent Ellen to tell him? Or did he not matter to her? He had to find out. Even if the news would tear him apart, he had to know.

On Saturday morning, Kagiso's father returned from work at eight with hard news. His brother Amos would have to come for her that noon, not Sunday as planned, because his mother-in-law was seriously ill.

Kagiso burned as he tried to announce the change gently.

"I won't go before one," she told him, defiant now that it was too late.

"You will go when I say," he replied, his voice softened by sadness.

Kagiso left the house. She had not packed a single belonging. She wasn't planning to make her uncle's house her home.

Was her aunt coming to say good-bye? Was there a chance that Peter would come? She hadn't called him or asked her aunt to tell him. She felt she had betrayed the struggle by indulging in his attention, his world. Forget it, she told herself. Don't cling to outside help.

At Palesa's, Kagiso blurted out the new departure time. They devoted their last hours together to planning for the meeting at noon with Soweto Civic Organization leaders Bertrand and Mary Khumalo. These were the allies Kagiso believed they needed – anti-apartheid activists whose commitment to the struggle could not be questioned. Kagiso and Palesa wrote nothing, for fear it could fall into the wrong hands – police or radicals. They wanted a critique of their ideas and backing by renowned activists as armor against those who instigated violence.

They collected Sonny Boy at eleven, then walked past the Mandelas' three-room home on the way to the Khumalos' house, a township house greatly improved by renovations and additions. Although they were early for their appointment, Mary Khumalo led them to the large living room in back where armchairs and sofas lined the walls.

"We are very much grateful to you," Kagiso began after the greetings. "We are sitting with this problem of student radicals."

"We have seen how brutally the police treat them," Bertrand Khumalo agreed.

"But the radicals are also brutal, killing families of police," she said.

"What's your point?" he replied, pulling back as if to distance himself from her ideas.

"We are all comrades," she defended her friends. "We are in every school boycott, at every funeral…"

"And?"

"They are seeking personal revenge instead of liberation for all," Kagiso struggled to convince them. How could they not see the difference? "If we say that we must be non-violent, they call us collaborators and target us."

"I see," Mary interjected.

Her husband nodded. "Yes, a more disciplined approach. It's more effective."

Kagiso breathed a sigh of relief that they understood. Mary even proposed that the student organization do a joint project with the civic association to reinforce non-violence.

At one o'clock, Kagiso apologized to their hosts. "Sorry for that. My father says I must go home."

The Khumalos said they understood and thanked her for coming.

Palesa looked up tearfully.

Kagiso laid a finger across her lips to signal that there was no need for words.

Palesa stood up, hugged her and handed her a folded paper.

Kagiso reached her home by quarter past one. Her uncle was waiting.

She threw her clothes into a pair of plaid bags along with a hair pick and a toothbrush. She rifled through her sister's bureau drawer and then her own in a vain search for her red-and-white earrings. Finding her sister's Hello, Kitty T-shirt still hidden among her own clothes, she folded it neatly and put it on her sister's bed. But still she put a note in her bureau drawer warning: *Tswaya!* She pretended to ponder what else she would need, hoping her aunt would come soon, hoping Peter would not be with her, and that he would.

Uncle Amos paced while she shuffled through items in the bathroom, living room and kitchen as if in search of essentials. She went to say good-bye to the neighbors, whom she didn't like. She hugged her sister, who clung, and her brother, who squirmed away. Finally, she had to say farewell to her parents – with unexpected tears for her mother and blistering looks at her father.

Amos placed her bags carefully into the back of his van, tucking in the garments that hung over the brims and zipping the bags closed. He settled into the driver's seat, on the right, and drove off as Kagiso looked hopelessly out the rear window.

Kagiso realized she had staged this exit with no fanfare, as if pretending it wouldn't happen would keep it from happening. But now she felt the loss. Why hadn't she let herself cry with Palesa, whose friendship had carried her through every trouble? Wasn't she going to miss a bear hug from Sonny Boy and a farewell from Lawrence? And why hadn't she told Peter?

Looking back over the rolling hills of Soweto as her uncle's van pulled onto the highway, she felt her life emptying out. On her way to purgatory in Mmabatho. Her uncle's house would be bursting with his four sons, ages eight to fourteen. For her: no friends, no way back, no chance to work for the freedom struggle, no life at all.

A half hour out of Soweto, Kagiso finally remembered the paper from Palesa. She pulled it out of her jeans pocket and opened it to find a detailed pencil drawing of the crèche, with children on the swings and climbing on the bars. It almost made her cry, but she refused to let it. She refolded the drawing and slipped it back into her pocket. Too hard to think about.

Kagiso was in no mood to talk. Neither was her uncle. They drove for four hours through prosperous white-owned farmland, until they reached his home, her place of exile.

"You are welcome," her uncle said as he showed her in. "A girl in the house is new for us, something good."

"Thank you, Uncle."

The long list of errands frustrated Peter: A stop at the ticket outlet, the automatic bank teller, the liquor store, the photo shop. It went on and on, none of them his tasks, all of them eating into the time he could see Kagiso before she was sent away.

At long last they reached the familiar Soweto house with its newly finished addition. Two o'clock. Much later than he had hoped. He blamed his ever-tardy mother again, though he knew it wasn't entirely her fault.

They knocked. Sally Mafolo answered, dressed this time. She was clearly upset but invited them inside.

Through the open back door, Peter could see a man painting the outside of the house. Short, with the arms of a bodybuilder. Just as Kagiso had described her father. Peter stared at the man who was sending her away, not wanting to meet him, and hoping he didn't know that Peter had kissed his daughter.

"*Dumela*," Ellen greeted her sister. "Kagiso?"

"Amos left early. Kagiso went with him," Sally explained. She bit her lip to keep from crying.

Peter could feel Kagiso's anger and despair haunting the little house. He could not linger there. He whispered to his mother that they should visit Sandile's parents. They said goodbye and got into the car.

Peter kept surveying the streets and backyards as if he might discover a girl in a red shirt and white jeans. Her absence made him sad; Sandile's made him afraid. He turned his thoughts to his missing friend when they pulled up at the Malindis' house.

"I'm sorry we missed her," Peter's mother said, breaking the silence of their drive home.

He couldn't bring himself to reply. The absence of his two friends felt like an amputation.

When they reached their house, he went to the garage to get a bucket full of old tennis balls and a racket, didn't bother to change clothes and walked to the tennis court. He reached into the bucket and hit those balls, one after another, not practicing his serve or improving his game but killing the balls, letting them have it with all his might. Then he collected them by the dozens and hit them over and over. Several of them got stuck in the wire mesh of the fence. He pried them loose and walloped them again.

As the shadows stretched across the tennis court and slowly engulfed it, Peter kept up his fusillade. By the time he heard his mother calling him for dinner, it was fully dark on the court.

"There in a minute," he answered, stopping to catch his breath. Then he rounded up the dozen or so balls he could see. He paused to think of that first day on the tennis court teaching Kagiso how to play. In her honor, he hit the balls, one by one, as high into the air as he could, watching as they soared through the glare from the outdoor burglar lights and disappeared into the night, listening as they landed with a plunk in the garden or a splash in the pool.

When all the balls had sailed away, he went limp. He could barely lift the racket as he dragged himself into the house.

Sandile languished in the foul cell for days. He thought perhaps twelve. There was neither daylight nor moonlight to mark the passage of time. He ate what scraps were shoved at him through a slot in the door. He woke to find two men putting a bag back over his head in the dark.

"No," he moaned, as if his voice could defend him while his hands were tied. His knees buckled as they led him out. They forced him to stand again. They asked him their questions again. Still he did not answer.

They dragged him back into the cell. He dozed off. Sleep had become a form of defense, tuning out the horrors that surrounded him, making them seem as if they were happening to someone else, even as every bruise and cut hurt him more each day.

He woke up again, vomiting. The little food they gave him – mostly cold cornmeal with a few vegetables – was scarcely enough to keep him going. His stomach had begun to reject it, violently. He could feel himself wasting away. Half awake, he heard the police outside his door discussing whether to get rid of him now, before he was too far gone. He dozed off again.

April 1989

"So we got Collins," Peter told Sandile's supporters at lunch. "Statement to the press about what a star Sandile's been here."

"Well done," Tom commended him.

"Not enough," Peter replied. "We gotta keep on it."

"How?"

"What about a strike?" Vusi asked.

"Doesn't seem to work even in the township schools. I was thinking more of a letter-writing campaign," Peter suggested.

"Who'd we write to?" Vusi asked.

"Ambassadors, the Commonwealth," Tom recommended.

"Anti-apartheid groups," Vusi offered.

"They're already involved. But we can keep Sandile's case alive," Peter continued, hoping maybe they could keep Sandile alive, "by keeping his name in the press. Personal letters from each of us who knew him – know him. Stuff about things he likes to do and how much we miss him. My mom's a journalist. Trust me. They eat this stuff up."

He urged them all to go home and write whatever came from the heart, and in the morning they'd share their work and fix it up and decide where to send it.

"This is yours," Vusi said as he handed Peter the blue bandana, clean and ironed.

"Thanks." Peter was glad to have back his one memento of Kagiso.

He started his self-assigned homework first when he got home from the cricket match. It gave him hope to think not about what might be happening to Sandile but about what he would like to say to him when next they met.

We missed your bat in the game against Redhill today, but maybe it was good you weren't here because Tom made a spectacular fielding play that you would have muffed ...

That was the only way he could write it without breaking down. Not something to send to a newspaper. He tried again.

My best friend Sandile Malindi is an ace at every sport...

Not great prose, he admitted. Later he would ask for his mother's help writing something that could get published.

And then he wrote his first letter to Kagiso to explain what they were doing for Sandile. Thanks to his nosey mother, he knew there was no phone at her uncle's house, but he also knew the post office box number where Kagiso could get mail. Rereading it, he wasn't sure he should send it. If she had wanted to hear from him, she would have called or gotten a message to him before she left, or something. Maybe he should let her be.

After three weeks, the police but a bag over Sandile's head again, dragged him out of his cell, shoved him into the back of a truck and sped off. The truck bounced over potholes and skidded around corners, throwing Sandile around the enclosed back of the pick-up and making him dizzy. It screeched to a halt. The police opened the back and dumped him out; he landed hard on his right shoulder.

The truck sped off. Sandile lay face first on the ground. He could taste the dust that sneaked in through the cloth bag with every breath. His hands hurt where the ropes chafed them. His shoulder ached from the awkward landing. His chin started to bleed. He fainted.

Stiff stems poked Sandile's face through the bag. They pricked him. They made him itch. They woke him.

He raised his head, groaned at the pain in his shoulder, then gently rolled onto his tender back and worked his hands, still tied together, down his bruised and swollen legs and up in front. When he had accomplished that, he sat up and fumbled with the cord that kept the bag over his head. He tugged at the bag itself, got it partially off his face and breathed fresh air for the first time in however many days. He gulped at it, thirstily filling his lungs and reviving his spirit.

Sandile sat still and peered around him in the dim light of morning or evening. He was alone. He did not know how long he had slept, how long he had been captive or where he was. Tall withered grass covered the gently rolling hills around him. Judging by the land, he could have been anywhere in the Transvaal, the province that encompassed Johannesburg, Soweto and Bophuthatswana. But he guessed that the ride in the police truck had not been long. He couldn't be too far from Soweto.

And then a whiff of coal smoke told him someone lived nearby. Leaning over onto bound hands for balance, he heaved himself onto his shaky knees and raised his head as high as he could. Pushing the bag back off his face, he scanned the treeless land and saw nothing familiar.

The sky brightened a bit. It must have been morning. Sandile leaned on his hands again and pulled his feet beneath him. Steadying himself like a tight-rope walker before a stunt, he rose slowly to his full height. And there, at last, over the crest of a hill, he could see it – the coal-smoke cloud over Soweto, or some other black township.

For the first time ever, he was pleased to see that smoke. Crumpling to the ground again, he lay in the prickly grass as the sun began to rise, and he laughed to be alive. The grass and stones hurt the welts on his back. He rolled over onto his stomach and kissed the dust and wept and laughed.

Finally, he sat up and searched for something to fray the ropes that bound his wrists. Crawling along with the bag slipping over his eyes, he saw little of use, just rocks worn smooth. Then he found a foot track and followed it until he noticed a small pile of litter. He tried a rusty can that proved too dull. Then he spotted a beer bottle, broke it, wedged a jagged piece between his feet and used it to attack his bonds as best he could, cutting himself slightly in several places.

It was a tedious process. The knots had been expertly tied. The bag kept slipping back onto his face. He persisted and at last freed his bloody hands, massaged his chafed wrists. He untied the cord that held the bag, then flung both to the ground and lay face down again, tired from the effort. He dozed.

The sun toasted his aching shoulders, waking him once more. Sandile told himself to get up. It would be a long walk, he counseled. Better to make it in daylight. Tenderly, trying to care for each of his pains, he maneuvered himself back to a standing position, took a deep breath and stepped toward the smoke of what he prayed was Soweto.

His former shackles lay in his path. Now able to think of the future again, he collected the ropes and stuffed them in the bag to carry back as evidence.

The first hour of walking was slow. Sandile had to learn a new gait that accommodated his aches and bruises, his fatigue and thirst and hunger. But that hour also brought him hope; it brought him close enough to recognize the western edge of Soweto. He even dared to dream that, if he could just stagger to the first streets, some driver would take pity on him and give him a ride across the vast township to his parents' home on its eastern border.

"God has brought my son back," Grace Malindi told Peter by telephone late that afternoon. "I thank Him. I praise the glory of His name."

"Wow," was all Peter could manage.

"I thank you, too, for all you did."

"I didn't do anything, really. But can I talk to him?"

"Not now. He is resting. I'll ask him to ring you when he's able," she promised.

Peter begged her for more information. He could hear the anguish in her voice as she listed Sandile's wounds, which George had photographed as evidence.

Grace said she did not yet have the full story of how Sandile had been abducted and all that he had suffered. He had been too exhausted to provide the details.

When they hung up, Peter ran through the house shouting that Sandile was free, shouting to his sisters and his mother and Ellen Dlamini.

Ann asked if the Malindis had thought about calling a press conference and finding a lawyer. Peter said he didn't think so. She gave them a ring to see if she could help. When she finished talking with Stephen Malindi, Peter called his father at work and all the loyal members of the Saint Andrew's student delegation.

What he really wanted to do, and could not, was to call Kagiso, to share with her his joy and astonishment that Sandile was alive.

Kagiso spent her first days in the Bophuthatswana capital, Mmabatho, with her mind completely shut to all around her. Her uncle's house was one of hundreds of matching bungalows built in neat rows and columns by the Bophuthatswana government, using apartheid money. The houses, newer than her home in Soweto, but not bigger, were uniformly painted a light tan with brown paint at the base, where the ruddy earth would splash onto the walls if it rained.

Amos was a kind man, she thought, not tough like her father. Ironic that he had helped her father to build the extra bedroom in Soweto that now sat empty. Here, his four sons crowded into one bedroom; her aunt and uncle shared the other bedroom. Her aunt's mother, struggling with an illness that was never explained to Kagiso, lingered in bed in an alcove extending from the kitchen. And Kagiso took her place on a sagging sofa in the combined living and dining room.

The family was busy attending to the grandmother. Kagiso was relieved to be forgotten. She wanted nothing but to sulk and pity herself, and dream of escape. At night, she had half the house to herself to let her thoughts wander beyond the confines of exile, out into empty streets, away into her old world. But it was all dreams and memories that disappeared with daylight.

"This came for you," Amos told her after she had been there a week.

When he handed her a letter, it caught her completely by surprise. Communication from the outside came as a shock. And this was a letter from Peter, who really existed, no matter how far away he seemed to be. For hours, she kept his letter unopened in her pocket, next to the drawing from Palesa, patting it repeatedly for reassurance, until she could find a moment to step out of the crowded house and sit alone on the front step in the early evening.

She sliced open the envelope with a kitchen knife, then carefully unfolded a piece of lined notebook paper covered in scrawl. She had never seen his handwriting before. It seemed strange to learn something new about him from so far away.

Peter's letter confirmed her worst fear – that Sandile had been abducted by the police. He wrote about all the things that he and his parents, Sandile's parents and classmates, and anti-apartheid organizations were doing to try to secure Sandile's release. He said they had even formed a student association at, of all places, Saint Andrew's Academy. It sounded so much like Peter, she thought, a boy who couldn't sit still.

He ended the letter by saying that he missed her very much. The words made her catch her breath. For the first time since she had left Soweto, she let herself cry. Quietly, so her uncle's family would not hear, and carefully, so as not to dampen the letter. Kagiso let the tears roll down her face and drop onto the step, dark polka dots in the reddish dust.

She wiped her tears and then shook her head jauntily, to pluck up her courage. She folded the letter, returned it to the envelope and slid it into her pocket. The letter and Palesa's drawing went to school with her each day that week, as comfort in her isolation, as promises that there was a world outside.

"Bad for business," George submitted as the extended Malindi family gathered at the dining table to discuss what to do.

"Not about business," his father responded. "It's about justice."

Sandile's thoughts drifted as his family debated whether a press conference was a good idea or whether it was better to keep quiet about his abduction by the police. The evening invaded the room. It pressed on his chest like the darkness in the police cell, pushing out the air he needed. His mother switched on a light. He made himself look around and realize that he could see; he was not hooded, a prisoner of the dark, but surrounded by those who loved him. He breathed deeply and tried to concentrate on the discussion.

"Consider the risk of going public," Grace said, glancing at Sandile with tears in her eyes. "He has been through too much."

"Uh-huh," one of Sandile's uncles agreed. "They could target him or any of us."

"It's already public," Stephen pointed out. "In all the newspapers here, abroad."

"We're targeted from both sides – comrades and police," George reflected.

"True," another uncle noted. "That's why we stand together."

"And speak the truth," Stephen added.

Sandile turned toward his grandmother, seated next to him, and asked quietly, "What's your advice?"

She pointed toward his heart and said, "That is where you must find the answer."

His mind slid away again. The police surrounded him in the darkness, unseen, beating him, grilling him, starving him.

He wanted to drink water, to lie down, to sleep. Swaying in his chair, sucked back into that horror, he waged a battle to drive them away, to return to his family, his freedom. So much had been beyond his control; he had had to learn to survive when no decisions had been his to make. Now, he needed to make the biggest decision of his life. He could not breathe.

Leaning back in his chair, he tipped his face toward the ceiling and swallowed the fresh air. Sitting up straight, he looked around at the faces of people who had prayed for him and worried and cried and done everything they could. His mother, with her pistol useless in this fight. His brother, the partying knocked out of him. His father, trying to take charge of a situation he could not control. His grandmother, steady, almost strong again. Uncles, aunts, cousins.

Listening as each one spoke, he tried to consider all their views. But he knew that he had to make up his own mind. What should he do? The question hammered at his brain like an interrogation. Every repetition of it made him wince. Only a decision could stop that pain. Sandile breathed deeply, steeled himself to answer.

"Thank you, all of you," Sandile said, nodding toward each of them. They turned to hear him out. "I would like to speak out." He paused to take a deep breath. "At a press conference. As *Tata* said, it's already public. They know who I am, who all of us are. I must do what I can to stop them hurting others."

"You are ready for that?" his mother asked. He could hear the worry choking her voice.

"*Ewe.*" The firmness of his answer surprised him. He was not that sure, but he tried to pull himself up into that posture.

Stephen got up from his seat at the head of the table and walked to Sandile, shook his hand, patted him lightly on his sore shoulder and announced, "Decided." Then he added, "Time to eat."

Just before the press conference, the Malindi family waited in a side entrance to the church nearest their shop. Sandile shifted slightly on his feet, trying to adjust to his aches, getting ready to talk, once again, about the ordeal he had suffered. Fear swelled up his throat, choking him. As he tried to swallow it down, he realized that, each time he had to tell the story, the fear lost a little bit of power over him.

Suddenly he saw Peter arrive with his parents. A huge smile softened the angles of his serious face as he thought about what Peter had meant to him during captivity.

"That hurts," he griped as they hugged. But he was still smiling broadly when his friend stepped back apologetically.

"Not so good for your cricket game," Peter said, glancing at Sandile's swollen hands and his bandages.

Sandile laughed and put his hands together as if to swing a bat.

Then he turned serious again and studied the crowd seated in the pews: On the far side, representatives of the organizations that had fought for his release. In the back, members of his extended family, plus Palesa and Sonny Boy, but not Kagiso or Lawrence. On the near side, journalists who would soon quiz him on his ordeal. In front of the altar, a row of chairs facing the crowd, with a pillow his mother had brought for him resting atop the chair in the center. He was ready to speak out against apartheid, ready to establish his own way to fight against it.

The risks were real, he understood. If the police wanted to detain him and brutalize him again, they could do that. Or they could get one of their henchmen to attack him. This crowd of supporters would not be present to protect him. But he had gained a sense of his own strength. He would face the challenge.

Nodding to his parents that they could start, he stepped into the church hall. The activists stood and cheered for him as he limped to his place.

Flanked by an attorney, Reeva Jameson of the Detainees Rights Committee, Mr. Collins from Saint Andrew's, his parents, his brother and Peter, Sandile recounted precisely what had been inflicted upon him.

True, he had not seen faces, Sandile admitted in answer to a journalist's question. But he was certain that it was Soweto police. He had seen parts of their uniforms, heard them talk in the truck and in the office, memorized some of their conversations, taunts and threats, and their orders from superiors to continue the interrogation. He quoted them at length.

The journalists dashed off to process their film and file their copy.

Mr. Collins greeted Sandile at the entrance to Saint Andrew's on his first day back. Mrs. Fielding's class gave him a standing ovation.

"Huzzah," Tom and Vusi led the cheers.

But then the teacher shepherded the students back to the task of preparing for a geometry test.

At lunch the talk was of nothing else but Sandile's ordeal. He noticed that a few students kept their distance, with Andre Malan and his crowd looking at him as if he were a proven terrorist. The rest, titillated by a true horror story that happened to someone they knew, wanted to hear all the gory, frightening, enraging details. Sandile said little, but those who had read the articles about his press conference recounted the tale and asked all sorts of questions.

Sandile was deeply touched not by the attention but by what he learned about the campaign Peter had launched to free him. Peter had said nothing about it, but Tom and Vusi and other classmates told him. Sandile wondered how he had ever doubted Peter's judgment.

When Sandile finally had a chance to ask Peter about Kagiso, he was shocked to hear that she had been sent away. Peter had said nothing about that either.

"You had enough to worry about," Peter explained.

But Sandile wanted the details. He got some of them — about her father and his relatives in Bophuthatswana. When Peter started to explain that he had reached Soweto too late to say goodbye, he just stopped.

Sandile looked at his friend in surprise. He was used to Peter's light-hearted jokes. But he suddenly caught on that Peter more than missed Kagiso, even if he couldn't quite say how much.

Sandile didn't press him. He had been thinking about her, too, thinking about her commitment to the struggle against apartheid. Having experienced the dangers that she and her friends faced, he felt uneasy taking shelter at Saint Andrew's. At school, and even at home, they might applaud him. But he knew that he was the boy who had lost his way, agreed to do something violent, lacked the courage to complete it, been caught and beaten. A survivor, not a hero.

The bruises and scrapes made it hard for Sandile to get comfortable, even in his own bed. He lay on top of the blue-and-green plaid quilt, so that it would cushion him, and folded the other half over him. But it was the darkness that kept him awake. Not until a sliver of moon rose later and he could see around him and see that he was safe would he be able fall asleep. Until then, he knew that he would have to lie still, trying to rest because his body needed it, but awake because his mind had so much work to do. It had to go through the catalogue night after night of the cruel words of the police, of their laughter as they beat him and the stench of their jail, of the rhythm of the blows that left welts across his back and legs, of the anger in T.S.'s eyes and the blood upon his face, of his own failings to discern right from wrong. All those images and sounds and smells prospered in the darkness, uncaged until he could put each of them in its place. It was time for him to take up his life again. He was not ready.

Peter, Christina and Megan hit tennis balls around in the cool afternoon air. Canadian doubles of a sort, with him taking on both his fierce littler sister and his very precise bigger one. Suddenly they heard a shout from inside the house. They rushed to see what the emergency was. Peter reached the house first and found his mother in her office, pacing furiously with a letter in her hand.

"You OK?" he asked.

She waved the letter at him angrily. "Work permit denied," she shouted.

"Can they do that?"

"Yeah."

Peter remembered seeing the government letter on her desk weeks earlier, with its official letterhead and its bad grammar. He had heard his parents mention journalists who had been thrown out of the country.

"Why?"

"Could've been reporting on funerals or organizing Sandile's press conference or anything else. They don't say. They don't have to." As the two girls ran in behind Peter, she shooed all three out the office door, saying, "Kids, I need to make some important phone calls."

Peter collected the tennis rackets and balls. Then he went to his room to start studying for the geometry exam. Hard to concentrate on his least favorite subject.

Later, after their father got home, Peter and his sisters could hear a big debate between their parents behind the master bedroom door. They stayed away, watching some noisy "MacGyver" episodes on TV to drown out whatever was going on back there.

Peter could feel the tension as they all sat down to dinner. His mother served up macaroni and cheese, with the usual triple portion for Peter. They said grace. Then Richard told them they had important news.

"The government denied your mother a permit to work as a journalist here," he announced somberly. "I'll ask for a transfer back to Nairobi, so we can all go back together."

Peter froze, a steaming bite of macaroni and cheese suspended on his fork. He put the fork down. He listened in shock as his father explained that it would not be fair to stay if their mother couldn't work, that they had tried every avenue they knew to get her a permit, that he didn't know whether they would go back to Nairobi or somewhere else. It all sounded like a voice from the other end of a long tunnel.

Unfair to her, maybe, Peter thought, but what about me? He ate nothing. He sat listening to words he recognized but couldn't absorb.

Kagiso's uncle brought her another letter from Peter. Sandile was free! She wanted to shout for joy, but felt she had to keep all her feelings hidden. If her uncle knew that she had a friend who had been detained by the police, he would surely tell her father, and she would never be allowed to return home. But he was free, and she was filled with relief. Peter reported all the details of Sandile's suffering and of the press conference.

And he added that he wished she were there. His words – scratched awkwardly in pencil on lined paper with three holes in it – echoed in her heart. He was the only one writing to her, aside from her mother, who sent one-sentence messages hand-carried by relatives. Those messages didn't count because Kagiso was still angry with her mother. It was Peter's letters that seemed like threads of hope, however fragile, that connected her to real life.

Thinking about Peter's campaign for Sandile's release, she began to wonder if she could support the struggle against apartheid, even way up here in exile.

The Mmabatho school was physically better than her high school in Soweto – newer building, newer desks, enough textbooks to go around. But a framed photograph of the Bophuthatswana dictator, Lucas Mangope, loomed over them. She remembered that Bophuthatswana troops had put Mangope out of office, briefly, the year before, and that South African troops had returned him to power, like Humpty Dumpty back up on the wall.

The students seemed OK, she thought, but no sign of a protest movement. Maybe they were scared, after the coup, or maybe she just didn't know them well enough yet. They were other people, strangers, not her friends. Could she talk to them about protesting?

To find out, Kagiso decided to check with her cousin Carleton.

"You know why I'm here?" she asked as they walked to school together the next morning.

"Yeah," he said, glancing sideways at her with a sly smile. "Why?"

He signaled for her to lean in close so he could whisper. "The struggle."

"Yeah," she nodded. "Anything here?"

He leaned in again. "A little. Underground."

"Introduce me?"

"OK. But quiet at home."

She nodded. He was short and stocky, like his father and her father, but on the right side.

It was another week of long school days and chores for her uncle's family and trying to be thankful for their home, of exchanging secrets with Carleton and trying to engage new school mates, all with only a tiny piece of her heart in it. A very long week in a sentence of exile that looked like it would stretch out forever. And at the end of that third week, another letter. One she could barely manage to finish. It read as if Peter had hardly been able to write it. Not a steady report on events, but an anguished cry of pain: that he was being forced to leave South Africa.

How could 'they' force him to leave the country? The cruelty of the apartheid government was always personal, she believed. It broke the spirit, one person at a time.

His letter jolted Kagiso into action. She asked her aunt if she could borrow money to buy a stamp.

Under orders to set aside the things he wanted to take on the plane, so that the movers could pack the rest, Peter looked around his room and found it hard to decide. He found it hard even to think about leaving, deserting his friends when they needed him. Or was it that he needed them? Choosing what to take seemed trivial by comparison.

He slouched on his unmade bed as he looked around. The three Orlando Pirates caps were still on his bureau, along with the tickets to the upcoming match. So was the light blue bandana Kagiso had given him as protection from tear gas, his one keepsake. He got up slowly and put two of the caps and the envelope with all three tickets on top of his school books to give to Sandile. Then he looked for his duffle bag. There it was, behind a box that he had never unpacked after they arrived in South Africa ten months earlier. He dragged the green duffel bag into the middle of the room and put the other cap into it, along with the bandana, washed and ironed.

He lay down on the bed and surveyed the walls. OK, the poster of Marco van Basten – that should come. He got up and took out the thumbtacks that pinned it to the wall, rolled the poster, tied an old shoelace around it and put it in the bag.

Peter's father leaned in the open door to see how he was doing.

"You'll need some clothes, too," he reminded Peter gently.

Peter nodded as if that were insightful and opened a bureau drawer. Everything in it had been folded and stowed by Ellen Dlamini. He didn't sort through anything. Instead, he took out a stack of shirts and one of shorts, as well as a clump of underwear and socks, and put each pile straight into his luggage. A sweatshirt, a pair of jeans, a couple of pairs of gym shoes, a toilet case, a swimsuit because they were going back to Kenya, at least for the time being. The bag was full. Peter zipped it closed. He had done all he had the heart to do.

Stretched out across the bed again, he stared at the ceiling for a long time. He tried to picture what he had loved about Nairobi, why he had been sad to leave it, why he was reluctant to go back. Old friends were still there. He would find them again running across the soccer field at the top of a hill with views over the coffee plantations, in the houses draped in bougainvillea vines along Loresho Crescent, on the school hike across the Maasai grasslands. People he liked, but not the ones who meant the most to him, the ones with whom he had shared danger and tried to do something to make the world better. Not Sandile and Kagiso.

Peter arched his back so he could get his only letter from Kagiso out of his jeans pocket and read it again. She sounded as lost as he felt. She asked only one thing – a chance to say goodbye.

He heard the thunder of Megan's feet as she ran around the house with a friend who had stayed for a final sleepover. Suddenly, his little sister popped in the door of his room.

"Look what I found," she taunted him, holding a pair of red-and-white beaded earrings up to her ears.

"Where'd you get those?" he demanded, leaping from the bed and chasing her down the hallway.

"Barbie basket," she shouted as she scurried away.

"Not yours."

"Not yours either."

"Give 'em back."

"Nah-nah-nee-nanny. Peter's got a girlfriend," she taunted him.

He trapped her in her room, put a hand on top of her head and repeated, "Give 'em back."

"Ask nicely," she demanded.

"Please."

She laid them in his outstretched palm, then escaped to run wild in a house crammed with mover's cartons.

Peter went back to his room and opened his luggage. He folded the bandana around the earrings, cradled them in the Pirates cap and zipped up the bag again.

The pale green Mercedes rolled swiftly along the two-lane highway, heading northwest out of Johannesburg.

"Thanks for taking me, Mom," Peter said, then yawned because they had left before dawn to be able to complete a round-trip in one day.

"You didn't really think we'd make you leave without saying good-bye?"

Yeah, he had thought that. His parents had seemed so caught up in their own problems that he didn't think they recognized what Kagiso meant to him. Rather than say that to his mother, he went back to staring out the window at the broad farmland and the towns that would have been quaint but for the clusters of shanties on their fringes. He wasn't really looking at them, though. They blurred across his sleepy eyes.

In about four hours, they reached the colonial town of Mafeking, with its white-pillared porches. Peter's mother mentioned that it had been the scene of a famous siege at the turn of the century when the British and the Afrikaners fought to control South Africa. Peter was not interested in history lessons.

They passed through to the adjacent town of Mmabatho, where every structure was new and modern – government offices, a university, a futuristic soccer stadium, a hotel with a casino. Tract housing and schools stood on raw earth, baked hard but with gullies to prove that it sometimes rained. Peter didn't care about any of it, except that she might be there. This was Kagiso's place of exile.

Street signs were a sporadic afterthought. Ann tried to follow Ellen's instructions and often stopped to ask directions. They inched their way along, searching among a collection of identical khaki-colored concrete houses positioned with oppressive regularity.

Kagiso balanced a large basket of groceries on her head as she returned from errands her aunt had assigned. She thought about nothing. A crowd of children swept through a cross street. A familiar sight, she ignored it. Then she noticed the distinctive color of the car they were following. Swinging a hand up to steady her bundles, she strode as swiftly as she could after them. It's not Peter, she warned herself against hopefulness. But she pursued them at a quickening pace all the same.

The driver stopped to ask directions of an old man. Kagiso caught up during his slow explanation.

It was him! She lifted the basket from her head, set it in the dust and waded through the swarm of children. She reached in the open window and touched Peter on the shoulder.

He turned immediately toward her and a smile broadened his face.

The car began to edge forward.

"Stop, Mom. She's here," Peter called out.

Kagiso trotted alongside the slowly moving car, not letting go of the window frame for fear that the car was a phantom.

When it stopped, Peter opened the door, squeezed out through the crowd, stood in front of her and hesitated.

Kagiso looked into his pale eyes, unsure how to respond.

The crowd pressed in, pushing her forward. Peter caught her. She relaxed against him. He slipped his arms around her. The small children giggled, cheered, dashed away to report events. Kagiso did not care what they thought. After a moment, she did care. Self-conscious, she stepped back, looking at his face for a clue.

"Sorry I couldn't tell you we were coming," he said just as she said, "I'm so glad you're here." Then neither spoke.

"How did you find me?"

"Auntie Ellen's directions."

Time cheated Kagiso and Peter. It sped up during the moments they had together. They raced through all the things they wanted to talk about – Sandile's ordeal and what the future might hold for Peter and what the present meant for Kagiso.

"You're amazing," Peter said. "A couple weeks and you're mobilizing the students."

"Not mobilizing, just talking to some who want change. My cousin helps. But I got the idea from you."

"Me?"

"I was too sad and angry until I got your letter. If you could start a student group at Saint Andrew's, then I must try."

He grinned. "That's me – student radical."

"At the end of the day, it's the only thing that keeps me going," she confessed, brushing away her doubts about whether they fit together or not. Here, cut off from her old life, his support meant the world to her, as long as she didn't have to admit that to him or to herself.

"Wait. I almost forgot," he said, fishing in a pocket for something. He pulled out the pale blue bandana and handed it to her.

Kagiso wasn't at all sure what to expect. She unfolded the cloth carefully to find the surprise – her favorite earrings. Smiling, she slid the hooks through the holes in her ears and tossed her head to make them shake. She felt like herself again, coquettish, bold. She twisted up the bandana and flicked it at Peter, grinning as she teased him.

He grabbed at the bandana. "That's mine," he said. "You can't take it back." But she flicked it at him three times before she let him catch it.

They walked around the reduced perimeter of her life in exile – the school, the shops, the neighborhood. She introduced him to Carleton and her younger cousins.

Ann kept out of their way. All too soon, she told them it was time to leave. She climbed into the car to wait.

Kagiso didn't let Peter speak. She placed her fingertips on his lips and told him, "Don't say good-bye. Say you'll come back."

He took her hand, kissed her fingers and whispered, "I'll come back." He kissed her on the mouth.

When he let her go, she turned aside so that he would not see her cry.

The world seemed to Peter to be clouding over, threatening to withhold the light for a long time. The fields and towns passed by meaninglessly as he and his mother drove back to a home they were soon to leave.

"I'll miss her, too," his mother said.

He just stared at the highway in front of them.

"It hurts when you find something you care about, someone you could help, then you're prevented."

He pondered her comment and his troubles for a while before answering. "I never could've made a difference anyway."

"You already have."

His silence said he did not believe her.

"Just by supporting your friends when they needed you most."

"But it's still their struggle, not mine."

"Of course. But believing in them counts for something," she added. "Doing good is the only thing worth doing."

Peter shook his head gloomily. His mother tried a different tack.

"You remember that rock you told me to go see in Namibia – the Finger of God?"

"Sure."

"It didn't just take a strong gust to knock it over, you know. It took centuries of little grains of sand driven by the wind eating away at the stone. We're like those little grains," she claimed. "We play a role, however small, in weakening apartheid."

He contemplated her metaphor, then rejected it.

"Come on, Mom. That's a corny little story to cheer me up."

She shook her head and said, "To cheer myself up."

Sandile paced around his bedroom in the early morning light. He didn't want to go to school. It would be Peter's last day, and he had no idea how to say goodbye. He didn't want to go to Saint Andrew's Academy anymore anyway, especially without

Peter. He wanted to do something more to protest apartheid, although he still wasn't sure what that could be.

He stood in front of his bureau, stepping from side to side in uncertainty. He thought about how Peter had fought for him when he was in police hands. Or was he just dawdling because he felt awkward?

Suddenly, he realized that he needed to dash to catch the bus.

Mrs. Fielding's class offered Peter a round of applause at the end of the day. He took a theatrical bow. Most of the students headed home, but Peter and Sandile walked to the locker room to change for their last cricket practice together. Peter handed him the two Pirates caps and the three tickets to the big match.

"For you and your dad and George," Peter insisted.

Sandile was overwhelmed. He nodded but couldn't manage a word.

In the locker room, Sandile did his best to ignore Andre Malan, who was taking his sports clothes from the compartment next to his.

Just before heading to the fields, Andre turned toward Sandile and said, "Glad you're OK."

Was that a real change of heart? Sandile shook off the exchange and sprinted out to the pitch.

When the practice ended, Coach Haverford gathered the team to wish Peter good luck in his next school. They gave him three cheers. The players lined up to shake his hand and say a couple of words.

Sandile waited, on his toes, at the end of the line. He still didn't know what to say. He stuck to concrete things. "We'll miss you on the cricket pitch tomorrow against Redhill."

"Not true now that you're back on the team."

"I'll miss you," Sandile said, surprised, relieved by his own words.

"I'll miss you, too," Peter mumbled into his friend's shoulder as they hugged each other roughly, briefly, "even if you can't catch a fly ball properly."

It wasn't much of a jest, but it allowed them to part without tears.

May and June 1989

A white professor fatally shot in front of his home. The assassination of David Webster, an anthropologist at the prestigious University of the Witwatersrand and an activist for the rights of people detained by the police, shook everyone at Saint Andrew's Academy. Sandile most of all. He had first seen the headlines as hawkers sold newspapers at the bus terminal that Tuesday morning. The news reawakened his fears. The invisible force that sought to strangle him returned, with renewed strength. He needed a strategy to drive it into submission.

At lunchtime, he asked the school secretary if he could borrow the phone book, then noted the number for the Detainees Rights Committee. Checking his pocket for coins, he made a plan. There would be time to call that afternoon, after cricket, while he was waiting for his brother to pick him up. No one would be around to hear.

"May I speak with Mrs. Jameson?" Sandile asked the woman who answered the phone. He stepped from one foot to the other as he waited in the covered passageway between school buildings.

"May I say who is calling?"

"Sandile Malindi."

"I'll fetch her now, now."

Sandile fidgeted, wondering if he was doing the right thing, very much afraid of the consequences.

"Reeva Jameson speaking."

"It's Sandile."

"Good to hear your voice."

"Thank you for what you did for me."

"We were glad to be of service. Are you well?"

"Yes." He hesitated.

"Do you need help?" she asked.

"No." He took a big breath and made himself go onward, "I want to know what I can do to help."

"Well that's grand, but best not to discuss it on the phone. Would it be possible for you to come see me tomorrow?"

"Yes. At four, after sports? Where do you stay?"

Mrs. Jameson gave him directions from Saint Andrew's to her home a short walk away.

Sandile rang the bell at the gate of one of Houghton Estate's finest homes. A wide driveway curved up to a Cape Dutch mansion with whitewashed ornate facades supporting a dark thatched roof. A pack of beagles rushed to the gate, wagging their tails and howling to announce his presence. The gardener asked his name, then ushered him in, shooing the noisy dogs away.

Dressed in a white silk blouse and trim skirt, Reeva Jameson came out onto the front steps to greet him and led him to a sunroom filled with blooming gardenias and a grand piano. They sipped tea as they talked about what Sandile could do to help detainees.

"Above all, we want to be sure that you are safe," she assured him.

Sandile nodded.

"This is mainly an organization of black South Africans," she explained. "They put whites like me out front not to run it but because we face less risk."

Sandile appreciated their caution, but the killing of the professor reminded him that even whites faced some danger, and that he would, too. "What can I do?"

"There are many ways to help: Visiting families of detainees, talking with detainees who have been released, answering phones, writing reports."

He listened but did not state his preference.

"You must give it some thought," she recommended. "And be sure you're quite ready."

"Thank you. I will."

On the walk back to school, Sandile considered what he might prefer to do. Not office work. Maybe talk with the families or former detainees. He hurried to reach the school before his brother, who had suddenly taken to arriving on time.

"Hey, George," Sandile called out as if he had been waiting patiently, although he beat his brother by two minutes.

"Hey, Sandile. Right on time."

"That's new."

"For you? No."

"For you."

"Just trying to take care of my little brother." George wheeled the red BMW around and headed out the gate.

"Thanks, but I can take care of myself."

George stopped the car and looked at him. "I know that, man. I saw how you handled yourself. Makes me proud."

Sandile was stunned by the respect. "Thanks."

Peter flew down the right sideline of the soccer field at the International School of Kenya, dribbling, dodging a defender deftly and then lofting the ball to a teammate at the top of the penalty box who headed it toward the post. The goalkeeper punched it away. Peter swooped in before any opponent could reach the rebound and hammered a shot just under the crossbar. The ISK team roared in triumph.

He was back as the star striker. He was better than ever. But it was no longer sports glory that he sought. He ran his heart out because it was the only way he could cope with leaving his friends in South Africa. Yes, it was good to see old friends and to play again on this hilltop in northeastern Nairobi. But it was not where he wanted to be. He missed Sandile on the field and in the classroom; he missed Kagiso everywhere.

At home, feeling the pressure of his father's advice that grades would matter when he applied to colleges in the United States, Peter tried to focus on his school work. But he couldn't get any of it done without first writing up the game details as if he were telling them to Sandile. Maybe not to send. Just a pretend conversation.

And then he tried to imagine doing the school assignments alongside Sandile. He plodded through Algebra II and French III and "A Child's Christmas in Wales," trying to muster the kind of academic dedication he had seen in his friend. Hard to do because he was off kilter again. The family had come back in May, at the end of the school year in the U.S. system, though it had been the middle of the school year in South Africa. ISK was familiar, of course, but the curriculum was American – stories of Lewis and Clark, not European colonizers driving Sandile's Xhosa ancestors to the edge of the earth.

The return to a house on Loresho Crescent was disorienting, too. Not the same house they had lived in before, but one just like it and only a few doors away. The same parquet floors in the living and dining rooms. The same louvered windows. The same bird-of-paradise flowers in the garden. Different housekeeper and guard, but relatives of the ones who had worked for them before. For Peter, it made life in Kenya seem like a videotape rewinding and playing repeatedly, like his sisters watching "The Princess Bride" for the fourteenth time.

After dinner and after all the homework was tucked away, whether it was well done or not, then he treated himself to private moments thinking about Kagiso in his room with the door locked and the lights off except for a flashlight. Pad and pencil in hand, he just lay there thinking about her. Stupid to write to her about sports. And there were only so many questions he could ask her about South African politics, since she was in exile and under her father's and her uncle's scrutiny. She wouldn't be able to write anything controversial, just in case they ever saw it.

For news about South Africa, he had other sources. He read everything he could find on it in the international publications his mother bought at the tourist hotels in downtown Nairobi – *Time* and *Newsweek* and the *International Herald Tribune* and even British newspapers – and in the anti-apartheid *Weekly Mail,* which arrived in the post office box of his father's charity several days late and only when the South African government allowed the newspaper to publish. The news was mainly about crackdowns on protesters and divides within the ruling National Party that had invented apartheid, and about the rise of even more extreme anti-black groups. Peter found it discouraging.

It wasn't news about the country he wanted so much as news about Kagiso. But he couldn't write a letter that just said, "How are you?" He tried writing her some poetry, but it sounded like greeting cards. Those pages were never going in the mail.

Then, remembering her questions about the "real" Africa, he decided to write about some of that. One letter at a time, he told her what they learned in class about Kenya history and culture, the plans for another school trip to a Maasai village, science classes about Rift Valley geology, family visits to wildlife reserves and to the Arab trading town of Lamu, with its miles of untouched beaches along the Indian Ocean. He thought she'd be interested, but he worried whether those stories would just make her feel more isolated. It was all twisted up in his head and his heart.

The cricket season ended. Soccer hadn't started yet. Sandile didn't let his brother know that he was finished with school earlier on those days. Instead, he went to Reeva Jameson's house whenever he could to call families in need. Speaking with them dredged up his fears, but he persisted, hoping the work would help him to conquer those bad memories. After a couple of weeks, he felt ready to visit a family in Soweto, choosing one at some distance from his home and his parents' shop.

Rising early on Saturday, he went to the squatter area where the Chikane family lived. With no street address, he had to ask neighbors which shack was theirs. Worried that even his questions could bring the family more trouble, he spoke only to children too young to be caught up in politics. They led him to the place and then dashed away.

"Mama Chikane?" he asked of a woman peeking out through a doorway.

"Who's asking?"

"Sandile."

She waved him inside, then shut the makeshift door behind him.

"Do you have news of my son?"

"Not yet. I'm sorry," Sandile replied.

She let out a long, low moan. "Thirty-eight days gone," she told him.

In the sound of her pain, he could hear the anguish his own mother must have felt.

The shack was dark inside, with no windows, just a little light coming through gaps between the corrugated metal panels. The place had the sour chalky smell of old trash and mud. Sandile could hardly breathe. His old fear tried to strangle him. Closing his eyes, lifting his head, he tried to beat it back with ideas. What was it Mrs. Jameson had suggested he say to families? Were there any words that could comfort this woman? He only remembered the first part: Ask what the detainee is like; speak in present tense. He would have to try.

"Mama, tell me what Moses likes to do?" he prompted the mother.

She paused a moment, as if surprised at the question.

Unable to see her clearly, Sandile worried that he had upset her. He felt himself choking.

"He is the best at sports – soccer, for sure," she declared. Mrs. Chikane sniffled, then hunted through something Sandile couldn't discern in the dark shack. "Here," she said, handing him a battered photo. She pulled the door open a crack to let in a shaft of light.

The fear lost its grip on Sandile's throat and receded toward the dark corners. In the faded picture, he saw a little boy in a huge and ragged Orlando Pirates T-shirt.

"When he was ten years," she clarified.

"How old is he now?"

"Sixteen years."

"Still a Pirates fan?"

"Yebo," she assured him.

They chatted on about Moses's sports achievements and his dreams of learning auto mechanics, though the family did not have a car. After half an hour, Sandile said he had to go. The thought of Moses as a soccer fan brightened his spirit; he made a mental note to bring the extra Pirates cap from Peter on his next visit, so she would have something to give her son when he returned home.

Here I can make a difference, Sandile told himself as he headed to his parents' shop. Not off at Saint Andrew's but here in Soweto, visiting families and detainees who need support.

Throughout the afternoon and the next day as he worked the cash register, he listened to the customers more than usual, chatted with them about what they were buying and whether they had found everything they needed. By Sunday evening, he was determined to talk with his father about transferring to one of the private schools in Soweto that were earning good reputations. Neither studies nor sports were fun for him anymore, but he couldn't make that argument; he knew that "fun" was not a priority for his parents.

"Saint Andrew's, that is the best place for you," Stephen Malindi declared.

"The Star School is just as good."

His father shook his head. "I want you in a school for all races. That's the future."

The answer frustrated Sandile not only because he didn't get his wish but also because he believed his father was right about the future. In a small act of defiance, he put his books away without studying for the chemistry exam. He spent the rest of the evening straightening up the cans and boxes on the shelves with Abel.

On Monday morning, he regretted not having studied and tried to cram for the test while standing up on the bus into Johannesburg and then waiting for the transfer.

It wasn't until June that Kagiso figured out how to earn a little money so that she could buy an airmail stamp to Kenya, and an envelope and paper. She asked the owner of the nearby spaza shop if she could work there now and then selling cold sodas and soap and cigarettes, and earning a few *rand*. She paid her aunt back and then bought supplies.

Peter had sent several letters. Sweet blunt boyish letters full of tales of wild animals and exotic beaches and soccer matches and declarations that he missed her too much. She felt bad that she had not been able to reply. It wasn't for lack of thinking about him. She had written her memories on scraps of paper and box tops, whatever was available, to prevent them from becoming imaginary. Those thoughts were a jumble. She needed to start again.

She began right at the top, in pencil in very small handwriting, so that she could get as many words as possible onto one page and wouldn't have to pay for extra postage. Half the front side was a long apology for not having written sooner. She explained about the money, not as a complaint, just as a way to say she had missed him.

Next she wrote in detail about the slow process of talking politics with students in Mmabatho. Even with Carleton's help, they were reluctant to speak up, being cut off from the main anti-apartheid movement and under the thumb of a dictator who did not hesitate to silence dissenters. But they dreamed of a time when apartheid would be gone and Bophuthatswana would be part of South Africa again and they could go where they liked and get good jobs and build better lives for them-selves and their families. She tried to talk with them about building on those dreams, quietly at first, but getting ready for the right moment to speak out. And secret talks with Carleton about politics kept her going.

Kagiso looked back over that section and began to censor herself. Why hadn't she been cautious? She knew better than to write down things that could be used against her. She went back over the words and erased anything that could be trouble, just to be sure, leaving just enough so that she hoped Peter would be able to read between the lines or through the smudges.

The details of daily life were too dull. One sentence was enough.

And then there was half the back side for everything she felt about him. And she couldn't get a word onto the page. She sat on the front step, leaning on a textbook for a desk and trying to harness her feelings about him. But her thoughts were like crickets hopping wildly at the least effort to catch them. The evening light dimmed. She gave up, folded the paper and slipped it into the envelope with the latest letter from Peter that she kept in her jeans pocket. The two papers would sit side by side until she could find a private moment to write again.

Lying on the lumpy sofa that night, she thought about the unfinished letter. She decided that if she couldn't say directly how much he meant to her, then she could show him. She got up and found a flashlight in the kitchen. The bulb was dim, but it cast enough light for her to write, recording the things they had done together, except for T.S.'s funeral, in case of censorship. She focused on the little things that she had come to treasure – the caviar he had tried to feed her and the sunscreen he had threatened to squirt onto her and the red-and-white earrings that now reminded her of him.

Peter and his parents debated the significance of events in South Africa at dinner: 'The Big Crocodile,' South Africa's State President P.W. Botha, had announced elections for September. It looked unlikely that he would run again, since he was recovering from a stroke. His government promised a five-year reform plan, but that announcement came shortly after it declared another twelve months of the national state of emergency.

"You think anything's really changing?" Peter asked both his parents as his sisters cleared their places and headed for the television room.

"Whites-only election," Richard reminded him. "So how much change can that bring?"

"And yet another 'reform plan,'" Ann added. "The last one tore the country apart."

"Guess you're right," Peter conceded, although he had hoped things would get better, at least enough so they could go back.

"But the *Weekly Mail* exposing death squads run by the security forces, now that's news," Ann added.

Yeah, but the kind of news that wasn't going to make it easier for her to get a permit, he thought. He was getting plenty of political updates, but what he really wanted to know was why Kagiso hadn't written back and whether he still meant something to her. He was glad his mother bought stamps and envelopes and took his letters to the central post office in Nairobi without asking questions.

Finally, a letter from Kagiso reached Richard Seibert's office two days later. Peter saw his father pretending not to look at the return address as he handed over the pale blue airmail envelope edged in red and navy stripes. Peter tried to act nonchalant as he took it to his room. Then he locked the door and sat on the edge of his bed, thrilled to touch something that she had touched, afraid to open it in case it said 'goodbye.' After a long moment, he told himself to face it, found a pocket knife to slice open the thin paper and unfolded a page covered in tiny handwriting. He held the letter near the window so that he could make out the words and decipher some of the smudges.

The whole last section knocked him over. He sprawled back across the covers full of delight to remember all those moments with her, joyful and relieved that they had been real, that they had been shared. He luxuriated in those thoughts until his mother called him to dinner.

"Either of you still have *rand*?" he asked his parents at the table.

"Just coins," his father answered. "Why?"

"I need to send them to someone," he said.

"I'll look for some. But don't just put them in an envelope. Tape them to cardboard."

"OK. Thanks, Dad."

Sandile stopped by Palesa's shack on a Saturday afternoon. He wasn't sure why: Maybe just wanting to commiserate with someone else who was missing a friend. She seemed surprised to see him, but welcomed him in for a cup of tea on a chilly day.

As she heated water on a kerosene burner and got out the mugs and tea and powdered milk, he looked around the one-room home, admiring the mosaic of folded magazine pages that covered the walls.

"What do you hear from Kagiso?" he asked as he warmed his hands around the mug.

"Nothing," she said.

"Really?"

"Just a word from her mother."

Sandile tried to figure it out. Her best friend was sent into exile, and they didn't call or write? Was there no phone in either home, no postal address, no money for stamps? Too delicate a question to ask her. Better just to share what information he had from Peter. He told her what he knew of Kagiso's situation at her uncle's house and of her efforts to talk to students at her new school about working for change.

"Want to write her a letter together?" he proposed.

"For sure," Palesa agreed. But she didn't bring out paper or pen.

Sandile searched in the pockets of his windbreaker and came up with a piece of notebook paper and a pencil. Unfolding the paper onto the rough table, he erased the list of homework assignments at the top of the page so they could begin.

Palesa told him to write about the latest meeting with the Soweto Civic Association, though she said not to use that name, just in case.

"We can say 'association,'" she explained. "Say they are supporting us."

"What else?"

"You can say for sure that the class is moving to that side. I mean, they are not going with the radicals, but you can't write that," she added.

"I understand," he agreed. "Anything more?"

"Lawrence is fine. Sonny Boy is fine."

He pointed at her.

"Me, I am fine."

"I should let you write," he offered, seeing that she was reluctant to say anything substantive to him. He turned the paper around for her and handed her the pencil. She filled up the sheet, stopping now and then to erase some errant words.

"You can get this to her?" Palesa asked.

"For sure," he said.

She turned the paper over and filled the back side. "Sorry for that. I took all the space."

"No problem. I can get another page at home."

They sat, unsure what else to say. Sandile thought he should go, but he was reluctant. Something in her quiet manner made him want to stay.

Maybe a little too quiet. The silence compelled him to come up with another topic of conversation. Reaching for something, he began, "We have this student group at Saint Andrew's. Peter started it. They wrote letters and petitions when I was detained."

Where was he going with this? What did it have to do with her? He tried to connect, without having thought it through. "Let me know if you want to get involved."

Her smile was unclear. Did she like the idea? Or was she too polite to tell him it was dumb? He wasn't sure why he had brought it up. Just because he didn't want to leave without a chance to see her again? Confused, he thanked her for the tea and promised to mail the letter.

July, August and September 1989

"Your mother has broken her ankle," Uncle Amos told Kagiso one evening when he returned from work at the furniture factory. "Your father says you must go that side to cater for her."

Kagiso wanted to shout for joy that her sentence of exile had ended. She clapped her hand across her mouth to stop herself. What would he think? That she thought her mother's injury was a happy event? That she was ungrateful for his home?

"Sorry for that, Uncle," she said from behind her hand. She wondered how long ago her mother had been injured and how Amos had gotten the message. Was it such an emergency that her father actually used the phone – to call Amos's boss? Whatever the story, the big news was that she was going home.

"I cannot take you until next week, when I have a delivery to make," he explained.

Anxious to go as soon as possible, Kagiso decided to investigate the cost of taking the bus. She had saved up a little money from her work at the spaza shop and she had the coins that Peter had sent. After school the next day, she checked on the bus fare, only to be disappointed. Her funds were well short of the price of the trip. Another week of exile suddenly seemed more oppressive than all the weeks before it.

But Amos had good news for her the next evening.

"The *baas* says I must make the delivery tomorrow. Can you be ready early?" he asked his niece.

"For sure." He must have been thinking of her chaotic departure from Soweto, Kagiso realized. This time, she would be the picture of efficiency. She folded her clothes precisely and placed them in the main compartments of a cloth bag along with her school notebook. Tucking her mail into a small pocket of the bag, she paused over the letters from Peter and wondered what address she could give him to write to her in Soweto. Something to think about on the drive back, she decided as she placed her red-and-white earrings on top of her luggage so she would remember to put them on in the morning.

At dinner, she thanked her aunt and uncle for taking her in.

"We are happy you came," Amos told her. "We need some girls here," he added, looking around at his crew of sons.

After she finished washing the dishes, Kagiso hugged her aunt, went to the kitchen alcove to wish the ailing grandmother well and stopped at the boys' room to say goodbye to them individually.

"Carleton, say goodbye to everyone at school for me?"

"For sure."

Stretching out on the sofa for one more night, she hardly slept. The exhilaration of freedom coursed through her.

As daylight slowly entered the room, she jumped up, put on her earrings, gathered her things, made tea for her uncle and herself, and then waited until he was ready. They climbed into his van and headed to the factory to load the items for delivery.

The chairs and tables rattled as the van sped along the highway toward Johannesburg. Kagiso was surprised to see how beautiful the countryside looked – broad green and golden farmland, little towns with whitewashed houses, rugged hills where the road passed along the top of a vast concrete dam. None of it had caught her attention on the drive up. The countryside seemed to flit by. The conversation with her uncle was sparse, but he turned the radio on. She tuned it to a station with all the latest music from Hot Stix Mabuse, Brenda Fassie and Lucky Dube. After a half hour, he switched to a station playing the Thulani church choir and Ladysmith Black Mambazo.

They stopped briefly to fill the gas tank and use the washrooms, then pushed onward. By one o'clock, Amos dropped her at her house in Soweto. She hugged him goodbye before he headed back toward Johannesburg to make the delivery. Fishing in her pockets for the key she hadn't used in three months, she dropped her bags on the doorstep.

"Who is there? Show yourself," her mother's voice commanded from the living room.

"Kagiso!" she shouted.

"Oh, my baby, you're home."

Kagiso heard her mother shuffle around inside and call out, "I'm coming."

"I can get it, Mama." Kagiso burst in the door, saw her mother trying to gather crutches and get up off the couch and rushed to give her a hug. "Sorry for that," Kagiso said, indicating her mother's white plaster cast.

"I am very much happy to see you," Sally said as she turned down the radio. "Even if this is the reason," she added, pointing at the bulky shield on her left foot.

"How did you break it?" Kagiso asked as she plunked down into an armchair.

"Stepping off the bus with a big crowd pushing from behind."

"Oh. Sorry for that. Are you feeling it?"

"Not much anymore."

Realizing that she was hungry, Kagiso asked if her mother wanted tea, then went to the kitchen to prepare some for the two of them. As the water heated, she hunted for something to eat. No biscuits. No bread. No leftover mealie meal in a bowl on the kitchen table. Nothing in the refrigerator. But there was tea and some sugar and powdered milk. That would get them through until she could go shopping.

Sipping their drinks, Kagiso and her mother went over the details.

"Thanks be, it was at the taxi rank. Someone helped me across the road to Baragwanath. I waited hours before the doctor set it."

"How did you get home?"

"I sent word to your father. He came for me."

"And the crutches?"

"Sonny Boy's father made them." She held one up to show the craftsmanship.

"Who's cooking?"

"Noma brings something when she can. Or I send Mike for bread and we just have tea for dinner. Now, even Tiny, she is making tea."

"I must go to the shops," Kagiso said as she cleared the tea things. The thought of the empty shelves intensified her hunger. She gathered some plastic bags and asked her mother for some money. The nearest shop would be best, as the list was long: a large sack of mealie meal, a pumpkin, onions, carrots, a tin of beef because the shop didn't usually have raw meat, and she wouldn't trust it if they did. Bread, of course, and a tin of margarine and a bottle of piri-piri sauce. The cooking oil and sugar were low, but they would have to wait or it would be too much to carry.

Soweto seemed fresh and bright on that winter afternoon when Kagiso stepped back into her world. Never mind the drab houses and the tawny, dried up grass on the open fields and the coal smoke drifting across neighborhoods. These were her neighborhoods. It was good to be back. She took a deep breath, smiled and set off. Trudging back with two heavily loaded bags, she greeted neighbors and small children.

"Do you need anything?" Kagiso called to her mother from the kitchen as she finished unloading the supplies and then cut herself a slab of bread.

"I'm fine."

"I am just going that side for a few minutes," Kagiso told her mother as she headed for the door with her snack in hand.

"No politics," her mother warned. "Your father forbids. And I need you."

Kagiso had already figured that was part of the deal, that she would be on a short leash – school and chores. But she winced to be reminded of it. "I must greet Palesa."

"Yes, but that's all."

Kagiso sprinted off toward Palesa's place, where she waited, nibbling on her bread and margarine, for half an hour before her friend arrived from school.

"Palesa," she shouted when she spotted her friend walking slowly in her black-and-white uniform.

Palesa looked up, then ran the rest of the way, dropping her books and papers on the ground to throw her arms around her friend. They hugged long and hard, shouting, laughing, crying.

"I am very much happy to see you," Kagiso said.

"And me, I am happy."

They stared at each other in disbelief for a moment.

"I heard your mother was hurt. I never knew she would call for you."

"Surprised me, too."

"She is OK?'

"On crutches. So I must do everything."

"Like before," Palesa reminded her.

"Yeah," she laughed. "How is Sonny Boy?"

"Very fine. We're reporting to the Civic on Saturday. Come?"

"Now they are really watching me."

"More?"

"Yeah. She's home all day."

Palesa nodded.

"And Lawrence?" Kagiso inquired, giving her friend a sly look.

"Fine. Still quiet."

Kagiso decided not to push her too far.

"Sandile came to see me."

Kagiso perked up.

"To write you a letter," she explained.

"You sure that's all?" Kagiso let her thoughts wander for a moment. Could Peter send letters to her through Sandile? No. Something too personal about that. What about Ellen's new employer? Could she trust her aunt to be the intermediary? Did she have other choices? Something sneaky about it, she felt, as if she were cheating on her friends, opting out of township problems by tethering herself to a white boy who lived far away.

"He said something strange about a student group at Saint Andrew's and did I want to get involved," Palesa said, dragging Kagiso back into the moment.

"Sweet on you?" Kagiso asked, a little smirk curling her lips.

Palesa shot her a sideways glance that didn't answer the question.

"I must go," Kagiso said.

"Kagiso's home!" Mike shouted as he came in the door after school. Tiny scooted past him, grabbed her sister around the waist and refused to let go.

"I was missing you too much," Kagiso said as she bent down and hugged them both. They pushed her over onto a sofa. Mike wrestled with her, crushing Tiny between them.

"Let me go," Tiny demanded.

"What is all the noise?" Patrick called out from the bedroom.

Tiny ran in to tell her father the great news.

The man emerged from his bedroom, slowly stretching his arms and yawning.

"Thank you for coming quickly," he said to Kagiso.

She got out from under Mike and stood up to face her father. This was the part of coming home she had not let herself think about – how to act around him. She was still angry and wanted to tell him he had been wrong to send her away; that was unlikely to go over well. He might even send her back. But she definitely didn't want to crawl around trying to stay in his good graces.

"*Dumela, Baba,*" she started, hoping he would show his hand first.

"*Ahe,*" he answered. "It's good to have you home." He moved to put his powerful arms around her, but Mike jumped in between.

"What's for dinner?" the boy inquired. "I am missing your special food! Look how skinny I got." He pulled up his shirt to show his ribs for inspection.

Kagiso looked at her father's eyes before she headed to the kitchen. Maybe there was a touch of patience there, a little room to maneuver. She would have to see.

The Malindis' store was busy in the early evening when Sandile spotted Kagiso among the shoppers in line at the cash register. After he rang up her purchases of beef and cooking oil, sugar and skin lotion, he asked George to fill in for him for a moment.

"Good to see you," he told Kagiso as they stepped outside.

She placed a hand on his sleeve and said, "Thanks God you're alive."

That took him back into the ordeal of detention and torture and recovery. He paused to push those memories into their caves. "How long you been home?"

"Three days."

"To stay?"

"Don't know. My mother broke her ankle, so I am just helping."

"Sandile," George called out the main door.

"Just now," Sandile answered him, then added to Kagiso, "See you sometime?"

"For sure."

Sandile went back to work in the shop, but he couldn't help thinking about Kagiso. He had many questions to ask her, many things he wanted to tell her. Better to go see her. Assuming it was OK to visit her, that her parents didn't think he was the one who connected her to trouble, when it was the other way around.

Sandile knocked on the Mafolos' door on Saturday. Kagiso welcomed him and introduced him to her mother, who was talking with her sister, Ellen Dlamini.

"Pleasure to meet you," Sandile said to her mother. "Auntie, how is your new job?" he asked Ellen.

"Fine," Ellen assured him. "But I miss my big boy Peter."

"Me, too."

Kagiso stepped into the kitchen to make tea for the four of them.

"How did you get hurt?" Sandile asked Sally.

Sally shifted uncomfortably, using her hands to lift the cast and reposition it on the couch. "Foolish," she said. "At the end of the day. Everyone pushing to get off the bus. I missed a step."

"Sorry for that." Glancing at the piles of unfinished clothes and sewing supplies near her on the dining table, he said, "I see you're still working."

"Only hand sewing. They pay very little for this," she said, flipping over a girl's flowered dress that needed buttons.

"Let's walk," Kagiso suggested to him, telling her mother, "I need to get some things at the shop."

They started on a stroll toward the grocery store as Sandile asked about her time in exile and listened as she described the incremental steps toward getting Mmabatho students involved in the struggle. He recounted his release from detention, the press conference and his work with the Detainees Rights Committee. He hadn't even told his family about that work, but it was important to him that she understand this new side of him.

"What will you do now you're back?"

"School, errands, cooking."

"I mean in the struggle."

"They are watching me too much."

"Who?" He thought immediately of the police and wondered why she would be on their list of targets.

"My parents."

"I see."

"But Palesa tells me everything." She faced him and said, "I hear you went to see her."

Embarrassed, he didn't know why, he tried to explain. "To write to you."

"Hmm. And something about getting involved with Saint Andrew's?"

He didn't answer.

"Maybe later for that."

He changed the topic. "What do you hear from Peter?"

She stopped and shook her head.

He wondered if he had asked something too sensitive. Switching topics again, he suddenly thought of a practical idea. "Could your mother still sew if she had a machine?"

"For sure. Only her left foot is injured."

"I think I can get her one." He planned to ask his mother if her friend who owned the dressmaking shops had an old sewing machine to lend

She gave him a big smile, tossed her head and turned toward home. "See you sometime."

Like playing a game, he thought. Talking to her was competitive, evasive, unpredictable. Not quite his type, but he could see why Peter was captivated. If he was still captivated.

Although Peter wrote to the address Kagiso had sent, at Ellen's new employer's office, he didn't hear back from her. Fearing that she had lost interest, he tried to move onward, but it was a struggle. Most of the students at the International School of Kenya went to their home countries for July and August, when the school was on vacation. Richard and Ann had decided they would stay put, except for a trip in late August to the Tivoli Gardens and Legoland in Denmark, where they planned to meet up with his grandparents.

Peter thought of the trip as a way to avoid thinking about South Africa, and about the PSATs and other exams – the start of the marathon project of applying to colleges in the United States. But, really a trip to two amusement parks – wasn't that something he would have liked five years ago, when he was little? In the meantime, he was home in Nairobi, bored and restless.

Richard knocked on Peter's bedroom door one evening.

"You can come in, Dad."

"Locked."

Peter got up off his bed, turned the key and opened the door a crack.

"I've got a great plan for you," Richard said.

Peter let him in.

"I went to visit one of our partner programs today – a boarding school for boys."

Peter rolled his eyes. His father was always trying to turn him into a charity worker like himself.

"It's called Starehe. The boys come from poor families all over the country. Really bright, motivated kids."

Trying to be patient with his well-meaning, clueless father, Peter kept waiting to hear what this had to do with him.

"To cut to the chase, they need volunteers to help the soccer coach. How 'bout it?"

"I'll let you know."

The first day without school, Peter sat around the house trying to think what to do. No tennis court or swimming pool, like their place in Johannesburg. He'd have to ride his bike up and down the hills of Nairobi to get to the school courts. Not sure the pool there would be open. The roads were pretty risky on a bike – no shoulders, erratic drivers, large potholes. He decided to stay home and relax. First, a couple of attempts at letters to Kagiso, just in case. Those ended up in shreds, even the one in which he admitted he had found her book in one of the mover's boxes. Then he pestered his sisters into a game of croquet that ended in a major dispute. He challenged Megan to badminton, then beat her so soundly it hardly seemed worthwhile. Sitting in a lounge chair to read a book, he found he couldn't focus. The old copies of the *Weekly Mail* contained nothing new when he reread them. Boring, boring, boring.

After dinner, Peter had a question for his father.

"So, when can I start?"

"What?"

"Soccer at whatever that school was."

His father put down the magazine he had been reading and said, "OK, great. I'll ask them in the morning."

"And what'll I be doing? Not like boys here don't know how to play." Peter had seen the skills of Nairobi boys playing with a dead tennis ball on a bare patch of earth.

Richard knocked on Peter's bedroom door at what seemed to Peter like the break of day but was actually eight o'clock.

"I called the school. The coach would be happy to have you today. Can you get up, please?"

Peter rolled over, tried to rise, shook his head to wake himself, and muttered, "Yeah."

"I need to go in fifteen minutes."

"OK. I'm coming. Ask Mom to make me some breakfast?"

He slipped into soccer clothes and sneakers, carried his cleats and headed to the kitchen for his take-out breakfast to eat in the car. His father drove him to the big stone arches at the Starehe entrance, asked the guard for directions to the athletics office and then introduced Peter to the soccer coach, Mr. Njoroge.

"Peter, you say? Very good. We have much for you to do." Mr. Njoroge kept him busy setting up cones for passing and dribbling drills. The boys came in groups by age throughout the day.

"What position do you play?" Mr. Njoroge asked him after a couple of rounds of practice.

"Striker," Peter replied, wondering if he was supposed to say 'sir,' too.

"Good. I have these ones who want to be keepers. Challenge them," the coach said, indicating a group of six boys who stood silently behind him. "Boys, this is Peter. He will work with you at that goal."

Challenge himself, Peter thought. He'd never tried to play goalkeeper, so he'd have to work from what he knew – how to outfox goalies.

"Hi, guys," he said when he and his six charges reached the goal at the far end of the field. "I'm Peter, like Coach said. What are your names?" He went down the line, shaking hands with each of them: Josephat, Elliot, Ishmael, Mwai, Raila and Silas.

"Good afternoon, sir," Silas replied.

Peter was shocked to be addressed so formally by boys just a little younger than he was. "You can call me Peter."

"If you want to be a keeper, you need to know how a striker thinks," he said, making it up as he went along based on vague recollections of what Coach Haverford had taught the

Saint Andrew's goalies. He wished Sandile were there to share his brilliant defensive techniques. Anyway, he'd have to do his best. This was much better than sitting at home with his little sisters for two months.

First, he positioned the six boys across the field, so he could show them how little space there was for good shots from the sidelines. Then he had them stand in the goal mouth, one at a time, to face a slow-motion attack from each position, urging them to move up and cut the angle to limit the striker's options. Then, they sped up the practice, rotating positions every five shots.

They were good, he thought. Raw talent – they hadn't been coached much – but quick and fearless. Especially Silas, one of the smaller boys, skinny, all legs and arms flying, but every ounce of him devoted to stopping the ball as he dived on the hard earth or flew toward the posts to grab or punch a shot.

Watching him, Peter couldn't help thinking about the boy he had met in Alexandra township, the one who called himself the best keeper in Alex. Why had he never gone back to find him? He would try to make up for that by giving everything he could to these boys. Kagiso would approve, he thought, if she cared at all.

Peter wrote all about the coaching – to Sandile. He did sometimes read back through Kagiso's letters, though, and wish that he had a photograph of her.

Ellen shared the new bedroom with Kagiso in September, but she brought no letters from Peter. Three months without a word. Kagiso felt betrayed, but she hid her feelings all weekend.

By Sunday evening when her aunt left, her silence had festered, turning from hurt into anger.

No one she could talk with about it. Not even Palesa would understand how much he had meant to her during her exile. And now he had abandoned her. At least he could have said goodbye. Was that something white boys did, walk away as if she meant nothing to him? Then fine, he meant nothing to her. No need for his support, now that she was back among her people.

Tossing her head, she decided to forget him and to focus on politics. The nature of the freedom struggle had begun to change, and Kagiso wanted to be part of that change, however small and hidden her role might be.

Her mother kept the radio on as she sewed, making it easy for Kagiso to keep up on the news. The civic associations linked up with the trade unions to launch the Mass Democratic Movement. Protests began around the country – at hospitals and other segregated institutions. For the first time, authorities granted permission for demonstrations and police showed a bit of restraint in reacting to protesters. Not exactly the end of apartheid, but an opening, Kagiso hoped.

Her friends kept her up on what the students were doing. She couldn't go to meetings herself, but she heard from Palesa that Sandile had come, even offered to get his parents and Saint Andrew's students involved. That reminded her of Peter, so she shoved the thought aside and focused instead on what seemed like a little romance for Palesa.

Returning from school later that week, Kagiso opened the door just as her mother sashayed into the kitchen – without crutches. She stared in disbelief.

Her mother turned and smiled at her.

Kagiso began to laugh, and her mother joined her.

"How long?" Kagiso asked her.

"How long for what?" her mother asked.

Kagiso didn't press her. If her mother wanted to keep a secret about being well and not needing Kagiso's help to run the house anymore, then she could stay in Soweto.

"Let me show you what I'm making," Sally said, walking back to the dining table. She set aside a boy's shirt she was sewing for her employer and pulled out a set of pillow covers in white cotton decorated with bouquets of appliquéd flowers in a rainbow of colors, the borders of the cases trimmed with ruffles.

"Who's it for?"

"Owner of this machine," she said, patting the old sewing machine that Sandile's family friend had leant her. "She has saved my job."

"Very smart," Kagiso praised the work. Then she tested their new understanding. "I am going to Sonny Boy's. OK?"

Her mother nodded. "If he wakes, I will say I sent you to the shops."

Kagiso slipped out quietly but filled with excitement. The bonds were loosening, with her mother's help.

Surprised to see her at a meeting, Sonny Boy jumped up and gave her a big hug.

"Sorry for being late," Kagiso said as she greeted Lawrence and Palesa and others. She couldn't stop smiling, despite the serious business at hand.

"What are we doing for the sixth?" she asked Sonny Boy, referring to election day.

"Stay-away – all the organizations are calling for it," he answered. "Of course, protest at school."

Kagiso nodded, but she was frustrated that they didn't have new ideas, and that she might not be able to join in the demonstrations.

Sandile arrived and greeted everyone. Kagiso saw Palesa shine at his arrival.

"We have approval for the information campaign," Sonny Boy announced.

"Thanks for that," Sandile replied. "I'll get these printed. We've got a good team, whites and blacks, ready to go."

Sandile, Tom, Vusi and others handed out flyers in the entryway at Saint Andrew's on the day before the elections for president – a vote from which all black South Africans were excluded. Their classmates took them. Many even read them.

"Be sure to give them to your parents," Sandile reminded them.

When he went to class, his teacher informed him that the headmaster wanted to see him.

"Yes, Headmaster?" Sandile asked when he entered the administration rooms.

"Please come in," Mr. Collins showed him into his office. "I have been reading your pamphlet. You must know that, personally, I agree with the sentiments expressed."

Sandile smiled, relieved.

"However, we cannot have direct political activities for any party here on the campus. We need to work to overcome differences, not heighten them."

"Thank you, Headmaster." Sandile walked back to class annoyed that a man who had spoken out for his release would wobble on an information campaign. He told the committee members, and they all agreed to work outside the gates at the close of the school day. Almost all their materials were gone by the time Sandile ran back in to prepare for soccer practice.

There was Andre Malan, dressing for rugby, right next to him, again. Not exactly the person Sandile wanted to encounter at that moment. He wished Peter were there to lighten the mood with some little joke.

"If you have any left, I'll like one," Andre said.

Distrusting his classmate's motive, Sandile slipped him a pamphlet anyway, in hopes of a change of heart.

"My father let all his workers off tomorrow," Andre said, "with pay."

Now that was news, Sandile thought.

Breathless, Kagiso huffed her way through the *toyi-toyi,* running in place and chanting, surrounded by her classmates in a big protest on election day. How long could people do this? How many times could they protest before their frustration boiled over into violence?

"I must go," Kagiso explained to Palesa, "before he wakes."

Palesa nodded but kept up the rhythm of the chants as she waved goodbye.

When Kagiso reached home, her mother showed her the finished gift for the sewing machine owner, then wrapped the pair of pillow covers in leftover fabric and tied them up with seam binding.

"Will you deliver for me?"

"Tomorrow? Because of the strike?"

"Sure, sure."

A few days after the elections, Sandile and his grandmother sat in the living room watching the evening news from the South

African Broadcasting Corporation, the television controlled by the government. To no one's surprise, the National Party had won the elections again. A new state president, F.W. de Klerk, would take over, but he came from the same stock that had created apartheid in the first place. Sandile wasn't expecting any sort of change.

He was more interested in the meeting his parents were holding in the dining room – a gathering of members of the Black Business Leaders Council. He could just hear their debate above the telecast, which his grandmother liked to play loud.

"International sanctions are destroying the economy," his father told the gathering. "We can use that to push for freedom."

Sandile was proud that his parents were taking on a more public role. Not because he had done it first, but because it showed that they had always been committed to the community. Together with their business friends, they might actually make a difference.

A voice on TV caught his attention, something about how unfair it was that hotels in the seaside city of Durban discriminated against blacks. Sandile turned his full attention to the SABC report. There he was, a reporter who had been one of the biggest propagandists for apartheid. And, suddenly, he was taking the other side, bemoaning the segregation that kept blacks from enjoying the beaches along the Indian Ocean.

How could that be? Sandile listened carefully, but when the report was over, he thought he must have misheard. He wished there was some way to rewind the news and hear it again. If the government was ready to turn its propaganda machine around, then it must be setting the stage for something big. How big? Sandile could hope but he could not yet believe.

October, November and December 1989

The invitation surprised Peter. The girl was new at school. He didn't really know her. But she asked him to come to her sweet sixteen party. Which reminded him that he hadn't had a sixteenth birthday party, what with Sandile detained and Kagiso sent into exile.

He had no interest in going. But his sister Christina's tart words kept echoing in his head: "Stop moping. Go out." Easy for her to say, Peter thought. She had her little gaggle of giggling friends in Nairobi who moved around together. But he had left his two closest friends in South Africa, and he had come back to Kenya different, with new ways of looking at life. All the same, he would have to find a way to make it through high school here. There was little chance they would be moving back to South Africa.

He said 'yes' to the girl. Jessica. He thought that was her name. It seemed rude to say 'no.' What if nobody went 'cause nobody knew her yet?

Fancy clothes not required, as they had been at the Miss Soweto beauty contest. He could just go in shorts and a polo shirt. Hadn't been to any parties since he moved back to Kenya. But now he was going.

His father dropped him off at the house. The guard opened the gate and directed him toward the loud music coming from the backyard.

COMRADES

"Hi. I'm Peter," he introduced himself, shouting over the music.

"I know," Jessica answered. "We're both on the tennis team, remember? Thanks for coming."

He drifted over to a group of students who were eating snacks and drinking out of plastic cups. They stood around a small swimming pool. The turquoise glow of the pool lights reminded him of his evenings with Kagiso. But those were over, he told himself. You have to move on.

"Hey, Peter," a soccer teammate said, slapping him on the back.

"How ya doin'?" he answered.

"We got some Tusker if you want it. Check out the bag behind that bush," another teammate said, directing him toward the stash of local beer.

Yeah, he did want it. Might make all this easier. He got a plastic cup and poured a beer into it. He took a drink, wandered over to the food table and filled a plate with a pair of hamburgers and some potato salad. A taste of home for American kids who weren't used to living abroad. Fine with him. He wolfed it all down and went back to the group of guys who were talking sports.

The music stopped and Jessica's mother announced that it was time for dessert. She carried a big cake frosted in pink and sporting the requisite sixteen candles out onto the terrace. They all sang 'Happy Birthday' to Jessica. Cheers as she blew out the candles. Cake for everyone. Peter watched as if it were a movie. But the cake tasted fine. He went back to talking sports.

"Wanna dance?"

The voice came from behind him. He turned and saw that the birthday girl was standing there, her long brown hair hanging straight down, and her pale face illuminated by garden lights of many colors.

297

"Sure," he agreed.

They joined a group of classmates dancing to "Born in the USA." Peter jumped and spun and shook to the music, beginning to feel like he belonged among them. He looked at Jessica as she shimmied with her arms stretched above her head. Nice body, sleek and sinewy. Good tennis player, too.

Sally Mafolo had the radio turned low as Kagiso prepared her brother and sister for school on a morning in mid-October, but still Kagiso heard the news.

"...release five African National Congress leaders who have been imprisoned for more than twenty years," the voice on the South African Broadcasting Corporation newscast said.

Could that be right? Kagiso dashed across the living room to turn up the sound.

"Walter Sisulu, Ahmed Kathrada, Andrew Mlangeni, Raymond Mhlaba and Elias Motsoaledi are to be released from Robben Island and Pollsmoor Prison..."

The news struck her like a splash of ice water in the face. Shocking. Exciting, but fleeting. She was sure she had caught the whole list, and Nelson Mandela's name was not on it.

What did it mean that they let the others go but kept Mandela in prison? One more promise half-fulfilled, a tease meant to placate but not free the people of South Africa?

She wanted to shout about it, but she kept her mouth shut. Her mother, already deep in her sewing projects, seemed not to have heard. Kagiso finished preparing Mike and Tiny for school and then sprinted to Palesa's.

"Did you hear?" she asked Palesa.

"What?"

"They are releasing them – all but Madiba," she explained, using Mandela's clan name.

"For sure?"

"On the radio this morning."

"No mistake?"

Kagiso shook her head.

"You think they will go all the way?"

By the time they reached school, the debate was in full swing.

"It's a trick," one of T.S.'s followers declared. Zwele and other followers were still in police custody.

"*Yebo*," Zwele's friend Thabo agreed. "They want us to come out, expose ourselves, so they can detain *all* the comrades."

"Me, I am going out to celebrate," one of the girls shouted, grabbing a friend and prancing away.

"It is nothing without Madiba," Sonny Boy declared. "We must keep up the pressure."

Lawrence nodded approval, as close to taking a position as Kagiso had seen him do in months.

Several students broke into protest songs and chants.

The teachers herded the crowd into the school, though some students filtered out through the gate.

Kagiso sat in their dilapidated classroom and thought over the news, trying to ignore the day's lesson on South Africa's role in World War I, except for the parts when they all had to stand and recite. What did the prisoner release mean? It could be a promise of more to come, but the government had done nothing that earned her trust. If they didn't let Mandela out soon, there would be an explosion of frustration, and violence. Kagiso was determined to be part of the final push for real change, for freedom. No matter what restrictions her father tried to apply.

"You think this is for real?" Peter asked his parents.

"Could be testing the waters," his father observed.

"Look what happened when they promised reform in '83 and left blacks out," his mother warned. "Worst violence in South Africa's history, economy in ruins."

"The ANC is still outlawed," Richard noted.

"Mandela and a lot of others still in prison," Ann added.

"But the government may be forcing its own hand," Richard said. "No way to back off now."

"So, how soon are we going back?" Peter asked. He tried to make the question sound hopeful, but he was entirely unsure. Just as he was beginning to feel at home in Nairobi again, to get interested in tennis with Jessica, the lure of South Africa retuned. The drama of protest and danger. The thrill of Kagiso's touch. All tempting him back toward a world he couldn't live in.

But he doubted that Kagiso would want to see him. And, anyway, he would have no say in whether they went back to South Africa. It would be up to his parents, and, even if they wanted to go, it would be up to some government minister who would or wouldn't grant his mother a work permit. So Peter would not have to decide anything, and that made his own uncertainty worse. Even if he made up his mind, he couldn't act on his preference.

With his thoughts tearing him in many directions, Peter needed some sort of activity to burn up his energy.

No tennis court at home, but the wall of the carport would do. He whacked hundreds of tennis shots at it.

That resolved nothing, but it calmed him enough to go to his desk and write to Sandile to congratulate him.

Moses Chikane was freed. Sandile learned about it through the Detainees Rights Committee and went to visit the family in the squatter camp three days later.

"Good morning," he said as he tapped on the makeshift door.

"They have gone that side," a girl standing beside another shack told him as she pointed down a path between the homes.

Sandile followed her guidance and reached an open area where a soccer match was under way. He spotted a player wearing a brand new Pirates cap and smiled.

"He *is* good," Sandile said to Moses's mother as they watched the game, though he could see Moses trotting gingerly as if his legs caused him pain. Afterward, he talked with Moses.

"First class," Sandile said. "A fine sweeper."

Moses grinned. "Thanks."

"You OK?"

"Just small, small pains."

"I mean after what they did to you?"

Moses looked startled.

Sandile knew that feeling. It was easier for him to ask that question than to answer it for himself.

"You know we can help," Sandile tried to comfort him. "The committee, even me."

"Thanks," Moses said. "Very much thanks." He reached out to shake hands with Sandile – a grip, then release as thumbs pressed together, then a grip again.

At midday, Sandile headed to Palesa's home, hoping to walk with her to the meeting at Sonny Boy's.

"Kagiso coming?"

"Meeting us there," Palesa replied.

Sandile was delighted to see Palesa alone. But what did he want to say to her? Did he have to say something? Wasn't it enough just to show that he liked her?

"You still with the Detainees?" she asked.

"Yebo. We are very busy with the ones released."

She nodded.

"I went to see Moses Chikane this morning. You know him?"

She shook her head.

"Some from your school?"

"Many of them. Even friends of T.S.," she replied. "Sorry for that."

"It's OK," he said, hoping he really had driven his worst memories into exile.

They walked a bit without talking. He wanted to keep up the conversation but he was having trouble gauging her interest. Was she just too polite to tell him to get lost? He had to find out. As they neared Sonny Boy's, he asked, "See you sometime?"

"For sure," she replied.

The smile that eased across her face reassured him.

At Sonny Boy's, they joined Kagiso and her friends in making plans to attend the rally for the African National Congress leaders released from prison.

"Can we come with you?" Sandile asked Sonny Boy.

"How many are you?"

"Twelve," he said of the group Peter had founded at Saint Andrew's. "But I don't think the white students will come."

Sonny Boy nodded in understanding.

"All together, we could be four or five."

"Let's start off from here," Kagiso suggested.

"My house is closer," Sandile offered.

They agreed.

As he walked toward his parents' shop, Sandile smiled with satisfaction. Funny to think what good had come of his confrontation with Kagiso many months before.

At the store, his father handed him the mail: a letter from Peter.

"You remember Soccer City?"

"Not sure," Peter replied into the telephone receiver.

"Where the Pirates play?" Sandile asked again.

"Oh, yeah."

"Full. Completely full. People singing freedom songs. Hundreds of ANC flags, even red Communist flags with the hammer and sickle."

"Yeah?" Peter tried to picture what Sandile was telling him. Their first conversation in months. He had wanted to call and hear about the changes in South Africa, and this rally in late October for the ANC leaders released from prison seemed like the biggest of all.

"A stage covered one end of the field and all the leaders were there – except Mandela. They said we must keep up the struggle until the ANC is unbanned and we are all free. Murphy Morobe read a letter from Oliver Tambo. Said it was a great day and all white South Africans should support."

"Wow. And police?"

"They stayed outside. No trouble. Every comrade was there, and dignitaries. Even Tom, though the other white students didn't come, and Vusi and few others."

"Sounds like Tom."

"And Palesa and Sonny Boy and Lawrence and …," Sandile paused, then added, "and Kagiso."

"Quite a crowd." Peter wanted very much to know how Kagiso was. But she hadn't written, and he felt a little guilty about asking, since he'd been playing tennis with Jessica now and then. So he didn't.

"*Yebo,*" Sandile agreed. "I bought you a T-shirt. Yellow, with a picture of Mandela and an ANC flag."

"Thanks, man."

"When are you coming back?"

"Don't know if we can."

The phone call to Sandile left Peter aching to be with his friends, adrift between two lands, neither of them his.

In need of some distraction, he flopped across his bed and landed on something hard and angular. American history textbook. Essay due on Monday for a competition in Washington. Big deal. Ten pages. Well, he could fill them. Keep himself busy. Finding a bunch of random words was never a problem. Words with meaning, that was another thing.

Stubby pencil in hand, he forced himself to make a start. Just fill up the pages. Get it done.

Nothing. He was lost in South African politics. No U.S. history in his head at all. He flipped through the textbook hoping for a topic that he could crank out. Washington, Jefferson, Adams, Lincoln, Wilson, Roosevelt. Old, old, old. Kennedy, Johnson. King. King – maybe something there. King and Mandela. What about that?

Really, what about that? He rifled through the pages on the U.S. Civil Rights movement. He took *Higher than Hope* from its prominent position on his bureau.

That put a stop to his project. Sitting cross-legged on his bed staring at the Nelson Mandela biography that he had failed to return to Kagiso, he thought about how she had blazed across his life like a shooting star. Brief. Beautiful. Beyond his reach. But thrilling. Not just because she was different from him, he insisted. He knew lots of black girls. No, something special about her. Had he lost her? Had he ever had her full attention? Or was it just when she was stuck somewhere – at his house over vacation, in exile in Bophuthatswana?

OK, this is going nowhere, and the damn essay needs writing, Peter lectured himself. He made an outline: similarities and differences between Nelson Mandela and Martin Luther King Jr. Dull, yes, but a start. Working until three in the morning, scratching out and erasing and rewriting, he wrote the whole essay. No one, perhaps not even he, would be able to read the mess on those pages.

As he typed the essay the next day in his mother's office, Peter thought it was not altogether horrible. He had made some good points. Two men whose greatness lay not just in their own actions but in the courage they inspired in millions of others, even when silenced – Mandela by jail and King by an assassin's bullets.

"Best work I've seen you do," his mother said when he finished typing.

"Thanks, Mom."

"Want some editing advice?"

"I guess."

She gave him some pointers. That meant painstaking re-typing. And then it was done. On to studying for exams. Sleep first, though. Sleep.

"My sister is very much happy with the new job," Ellen told Kagiso as they got out of their beds in the shared new bedroom. "Thanks to you."

"Thanks to Sandile," Kagiso replied. She couldn't take credit; it was her mother's needlework that won her a job among the seamstresses for Sandile's mother's friend. Beautiful dresses custom made for the elegant women of Soweto. Better pay. A short walk from home, though her mother was still pretending to need crutches.

"Your father is happy with it, too," Ellen added. "Will he let you stay?"

Kagiso shrugged. "*If* I stay out of politics." She gave her aunt a knowing look, trusting that she would keep the secret: Of course she would not shun politics, especially not with the chance to force real change hanging in the air.

"Our children will set us free," Ellen whispered.

Kagiso mouthed the words "thank you" as she dressed for the day in black jeans and a yellow T-shirt.

After serving bread with margarine and tea with milk and sugar to everyone who was up – her mother and aunt, Tiny and Mike – she said she had to meet friends.

"Wait," Ellen said to her, signaling that Kagiso should follow her back to the bedroom. Ellen reached into her plaid bag for a pile of letters that she handed to Kagiso. "My employer said she found these in her secretary's desk."

Ellen went back to the table. Kagiso stood with her mouth hanging open as she read the return addresses – all from Peter. A dozen letters marked "personal" and "private" with her name on them above the office address. She tucked them, unopened, under her mattress and went out.

The string of red-and-white beads around her wrist felt like a heavy weight. Kagiso set off to visit the homes of T.S.'s parents and his lieutenants. The boys, detained since the burning of the policemen's homes, had been released along with other prisoners. What they had done was wrong, she maintained, but they had suffered too much for it.

"*Sawubona*," Kagiso greeted Zwele when he answered the door.

He glared at her.

She saw more fear than anger in his eyes. She waited. After a minute, he opened the door wider and pointed to an armchair where she could sit.

January and February 1990

Sunshine flooded in the windows of the bus as Sandile rode up through the canyons of the Drakensberg. A midsummer day filled with heat and light and anticipation. Leaving the emerald hills of the Transkei behind, he was thinking about Palesa. The quiet way she listened with her eyes wide, the smile that spread slowly across her round face, her body lean and long.

Sandile thought back to the first time he had visited her home – a shack with no windows. She had let him in and shared what food they had. He had asked her a weird question about getting involved with Saint Andrew's students. And yet she had not seemed to mind that he stayed to watch her write to Kagiso.

What had she thought about his house when she saw it for the first time, in the middle of his argument with her best friend? The living room alone was bigger than her home. Yet she had chatted easily with his grandmother in Xhosa, not her own Setswana.

"That one is very sweet," his grandmother had said afterward.

Sandile didn't need advice on this. It was Palesa's grace in the unexpected that he remembered, her willowy walk, her hands moving softly.

Once he reached his home in Diepkloof Extension that afternoon, and greeted his grandmother, he set out for Palesa's. No idea what he would say to her, but a magnetic pull in her direction. He spotted her bent over a bucket of suds set on the bare earth. He watched for a moment as she scrubbed the laundry, pulling each piece out of the soapy water, twisting it to squeeze the water out, then plunging it back into the suds. The strength of her thin hands fascinated him.

He must have made a sound. She leaped to her feet and turned to see who was watching her.

"*Dumela,*" he said quickly in her language, to try to hide the fact that he had been staring.

"*Molo,*" she replied in his.

"Want to come over later?' he asked. "I mean, when you finish?"

"For sure."

Sandile wandered away, feeling like a fool. He was surprised when she knocked that evening, while he was watching the news with his grandmother.

"Please come inside," he urged.

Some big news screeched from the television. Something about the end of the state of emergency in the Transkei. His grandmother was clapping and calling out, "Praise the Lord."

He was trying to think of what to say to Palesa.

"Thanks for carrying that," Ellen said as Kagiso lugged a bag to the bus terminal.

"I'll miss you, Auntie." They hugged, and Ellen set off on her journey back to her employer's house.

Walking home, Kagiso remembered the letters, still unopened, under her mattress. She had sent Peter a message. Maybe now she could find a private moment to read his letters.

After her father left for the night shift, and the others went to bed, she took a table knife and a flashlight into her room. With the sheet over her head like a tent, she opened the oldest letter, from July. He was so happy for her to be back in Soweto.

She had decided not to cry, but the tears didn't listen. They just kept coming. They were more than a match for the corner of the sheet she used to wipe her eyes. She gave up stopping them and just let them flow, careful not to get the letters wet. One after another, his letters talked about his life in Kenya – following the changes in South Africa, coaching soccer at Starehe school, playing on the tennis team, missing her. Missing her. Missing her.

And then they stopped. In October. Because she hadn't written? Because he had found another girl?

The moments with him had been real, and suddenly she missed them again. She felt a void where something good had grown. She felt him lift her again out of the pool, over the fence. But then she fell. He was there. She was here. It was gone.

"This is the real thing," Sonny Boy told his friends in the workshop behind his house.

"They can ban them again," Kagiso warned. She dared not let herself hope too much.

"Not without a revolution," he replied. "I can feel it. This is real."

"We cannot go just on a feeling." But secretly, she wanted to believe, wanted to forge a different future for herself, too: University maybe? Forget about studying history. What about law, like Mandela? Don't get ahead of yourself. Don't jinx this, she admonished.

"They unbanned all of them – ANC, PAC and others. He told Parliament."

"What if they throw de Klerk out as president?" Palesa asked.

"A coup, like in Transkei and Bop," Kagiso added.

"I just know," Sonny Boy reaffirmed.

Lawrence seemed to lean first to one side, then the other.

"We can still plan, in case," Kagiso suggested. That was the best compromise, she felt: Hope, but not trust.

They agreed that the four of them wanted to be together to celebrate.

"And Sandile?" Kagiso whispered to Palesa.

Palesa smiled.

"OK, five of us together, and our families," Kagiso announced.

"Television. That's what we need. To verify," Sonny Boy said.

Kagiso knew hers was the only home with a television among her friends. "OK, my house," she said, not at all confident that she could talk her father into letting them gather to watch 'politics.' She would have to work on him; even he might be coming around.

"Sandile has TV," Palesa mentioned.

"Too far," Sonny Boy judged. "When Mandela walks free…"

"*If* Mandela walks free," Kagiso interrupted.

"*When* Mandela walks free," Sonny Boy insisted, "we want to celebrate …."

"…by watching at my place," Kagiso concluded.

The announcement surprised Peter most of all: His was one of the top two essays on American history at the International School of Kenya, and it was on its way to Washington to compete with compositions from high school students around the United States.

Something new for him – a star performance on schoolwork, a hint that writing might be an area where he could shine. He couldn't wait to tell his parents that evening.

"Peter, that's fantastic," his father said, clapping him on the back.

"Told you it was the best thing I'd seen you write," his mother added.

Still, his triumph was overshadowed by the news from South Africa: The government had unbanned the anti-apartheid organizations.

And his mother said she had applied for a permit to work there.

"Story of a lifetime," she called it. "When Mandela gets out."

"So we're all going back?" Peter asked. The changes were sudden, fluid, unpredictable, like a breakaway attack in soccer.

"We don't know if any of us can go," she replied. "But, if I can, do you want to?"

"Of course," Peter shouted without thinking.

"Just for a visit," Richard noted. "We're not moving again."

"Be quiet," Christina demanded from the television room. "We can't hear."

Excited to think of seeing Sandile, unsure what to think about Kagiso, Peter jumped up and went to annoy his sisters.

Auntie Ellen gave me all your letters just now. I am very much sorry for that.
    Wishing you and your family happy Christmas,
Kagiso

That was it? Months of waiting and that was all she wrote? But she did write. That was something, though Peter struggled to figure out what sort of something it was. Should he write back? To say what? A pile of halfhearted attempts at letters already stuck out of her book on his bureau. No use any of them, he decided.

Maybe he should just congratulate her on the progress in South Africa. That would open the door a little. Or would it? He scribbled something on a piece of notebook paper. Then he tore it to bits.

"What exactly are you looking for?" Peter's mother asked as she dropped him at the main market in central Nairobi.

"A red-and-white bracelet."

"Some nice Maasai crafts in the balcony on the far side. Leather bracelets with beadwork. And they love red."

"Thanks."

"But she might not be into red anymore," Ann advised. "Better get a bunch of colors."

Embarrassing that his mother knew who the bracelet was for, though at least she didn't say the name out loud. And confusing advice, he thought. Why would Kagiso change her mind about her favorite color? But the bracelets wouldn't cost much, so he bargained for a half dozen in different color combinations, all bright beads in geometric patterns.

Jewelry was hardly a concern compared with figuring out whether to try to see Kagiso. Her note could be her way of telling him 'goodbye.' Sandile was his source for information about her, so maybe they were together and neither of them wanted to break that news to him. He tried to tell himself he could hardly blame them – she was so beautiful that someone would step in. How could he compete when he was far away?

Not wanting to dwell on doubts, he kept busy, in case they could go – what to pack, school assignments, promising his teacher he would write a report on Mandela's release, if he were released. Would he need a blazer and tie to visit Saint Andrew's? Should he take his tennis racket? A bathing suit, sure. Didn't require much room and the hotel was certain to have a pool and it was, of course, summer. Some polo shirts, a decent pair of slacks, the bracelets, *Higher than Hope* and the pale blue bandana from Kagiso, for luck.

Peter and his father and sisters set out in a rental car in Johannesburg on Saturday morning. They were supposed to drop the girls at their friends' homes for sleep-overs, but it took forever – chatting with the parents, getting stuck at lunch at the second house. The highway was clogged all the way to Soweto.

"Can you help me out?" Richard asked. "We're really late."

"Sure, Dad," Peter sighed.

Late. Like that was something new in his family, Peter thought. They wouldn't have time to call on Kagiso. Just as well he hadn't mentioned it to his father. If fate was keeping him from seeing her, maybe it was sparing him rejection.

They stopped at International Child Aid's two biggest projects in Soweto to drop off paper plates, napkins and plastic cups and to help set up chairs and tables and television sets for the community celebration on Sunday, assuming Mandela really would walk free. Busywork for Peter, but it kept his mind off his uncertainties. When they finished, after sundown, his father drove him to the Malindis' store.

"Welcome, welcome," Grace greeted the two of them with open arms. "We are very much happy to see you. And on such a day."

Sandile interrupted his work with customers and came over to shake their hands. The store was in a flurry of activity, with everyone preparing for a feast.

Stephen came out of the office to greet the Seiberts. He asked about the family and whether they were back to stay and what they thought of the changes. After a chat, Richard said he had to head into town.

"You beat Redhill at football?" Peter asked as he and Sandile restocked shelves.

"No one scores on me," Sandile boasted. "And your team?"

"Star striker," Peter bragged, pointing at himself. "But no cricket team this year, so I'm playing tennis." He thought about Jessica fleetingly.

"Malan is playing cricket now," Sandile announced.

"You're kidding." Felt like home to talk to Sandile again. Peter wished he could go back to Saint Andrew's, jacket and tie and all.

"Excuse me," a woman said to Sandile. "Where is the meat?"

"Sorry for that. It's finished."

No more beef or lamb. Latecomers had to settle for chicken. A vast pile of pumpkins disappeared along with five- and ten-kilogram sacks of cornmeal, boxes of Red Rose teabags, cans of *phane* and tins of margarine. Sandile's grandmother sat near the cash register advising shoppers on where to find the goods on their lists. Older women shuffled through the aisles humming church hymns and stopping to do a little dance step or two. They had grandchildren in tow to carry home the bounty.

As the Malindis closed up, two hours later than usual, people kept knocking on the door. At Stephen's direction, Peter and Sandile and George piled supplies on the front step for late arrivals. Then they locked the doors and the burglar bars and headed home.

Kagiso hummed the African National Congress anthem *Nkosi sikelel' iAfrika* as she walked back from church on Sunday with her family and what seemed like the whole neighborhood. The tune buoyed her hopes but didn't erase her fears. What if they had been tricked into trusting government promises when they should have known better? Why hadn't she asked her father sooner about her friends coming to watch television?

Taking a deep breath, she moved over to walk beside her father.

"*Baba,*" she started.

He looked down at her.

"My friends have no telly. Can they watch with us?"

He paused and then said to her mother, "Let's go that side," pointing down a secondary street. Her father stopped at the home of a friend, exchanged lengthy greetings and came back with an electrical cord.

Kagiso feared they would miss the moment of Mandela's release, so she took big strides, trying to speed the family home. But the adults were moving slowly, chanting and clapping in premature celebration as they shuffled along the street.

"Mike, Kagiso, come give me a hand," her father said as they entered the house. He walked into the kitchen, a room he rarely entered, and pointed to the table. "Take this outside."

Kagiso was starting to get annoyed. She just wanted to watch the television, even if her friends were not welcome. But she and her brother did as they were told, carrying the table out the front door and onto the flat concrete beside the front stoop.

Her father repositioned it. Then he went back inside and came out carrying the television. He took his friend's extension cord, attached the TV cord and went back in.

"How is the picture?" he called out the window.

"Fine, *Baba*," Mike replied.

Kagiso was too stunned to speak.

Patrick came to the door, smiling triumphantly at Kagiso. "Now all your friends can see."

She ran to her father and hugged him, for once letting his powerful arms shelter her.

At the church where Sandile had spoken to the press, Peter kept checking under his seat for his backpack with the bracelets and the book. Sandile had said they would stop by Kagiso's after the service. Peter heard not a word the preacher said nor any of the hymns the choir sang as the congregation ambled out.

Would she be glad to see him? Or indifferent, like the first time they met, at her house? Or what? He fought with himself over whether to think it through or block it out.

Suddenly, they were up in the aisle and then out in the glare of the sun. No more time to think. Probably better that way. Face your fate, whatever it is, he told himself. Be a man about it.

As he and Sandile approached the Mafolos', Peter spotted Sonny Boy and Lawrence in the crowd in front of the house. Then he saw a soft Afro shake, a pair of earrings dancing beneath it.

"Kagiso," Sandile called out.

She turned, flashed a smile at Sandile, caught a glimpse of Peter, froze. Her face became a blank slate that he couldn't read. Had Sandile not told her he would be coming? Why did that upset her?

Falling back on habit, he put out his hand and tried a jest, "Hi. Remember me?"

She looked up at him and asked, "You will stay?"

"I can't."

She shook hands briefly, then withdrew hers.

"Palesa here?" Sandile asked.

Kagiso pointed to her friend, who was carrying dining chairs outside. Sandile went to help her.

Groans from the group watching television. Kagiso and Peter stepped closer to find out what was going on. Looting, clashes between police and black demonstrators, and even deaths, in the Cape Town area. The government announced that Mandela's release would be delayed an hour or more, as if twenty-seven years in prison had not been long enough.

Friends and neighbors shouted at the television, demanding Mandela's release.

"Now I don't believe they will set him free," Sonny Boy lamented.

"They must," Ellen insisted.

Finished with the chairs, Sandile and Palesa asked for an update. As Peter turned to answer them, he noticed that they were holding hands.

The crowd stepped back to wait and fret, unready to believe until they had seen Mandela with their own eyes, or at least an image of him on TV.

Peter felt their anxiety, but he knew he had only an inkling of what liberation must mean for Kagiso and Sandile and all these people. He studied Kagiso, who was standing near him but watching the TV.

Suddenly, she turned toward him and spoke urgently. "Come that side?"

"Sure," he said, hoping she hadn't seen him stare.

Kagiso headed to the kitchen, but it was crowded with women. She motioned for Peter to follow her into a small bedroom where she turned to face him.

"I didn't know what to say...," she began.

"About ...?"

"The secretary kept the letters. There were so many and..."

"It's OK." Was she really apologizing to him?

"...and I was very much sorry I didn't..."

"Really, it's OK." Why was she trembling? He wanted to comfort her but thought that would be out of line.

Mike and three of his friends ran into the room and out again.

Peter used the interruption to collect himself, try to build on whatever hope she was giving him. He pulled the pack off his back, fished out the copy of *Higher than Hope* and handed it over, saying, "I came to return this."

She put her hand over her mouth.

The book looked a little dog-eared and bent, he thought. Did he do that? Guess he had read it too many times. Her silence made him nervous; he tried to fill the gap with words.

"It helped me write an essay and win this contest in Washington. My parents think it'll give me a better chance at a good college in the U.S. so I can..." He realized he was rambling and tried to bring it to a halt.

"Thank you." Her voice wavered. Her focus stayed on the book.

"Well, it's yours anyway."

She didn't seem thankful. He thought she was about to cry.

His mind jumped in all directions trying to figure out what to do, say, think, feel. The backpack slipped from his hand. That reminded him about the bracelets. He pulled them out one by one and handed them to her.

"From the 'real' Africa." He smiled in an effort to raise her spirits.

She glanced up at him briefly, then slipped them onto her wrist. "Which one?"

"All look good on you."

"This one," she said, selecting a yellow-green-and-black band to match her earrings.

"They're all yours."

"I'll share." She darted away like a bird freed from a cage.

"Sure," he said after she had left. Anything she wanted. He felt as if he were dangling at the end of a string that she controlled. But that was far better than a free fall.

Kagiso ran to the front yard to give Palesa a bracelet of light blue, orange and green, and to slide the smallest one onto

Tiny's upper arm. She came back through the kitchen to hand one each to her mother and aunt. But her real destination was the back of the house, where no one was around.

Leaning against the outside wall, she let herself go. Shaking, choking down sobs. She had worked it all out. She did not need him. And then he showed up, looking deep into her with those pale eyes. And she fell apart. She did not *need* him, but she did want to be with him. That was plain to her, and yet she could not have that.

This was supposed to be a day of hope and promise. Everything she and her friends had worked for. And now, even before the promise had come true, it was to be bittersweet.

Closing her eyes, tipping her head back against the wall, breathing slowly, as if it pained her, she stood for a long time paralyzed by the truth. It would have made no difference if she had received his letters on time and answered each of them. He would be there. She would be here. It was gone.

A single tear meandered down her cheek. When it neared her chin, she reached up to wipe it away. The bracelets slid along her arm.

Sweet that he had been thinking of her 'real' Africa. And yet she had run away from him. She tried to think back to what he had said. Not staying, that she had heard. And then something about writing and going to university far away in America.

And he had smiled at her as if there was something to hope for. She let that buoy her. A little hope began to grow. She would think of something, or at least make this a good day.

The throng in the front yard began to shout. She rushed through the suddenly empty house to see what was happening. Just images of crowds waiting impatiently in central Cape Town. She worked her way out of the crowd toward her friends.

"Come inside for tea," she said to all of them, but she was looking only at Peter, smiling at him, surprising him.

They followed her into the kitchen. She put a kettle on a back burner and, with no table available, balanced the cutting board on a shelf so that she could slice a loaf of bread in six thick slabs, and spread them with margarine and a lot of strawberry jam because it was a special occasion.

The shouting started again. They each grabbed a slice and dashed out.

The cameras of the South African Broadcasting Corporation were fixed on the entrance to the Victor Verster Prison near Paarl, not far from Cape Town. The announcers sounded breathless, but they had sounded that way all afternoon. Still, Kagiso felt the excitement building.

Suddenly, there he was, Nelson Mandela, in the distance of the camera shot. At least she thought it was Mandela. A tall man in a gray suit, with a number of people buzzing around him. Looking much older than the photo of him in her book. Holding hands with his wife, Winnie.

Kagiso and her friends began to shout. A roar rose across the vast township of Soweto. Yes, Mandela walking free, his right fist raised to salute the people of South Africa. Yes, yes.

Keeping their eyes on the television but jumping and shouting and hugging one another, the whole gathering began to celebrate. Kagiso felt time shift into a lower gear so that she could savor the moment.

The procession led to a convoy of vehicles to take Mandela to the center of Cape Town. When he and the others had slipped into their seats and begun to drive away, Kagiso turned toward her friends.

"Let's go around," she urged them. Maybe this would be her last chance to see Peter, but let it be a celebration. She grabbed his hand and Palesa's and began to move out. Palesa grabbed Sandile's hand. Lawrence couldn't stop shouting for joy; Sonny Boy tugged him along.

They slipped into a stream of people flowing toward Orlando West. The six of them tried to stay together, though young boys dashed through the crowd, shouting, chasing each other.

The streets were clogged near the Khumalos' house. They tried to take a back route to Albertina and Walter Sisulu's house, but it was surrounded by television crews and walls of people on tiptoe.

Kagiso could just make out the corner of the roof. She tugged on Peter's hand and asked, "What do you see?"

"Backs and tops of heads," he laughed.

"Let's try Mandela's."

But the six of them couldn't even get into the street that separated the Mandelas' modest red brick home from Archbishop Desmond Tutu's house – even though all of those people were in Cape Town.

"This way," Sandile called out to Kagiso and the others.

"Where?" she asked once she had tunneled her way out of the crowd.

"To the shop."

The crowds thinned as they walked east. At the Malindis' grocery, they found Stephen and Grace handing out cold drinks to everyone who came by. They had put a television in the big front window, facing outward. Sandile went inside and came back with cold drinks, biltong and biscuits for all six of them.

Television cameras were trained on the crowd in central Cape Town awaiting Mandela's arrival. Kagiso and her friends watched as the vehicles drove up and the great man emerged. So it was not all a dream; he really had walked to freedom and here he was again, ready to speak.

When Mandela finished, Kagiso tried to absorb his first message to the people in her lifetime. She had expected heroics, personal triumph. But when at last he could break twenty-seven years of silence, he chose to thank them, the ordinary people, the comrades and the "endless heroism of youth." He called himself the humble servant of all who had sacrificed for freedom.

Kagiso took that lesson to heart.

She did not know where the song started. She heard it behind her, like a thought in the back of her head. *Nkosi sikelel' iAfrika.* It spread among her friends and the Malindi family, throughout the yard surrounding the shop and across the township. "God Bless Africa."

As the song finished, she turned to Peter and said, "Thank you for coming back."

He gave a half smile and answered, "Wouldn't wanna miss this."

"You should stay."

"My parents don't want to move again.'

"But you can come."

He looked doubtful.

"You *could* go to university in America," she paused to emphasize her point, "or you could come and study in the new South Africa with *me*."

She turned slightly, pretending not to see the surprise on his face that quickly broadened into a smile. With a toss of her head that made her earrings shimmy, she took his hand and Palesa's and began to dance, adding a whorl of dust to the prancing, chanting, celebrating crowd outside the Malindis' shop and around the world.

About the Author

Barbara Borst teaches at New York University in the Journalism Institute and in the master's program at the Center for Global Affairs, where she leads study groups to Ghana, South Africa, Tanzania and Uganda. Previously, she was an editor on the international desk at The Associated Press and frequently reported from the United Nations. While based abroad for a dozen years, in Nairobi, Johannesburg, Paris and Toronto, she wrote for Newsday, The Boston Globe, The Dallas Morning News, The Los Angeles Times, Inter Press Service news agency, and others. Her recent work appears on her website CivicIdea.com as well as on The Huffington Post.